I0818067

PERPETUAL CHECK

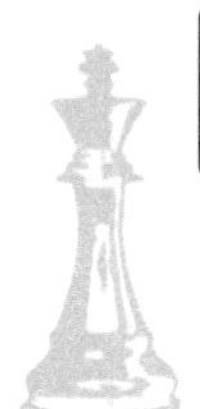

PERPETUAL CHECK

F. NELSON SMITH

Perpetual Check is a work of fiction. Apart from events and locales that figure into the narrative, all names, characters, places, and incidents are the products of the author's imagination or used fictitiously. Any resemblance to people living or dead, is entirely coincidental.

2019 Bear Hill Publishing Hardcover

Published in North America by Bear Hill Publishing
1843b Kelowna Cres.
Cranbrook, B.C.
Canada, V1C 6L6

bearhillbooks.com

Hardcover ISBN 978-1-7750741-7-5
Ebook ISBN 978-1-7750741-8-2

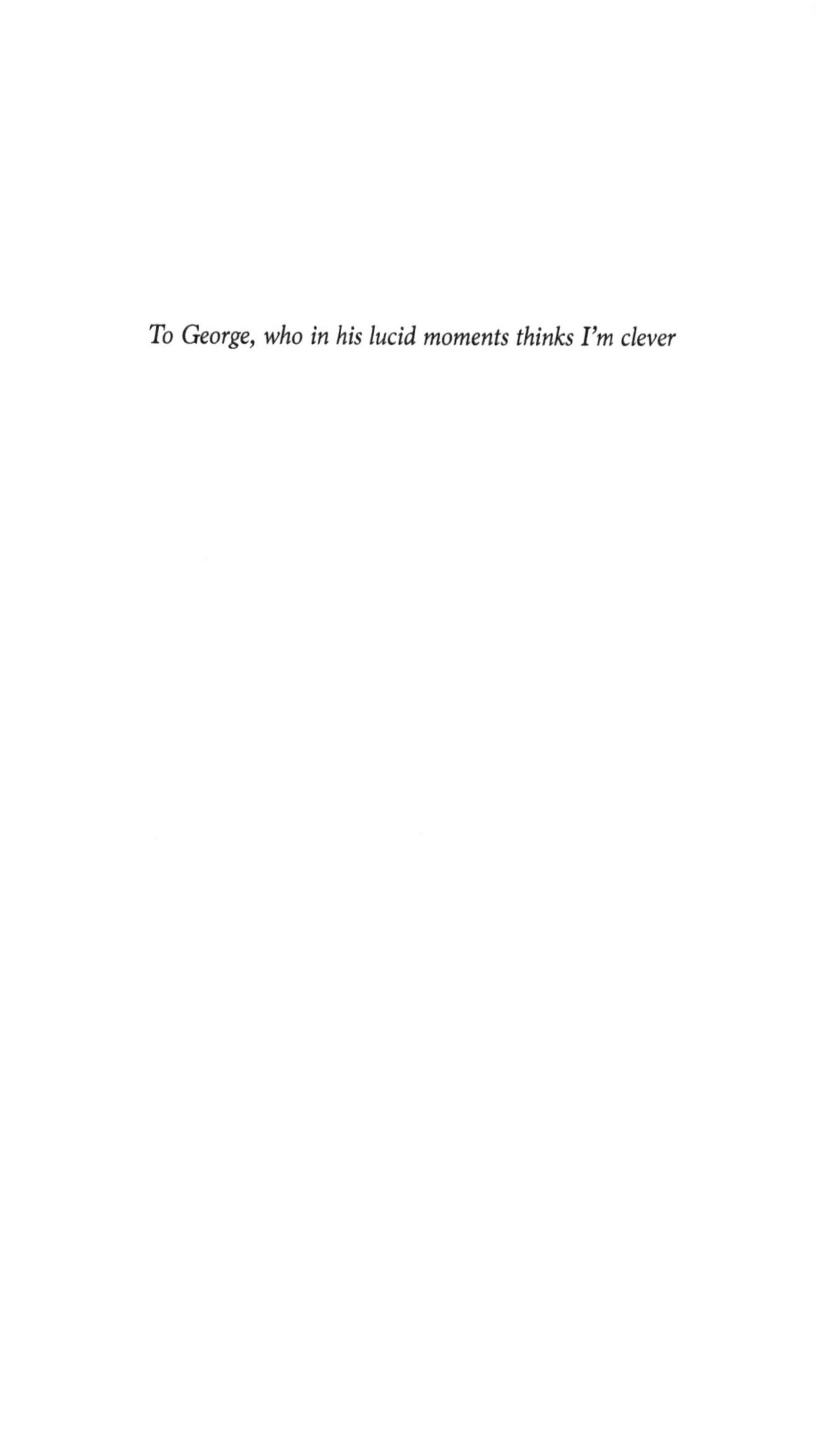

To George, who in his lucid moments thinks I'm clever

perpetual check */pər-pet`ū-əl chek/ noun* in chess, a situation in which one player's king is continually placed in check by the other player who may thereby claim a draw

One 1

JUNE 1985, STUTTGART, GERMANY.

The man standing in the hallway outside Ida Schiller's door looked more like a Sumo wrestler than a policeman. His bulk strained the seams of his suit to crucial levels, and when he used his handkerchief to mop his damp face, she swore she heard the seams creak. She backed into her neat front hall as Sumo Man stepped in and seized the space. Face red, sweat stains marring his jacket, his breath made whistling noises through his teeth from the effort of walking up the flight of stairs to her apartment door. For a second, she wondered if he might have a heart attack.

Another policeman, this one in the immaculate green and tan uniform of a municipal police sergeant, managed to squeeze by him, and she learned Sumo Man was Herr Mueller from the *Landeskriminalamt* or *LKA*. Miss Schiller compared the face on the ID card with the one before her. His eyes, almost hidden in the upper folds of his cheeks, regarded her with ill-concealed impatience, so she deliberately held the card an extra few seconds to show him that she may be a spinster *privatsekretär*, but she was not intimidated. Finally, curiosity took over, and she returned his worn leather folder. "What do you wish, Herr Mueller? Important items are waiting at the office. I don't wish to be late. It sets a bad example for the others."

"Please, Miss Schiller, I think we'd be more comfortable if we sat." He studied her face, and she grimaced, not hiding her distaste for dealing with a *Kripo*. "If you don't mind?" His voice was surprisingly tenor for such a big man.

Floorboards screaming, he followed her into her sitting room and waited while she sat in an armchair, its seat covered with embroidered velvet upholstery.

Mueller declined to sit, perhaps noticing her lack of hospitality or not trusting the chair to remain in one piece. The young sergeant stood with military correctness by the door to the hallway.

"Your employer is Joseph Dittmahn, vice-president of Redstadt Electroniks. With offices in the Schlossplatz."

Ida nodded in reply, though the statement made it clear he wasn't looking for confirmation. Mueller's bulk spread out in front of her, his expression that of a jovial shopkeeper about to take her order.

"You said he's away. Where was he supposed to be, please?" Fingers like sausages held his pencil to his notebook.

Her chin jerked-in reflexively to the question. She raised her eyebrows then cinched them together between her pale blue eyes. "He's in Munich. Until the day after tomorrow. Friday."

Mueller waited, as though expecting her to ask the obvious. Abruptly, he smiled, showing an unexpected array of white, even teeth. "His wife accompanied him?"

"No. She's visiting relations in England," answered Miss Schiller, her eyes glinting. "Has something happened to her?"

The policeman pursed his fat lips in a gentle reproof, then let the air wheeze through them as though regretful of what was to come.

"Not his wife, Miss Schiller. We were unable to locate her,

and that's why we've come to you. Early this morning, Herr Dittmahn was found in his car. Unfortunately, dead."

He waited, watching shrewdly from under sleepy lids. Miss Schiller's face turned white. One hand reached out as if to push his statement away. Her grip tightened on the arm of the straight-backed chair.

"In his car?" she mumbled, snatching at the detail.

"A highway maintenance crew found him at the side of the road, forty miles north of Stuttgart." He inhaled another labored breath and added, "He'd been shot twice in the head. At close range."

Miss Schiller choked off an incredulous cry. Her face twisted at his blunt words. "No! He's in Munich. He had reservations on the train from Stuttgart." Her expression obstinate, she repeated, "No. It's a mistake."

"There is no mistake," said the detective, his tone gentle now.

She endured his sympathetic murmurs with the same impatience of one forced to listen to a bad sermon. He required her help. Time was important. Robbery could be a motive. Did she have objections to a few more questions?

"Did Herr Dittmahn carry large sums of money or other valuables on his person? Was he in the habit of picking up hitch-hikers?"

"Robbery!" Ida Schiller dismissed the word like a puff of steam. "But whatever was he doing in the North?"

Mueller waited while she stared at her hands, forehead creased.

Finally, she sighed. "Perhaps he did pick up someone and offer to drive out of his way. It would be like him. Charitable, but foolish." She pressed her thin lips together. "Well, a robber wouldn't get much. Herr Dittmahn carries little money. He uses credit cards. Easier to account for his expenses if the banks do his bookkeeping for him."

The policeman shifted on his dusty shoes. "Miss Schiller, you've been with the company how long?"

"Twenty-one years."

Mueller's tone turned admiring. "I imagine Dittmahn left many things in your care, and you must know a great deal about the company's affairs. Everything was going well there?"

"You suspect a person in the company shot him?"

"I'm trying to get a background, that's all. Every possible angle, you understand."

Miss Schiller gazed back at him with penetrating eyes. "Everything is operating smoothly at the company."

"The company deals in electronic components only?"

She nodded.

"You do not deal in tractor parts?"

Her hand waved the remark away. "Tractor parts? Of course not."

"Yet, there have been shipments of tractor parts that disappeared after they'd arrived at their destination."

Miss Schiller's expression cleared. "Ah, you have tractor parts confused with electronic components. Herr Dittmahn mentioned that a shipment of computer components went to our subsidiary in Austria by mistake. But somewhere along the way someone had stolen the equipment and filled the crates with sand. It's odd, but . . ."

"Yes?"

"Nothing." Miss Schiller slumped in her chair. "It's nothing to do with us. Herr Dittmahn . . . I can't grasp it. It seems impossible."

"Indeed." He stared at her for a moment longer. "Maybe

something else occurred to you? About the shipment of components, perhaps."

Mueller pushed his head forward and sideways, exposing his right ear to her as if waiting for an answer from an addled toddler. It was patronizing even if encouraging, and she resented it. She pursed her mouth, looked past him, and ignored him.

He tried again. "Redstadt Electroniks receives shipments of computer components from Britain and the United States, does it not, Miss Schiller?"

Miss Schiller shrugged, then as if realizing the direction of his questions, narrowed her gaze on him. "Why are you asking these questions, Herr Mueller?"

He held up his pudgy hand, palm outward. "Please, Miss Schiller, only a few more minutes." His voice hardened. "The company's business is computer components. Yet some of the customs declarations on shipments arriving from Britain and the US state the containers hold tractor parts. You are perhaps not aware that your company forwards these particular crates on to Austria. It is strange, is it not, Miss Schiller? Now you say one of the same shipments contains only sand. Shortly thereafter, Herr Dittmahn is murdered."

"Rubbish!" She smiled, mocking him. "You are saying there is something untoward going on with the shipments. Secrets. But he doesn't approve of secrets. You don't know him. He believes in fairness and justice. Always. I would know if it were otherwise."

Suddenly aware that she was speaking of her employer as though he were not dead, emotion boiled up. She pressed her tongue against the back of her teeth to keep her jaw from quivering.

"What was Dittmahn's business in Munich?" persisted Herr Mueller, either oblivious to, or ignoring her obvious discomfort.

"He told me he was going to meet with a representative from head office," she said, regaining control.

Mueller raised his eyebrows and licked his pencil again. "He told you? You don't arrange his appointment book?" He didn't so much as a glance up from his notebook.

She flushed. "It was last minute. He took the notification himself and then told me. Did you think there was something furtive about it?" When his flickering eyelids betrayed his line of thought, her lips twitched an almost imperceptible smile at catching him off guard.

She answered the rest of his questions—Dittmahn's business acquaintances; the address of his wife's relations in England.

Only when she was sure the two policemen were not coming back did she permit herself to shed bitter tears. After a phone call to the office, she did an uncharacteristic thing. She slipped into her bedroom like a ghost and pushed the door closed behind her with the very tips of her fingers, listening for the soft click of the latch. After a moment, she moved to the bed where she stretched out and stared at the ceiling, uncaring that her shoes marked the white bedspread.

Later that same evening, she went downstairs and found a bulky brown envelope on the floor under the mail flap. She took it into the sitting room and with a small knife from her corner desk, slit the envelope in the same way she had opened a thousand like it before. Turning it upside down, she tapped the open end on her palm. A letter with the handwriting of her late employer slid out. Another shake of the brown envelope and a wad of money, followed by a square of microfiche, tumbled to the floor at her feet.

The letter explained the envelope's contents and outlined detailed instructions of what she was to do. A scant two hours later, she backed her Volkswagen from its parking place and sped off into the darkness. For the first time in her life, she knew real fear.

Far across Stuttgart at that exact moment, in a hotel suite with windows facing a spacious green park, a man spoke on the telephone. Thin parchment-like skin barely covered the knuckles which stood out on the hand holding the receiver. The same economy of skin, covering high cheekbones, stretched the man's mouth to a thin slit. Lustrous brown hair combed back from his forehead only served to emphasize his death's head appearance.

"Nothing was found in the office?" His quiet voice faded as he paused to listen. "And you searched his home . . . ? No—my informant is certain the document was in his office two days ago. . . . He didn't go near a bank. You found no receipts for packages or envelopes?" This time he listened a moment longer. "Ah, so? Herr Dittmahn was shrewd, but how careless to not destroy an invoice for a microfiche. A thick package becomes a thin package. Now, where would he hide it . . . ? He has a secretary who's disgustingly loyal. In love with her employer, I suspect." His lips twisted in a sneer.

Then his voice sharpened, the words insistent. "Go to her place. But be sure you have the documents before you tidy up the loose ends. Do I make myself understood . . . ? *Gut.* I will await your report."

The man replaced the receiver then poured two drinks from a crystal decanter placed on the sideboard. He picked them up and offered one to his companion.

Two 2

DANI MORDEN WATCHED HER AUNT LUCY walk a vague line toward the immigration area at London Heathrow Airport terminal. Her manner gave the impression a navigation mistake might have brought her to England, but now here, she would make the best of it. Two businessmen, fellow passengers off the airplane, came forward and guided Lucy to the line for passport control. In a frame of mind somewhere between derision and amusement, Dani ambled along in slow pursuit.

"Cute. Real cute," she muttered, moving up to stand beside Lucy. "Anyone would think you'd never traveled in your life. I'm glad Mother can't see you now."

Dani grinned at the prospect. *A real twit*, was her mother's favorite summation of Lucy's character. Aloud, she said, "You're not alike at all, are you?"

Lucy slowly turned her hazel eyes toward Dani and looked down her nose, as if she had suddenly been accosted by a strange man looking for company. "I should hope not," she said, voice dripping with ice. She opened her handbag and peered into its depths. A plump arm plunged in, almost to the elbow. "Drat. I can't find my passport." She extracted a guidebook with *Britain* printed in bright red letters on the cover. She handed it to Dani. "Just hold these a minute, would you, dear?" Next followed a large pair of scissors, more suitable for cutting ceremonial ribbon than anything else, and a puffy makeup bag. The two men standing behind them shifted forward, curious.

Lucy continued to talk, her conversation a confusing mixture of thoughts spoken aloud and words directed at her niece.

"Nobody ever accused your mother and me of being alike. Helen spent her life shouting about women's rights." She pulled out her reading glasses and put them on, making her round face rounder.

Peering more confidently into her bag, she pulled out a street guide to London and gazed at it as if it hid the route to her passport. Finally, she pushed the map at Dani. "I never could see the advantages, myself."

The corners of her mouth turned upward, and her eyes twinkled as she peeked over her glasses at Dani. "Too many drawbacks. Imagine, always being destined to carry your own luggage."

In spite of herself, Dani burst out laughing. Lucy handed her a small bottle of brandy.

"Aunt Lucy, how could you?" Dani's laughter turned to dismay. "You're supposed to drink it on the airplane."

"I didn't want it then, dear," replied Lucy, intent on the contents of her bag. "Seemed a shame to leave it. It may come in handy sometime. Here we are!" Rings sparkling, Lucy waved her passport. A small tin of hard candy fell out of her bag, followed by an orange, both going on a roll between the feet of the passengers in front of them.

The men moved back in line. "Wonder why she bothers with a suitcase," one said to the other.

Dani bit back a retort. Face red, she retrieved the orange and tin. The line crawled forward. She gazed at four girls over in the blue line in their mid-twenties, all chatter and excitement. A familiar feeling of aloneness flooded through her. *My first trip to England, and I get stuck with Lucy.*

The thought of spending the rest of the four-week trip with her old aunt didn't exactly conjure up images of exciting adventures. Lucy's letter asking for her company on a grand tour of Britain had come when Dani was in low spirits—dissatisfied with life. Any vacation, particularly one out of the country, was a welcome diversion. She was tired of Edward too, bored with his predictability. Nothing exciting there, just the same old dates. Dinner out—a movie. Now and then, a live concert in Calgary. A variation of their middle-aged fun. More nights than most, he'd end up impatient with her quickness of mind.

"You could at least let me state my next thought before telling me what it is," he'd say and smile indulgently at her. He should have been her mother's boyfriend. An image of Edward and her mother as partners prompted a choked-off snort. Then again, he sent more flowers to her mother than to Dani, saying it was only polite to keep in good with his future mother-in-law. Her mother said it showed old-fashioned respect. Dani accepted the explanation at the first bunch he brought, but by the arrival of the third delivery, the words bribery and collusion leaped into her mind. Still, she had hesitated about the trip with Lucy but had let her mother persuade her. Irritation flooded her. Why did she allow her mother to make her decisions as if she were too juvenile to make her own? No, her mother's life's purpose was to arrange Dani's. She could still see her mother's shocked face, as she had yelled the accusation at her.

"That's not true, Dani," her mother had answered. "I only try to help when you can't make up your own mind."

"Don't hang that one on me," Dani had shouted, letting it all pour out. "Go on! Admit I'm a disappointment. I try damned hard to be who and what you want, and I never succeed." Dani laughed a wild bitter laugh. "Have you ever tried to live someone else's dream, mother? Pushed into doing what they were afraid to do themselves? I can't give you the rewards you think you never had, don't you see that?"

"I see more than you know." Her mother's set face was ashen.

No, thought Dani now, *when she looks at me, she only sees herself. Her own image. Now she's angry because I didn't turn out to be the daughter she thinks she deserves. We've failed each other.*

Dani forced her derision down into the pit of her stomach where negative thoughts regarding her mother dwelled, feeding on each other.

Lucy touched the back of her elbow to coax her forward. "Our turn."

"I know," Dani snapped, transferring her resentment to her innocent aunt before realizing who she was talking to. If Lucy was offended, she didn't let on.

Passports and documents inspected at Immigration, they headed toward the baggage pickup carousels. Dani caught her suitcase on the first round. Lucy made an ineffectual reach as her own tumbled down the luggage chute, and she heaved an exasperated sigh as they both watched the bag start another journey around the carousel.

Lucy ignored Dani's grin, turning away to stare with curious interest at the people milling about. Her hair, still bright with natural gold and red highlights, shone as she turned her head.

Dani rubbed her neck with one hand and stuffed the other in her pocket. She softened her gaze and let out an imperceptible groan. *Lucy isn't so old,* she conceded. *Is she even fifty yet? Her pretended confusion is fun too. Maybe this trip won't be so bad if I just ease up.*

Her eyes followed Lucy's stare to a woman wearing a rumpled

but fashionable suit of superior cloth, standing beside the girls. She had to be European to be in that line. German most likely. She seemed restless, impatient with waiting. Periodically, she'd lift herself up out of her shoes to glance further down the luggage carousel then scan the surrounding area. Her eyes flickered over one individual before inspecting the next. Was she searching for someone? Dani watched as the woman reached up to tuck a stray piece of faded blond hair back into the bun she wore. Her pale blue eyes met Dani's, who lowered her head, dismayed at being caught staring.

"She's frightened."

"What?" Dani turned to her aunt.

"The woman in the camel suit," explained Lucy. "She's frightened. And a man is watching her. Over by the pillar."

Dani stared in that direction. People swarmed about the baggage carousel talking to others and rolling claimed luggage away toward the customs doors. Everything from understated suits and ties to blue jeans and bright shirts. A customs official? She saw nobody in uniform.

She shook her head, decided. "She's just a tired traveler."

"No. He was watching her." Lucy leaned closer, her voice insistent. "He kept comparing her to a picture."

"This is a restricted area, so he must be an airport official." Dani made her voice melodramatic and wiggled her fingers. "A policeman looking for a fugitive."

"I'm not wrong, Dani, in spite of your theatrics. When she looked his way, he disappeared so she wouldn't see him."

"You noticed all that?" said Dani.

"People who live alone notice other people all the time," replied Lucy. "It's our way of becoming involved socially, I suppose."

Do lonely people also imagine stories about the people they . . . *notice?* Would Lucy? Disturbed, Dani glanced at the woman now busy sorting out her baggage, at her confident manner as she searched for the correct customs hall, then marched toward it. *Nonsense*, Dani decided. The man had probably looked past the woman's shoulder at someone else. Travelers always watch other passengers at airports. Turning her attention to the carousel, she recognized Lucy's bag and made an ungraceful dash for it before it began a solitary second trip.

"Thank you, dear." Lucy smiled. "I quite forgot why we were standing here. Ah, there we are, the green door I think." She unhooked one end of the strap from her suitcase and walked off, pulling it behind her.

In spite of herself, Dani's eyes slid toward the pillar and searched around it for someone out of place in the crowd.

"Lucy always was a puzzle," she heard her mother's voice. "She was the brightest of all in school, and why she puts on that helpless act is beyond me. But don't let her fool you, her brain is ticking over all the time. I couldn't be bothered myself," her mother's characteristic expression rang in her ears. *I wish I had a nickel for every time I heard her say she couldn't be bothered. Too bad she couldn't be bothered giving me advice.* Warning herself to cut off those destructive thoughts, Dani straightened up and followed her aunt.

The customs officer smiled at Dani. "Anything to declare miss?" He inspected her customs declaration.

"Well, I came through the green door," she replied, then bit her lip. Instead of emerging as a joke, it sounded sarcastic. Ahead of her, waiting, Lucy let out an exasperated sigh.

The friendly grin faded from the officer's face. "Are you carrying any food, cigarettes, or drugs?"

Red-faced, Dani shook her head and wondered if she should have mentioned the bottle of brandy in Lucy's bag. She shook her head again at his question of the amount of cash.

He motioned her on and turned to the next in line.

A fine beginning, thought Dani, almost running down the corridor following the arrows toward outside.

"You aren't alone, you know," she heard Lucy say from behind her. "I did things like that too."

Dani only gave her aunt a scornful glance and quickened her step. "Right," she breathed.

Lucy sped up too, her suitcase teetering on its wheels. "Believe me, the first time I left home, I outdid anything you can think of. Things that still make me shudder when I remember." Lucy's suitcase fell over on its side. "Dani—slow down, for heaven's sake! I feel like a Pekingese running alongside a giraffe."

Her niece stopped in her tracks and swung around, almost bowling Lucy over.

"There, you see?" Lucy righted her suitcase, while she regained her breath. She fanned her face with her hand. "If you had waited, we could have found a luggage carrier, dear."

Dani blinked at her aunt's logic before a round of guilt washed over her for the third time since they'd landed. This was going to be a long trip.

"I'm sorry, Aunt Lucy," she said. "It's not that customs guy. It's me. I feel like a damn fool, always lousing up. I promise to lighten up, okay?"

"Take it all in stride, dear. Things are never as dire as we want them to be."

"What?" Dani asked, but Lucy gave a regal wave to a porter and spent a fussy few minutes handing over their luggage. They continued along the corridor toward the exit.

Dani's five-foot, nine-inch frame reached over Lucy's by at least six of those inches. She shortened her steps to match her aunt's now leisurely stroll, while Lucy ignored the suggestive hurry of the tall porter striding before them. An onlooker might have smiled at the *Mutt and Jeff* picture they made.

The German woman, hurrying along behind, did not smile.

The man, intent on watching the German woman was not concerned with them at all.

Lucy marched toward the head of the taxi area, all the while smiling and ignoring the ominous rumble in the long, impatient line. A man, luggage at the ready for an approaching taxi gave one despairing look at Lucy and handed her into the next one that came along. Dani stumbled in after her, resisting an insane desire to giggle.

"*Ach*, one moment, please. I overhear your hotel destination. Might I ride with you as that is my destination also?"

It was her. The woman they'd been watching. She didn't wait for a reply. In one hasty movement, she thrust her bag in front of her, sprang into the taxi and pulled down the little jump seat. The taxi tore off with that swift, sure speed only London cabbies can manage. The woman craned her head, staring out of the window at the terminal behind them. She pressed her thin lips together as though biting back a protest.

Aunt Lucy was right. She's really scared.

The woman turned from the window and closed her eyes. In a moment her head, nodding in motion to the taxi, drooped to her chest. Lucy and Dani kept silent; Dani watching the streets of London fly by in a dizzying whirlwind, and Lucy contemplating the sleeping woman. With a moan, the woman gasped and opened her eyes, her head swiveling in startled awareness.

"My dear," said Lucy, leaning forward, her hand reaching

out, ready to help, "are you ill?"

The woman glanced at Lucy, appraising her—the plump figure, the genuine concern worrying at hazel eyes, mouth tucked in at the corners, ready to smile. Next it was Dani's turn. She met the woman's suspicious stare with directness of her own brown eyes. The woman looked Dani up and down, taking in her trimmed nails, clear polish; no jewelry, only a watch. Her expression seemed to approve the classic lines of Dani's shirtwaist dress, open at the neck.

The woman's pale eyes swept to Lucy again, and she smiled. What could only be relief, washed over her face.

"No, no," she said, "I am fine, thank you. Only that I am tired from three days traveling. Also, it is hot for so early in June, *ja*?" She considered Lucy's spring print with the frilled collar and sleeves, then looked down at her own rumpled suit. "My clothes are not appropriate. For business yes, but not for the tourist."

Lucy weighed the woman's statement for a moment, then smiled. "I suppose you had to leave in a hurry?" The woman stiffened, but Lucy continued her chatter. "Starting a holiday is so hectic, isn't it? A dozen things to do at the last moment. There's never enough time when you have to catch a plane. And you've come all the way from . . . ?"

"*Ach*, you know how it goes, yes." She relaxed again. "I started from Stuttgart."

"The city of incredible greenness," said Lucy, "parks, forests, and mineral waters."

The woman's eyes lost their wary expression. "You are both here on holiday? Americans?"

"Canadians." Lucy's voice remained soft, but decisive.

"Oh! I beg your pardon. I know Canadians shouldn't be mistaken for Americans."

Lucy's eyes crinkled at the corners in appreciation. "My name is Lucy Trumble. I'm from Montreal. This is my niece, Dani Morden. She lives in Alberta."

"A teacher, yes?" replied the woman. "The pale skin tells me you are a bookworm, *ja*?"

Dani nodded, not sure how to politely respond to such a question.

"So! I have a sister in Canada. She is there for twelve years already. In a place called the Moose Jaw. You know it? Such a big country is Canada. Oh, I forget to introduce myself. I am—" She broke off and patted her escaping hair again then looked at her lap and fumbled for her purse. "Ah, here is our hotel. Perhaps we shall meet again."

Dani reached into her handbag.

"No, no," the German woman said, "you have been most kind. Please, I pay the driver. I insist. But please, you may send a porter for the luggage? I take care of everything here." She seemed used to giving orders.

Obedient like well-trained poodles, Dani and Lucy marched up the steps of the hotel.

The German lady's smile faded as she watched them go. She searched the street in both directions, then turned and gave brisk orders to the bellboy who appeared at her side.

The suite Dani and Lucy had reserved wasn't ready. A harried reception clerk advised them it would be at least an hour yet. He snapped his fingers at the bellboy, pointing to where to deposit the luggage, then suggested they have lunch in the restaurant.

"I can't face another cup of tea," said Dani, not caring if she sounded ill-humored. "It may be lunchtime to him, but for us, it's the middle of the night. I noticed he didn't turn away the German lady."

"She only wants a single," replied Lucy. She took out her map and pointed a finger at their location. "What about a walk? Holly Tours isn't far. We can check on our tour. After, we'll have plenty of time for a nap before dinner."

Dani brightened at the prospect of fresh air. "Hey, I'm with you."

They started down St. James's Street, crossed Pall Mall, walking down Marlborough Road toward St. James's Park. Dani gazed around and let her problems fade into the background. The multitude of noises, the swarming traffic, even the smell of gasoline fumes brought excitement. *London.* She was at the start of two weeks touring the West Country, then two weeks back in London: theatres, art galleries, museums, and history. Lots of history. She turned her face to the sun and felt the heat flood her body.

A police constable pulled her back to the sidewalk as she and Lucy were about to cross The Mall. "Look right, *then* left," he admonished, grinning with good nature. "If you don't, you'll be looking up."

They entered a path leading into St. James's Park. Ducks paddled in the lake, and people strolled along beside masses of spring flowers. They stopped to enjoy the antics of two children playing with a small terrier scrambling between their legs, barking furiously. From a nearby bench, a woman cautioned them to stay within shouting distance.

"Yes, Grandmother," they chorused and fell into a fit of giggles. Their grandmother tried to affect a stern presence, then gave up and grinned at Lucy.

"Wish I could bottle all that energy, I could do with a bit myself." She picked up a book from her lap and opened it. Dani and Lucy crossed a low arched concrete bridge, admiring the bird life and pelicans on the water. Halfway, Lucy pointed out a large building to their left, much of it hidden by trees. Dani consulted her map.

"That's the Horse Guards Parade," she said.

"Lovely," agreed Lucy. "When we come back to London, we'll take a closer look."

Thirty minutes from starting out, they emerged at Birdcage Walk and continued around Queen Anne's Gate to Tothill.

At the tour office, a middle-aged man in a pinstriped suit with a white rose in his lapel, eyed Lucy and took over from his clerk. He introduced himself as Mr. Holly, the manager, and ushered them into his private office. Half an hour later, they emerged loaded with sightseeing documents and explicit instructions regarding time and place of their tour.

The manager spoke to Lucy in steady, careful tones. The way he stressed each syllable, emphasized to Dani his doubts about her aunt's ability to manage so much information at one time. Dani's suspicion was confirmed when he whispered the same instructions to her as they left his office.

"Is that going to happen every time we meet someone?" she asked when they were outside. "How are you not irritated?"

"Pay no attention." Lucy patted Dani's arm. "They would be so unhappy if I let on that I understood them the first time. How could I cheat them of the satisfaction?"

Dani gaped at Lucy. "I can't believe I'm hearing this."

"Later, dear . . ." A puzzled expression appeared in Lucy's eyes as she studied the space beyond Dani's ear.

"What's wrong?" Dani twisted her head to stare behind her, half expecting to see Mr. Holly running after them with some forgotten folder.

"I'm sure it was him," began Lucy. "I mean, for a moment I

thought . . ."

Dani squinted at her aunt, trying to make sense of her mumbles.

Lucy shook her head as if to clear it. "Never mind, he's gone. Now, are we ready for that nap? I'm feeling the effects of jet lag. Thank goodness we still have a day before the tour leaves on Monday." Her eyes turned in the direction of the imagined sighting one last time before pushing the tour documentation into Dani's arms without warning. Dani's knees dipped as she struggled to keep the unruly bunch together.

"Lead on. I'll try to cope," she replied and followed Lucy across the street. "How come Sir Galahad never materializes around me?"

"Damn and blast." Lucy heaved up the brown case and headed into the sitting room.

Dani dropped her tour folders on the couch, startled into attention by Lucy's uncharacteristic outburst.

Lucy held up the case. "These dreadful hotel people have sent up the wrong luggage. This belongs to that German lady." She put the suitcase down and went to the phone. "First our room wasn't ready, and now this. It's too pathetic. Hotels have deteriorated in London. Years ago—"

"It can't be too far away," interrupted Dani. "Maybe the bellboy mixed them all up when he brought them in from the taxi. Hang on, I'll straighten it out. She may have even tried to return it while we were out." Dani left, carrying the suitcase.

Twenty minutes later, she was back, this time with Lucy's case. "That's what happened, all right. She couldn't apologize enough, even though it wasn't her fault. She was as shocked and surprised as you were."

"No harm done, I suppose," said Lucy, relieved. "Still, I don't like it. The name tag is plain enough."

"Well, it's not the end of the world," said Dani. "She couldn't open it without the key anyway."

Lucy averted her face from Dani's hard stare too late. Daylight dawned.

"You didn't lock it. Couldn't find the key, I'll bet."

Lucy drew herself up and with her down-the-nose attitude said, "The taxi came before I had time to lock it."

Dani put her hands on her hips, returning Lucy's indignation a moment longer, then grinned. "Well, you're lucky. As usual. She said she hadn't even noticed the switch. She took a nap the minute she got in her room. Poor thing was exhausted." Dani bent and picked up a travel folder, adding as if in afterthought, "The next time you see her, don't let on how upset you were."

This last comment piqued Lucy's interest. "Does it matter?" Dani didn't seem compelled to answer the question. Lucy persisted. "There's something you haven't told me."

"Her name is Miss Schmidt, and she's booked on our tour. We had a long talk. I tried out my German on her. It's impossible for her office to bother her if she's on a tour, and she wants privacy to enjoy her holiday." Dani paused, her smile fading into a puzzled frown. "Miss Schmidt says she doesn't know a soul in England, but I just remembered—there was an Englishman in the lobby. He knew she was German. I wonder how?"

Lucy peered into her opened case. "What was that about?"

"Well, when I asked the clerk for her room number, a man pretended to know me. He said we'd met before when I was with my friend, the German lady. I dusted him off for trying to pick me up, but now that I think about it, he knew she was German.

You don't suppose he may have been genuine after all?"

Lucy straightened. Her stare sharpened on Dani. "What did he look like?"

"In a word . . . a big freckle. Red hair, and covered in freckles." Dani dismissed him by opening a tour folder. "No. It was only a fishing expedition."

"A what?"

"You know, the old pick up routine. Hey, it's okay," she said, laughing at Lucy's worried expression. "I told him we'd met her at the airport and didn't even know her name. I offered to get her for him. At that, he decided she wasn't the right person after all." Dani bent her head to the folder, still smiling. "Some people aren't original thinkers, are they?"

Lucy said nothing in reply. For a long moment, she contemplated a picture of Tower Bridge hanging above the sofa, then switched to ponder the telephone. She sighed and decided she needed a nap.

Awake at once, Lucy stared at the ceiling. For a puzzled moment, she thought she was in her apartment in Montreal and had fallen asleep again in front of the television. She turned her head to peek at Dani, asleep in the other bed; dark hair tumbled across the pillow.

Youth. They take themselves so seriously. What's gone wrong, that the ability to laugh at themselves has disappeared? Has the world become so arrogant that humor, the one thing which breaks down barriers and binds people together, is snatched away?

Dani shifted, turned on her side to face Lucy, sighed, and slipped back into an easy sleep.

Lucy thought about the call from Helen, asking her to include

Dani in her plans for a trip to England. "Someone or something has to shake her out of the life she's living, Luce. She's intelligent but doesn't want to use it. All the time she was growing up, she buried it, to be like other girls so they'd accept her. It never lasts, and she blames me because I try to steer her to places and people she would appreciate. She's holding herself back with no purpose, and her decisions always make her unhappy. Mark my words, Luce. Someday, one of those wretched decisions will bring her to disaster. I'm at the end of my patience, and I'll go screaming bonkers soon. Please, say you'll take her."

Lucy sat up and punched at her pillow then laid back again. She hoped Dani's mood at the airport was behind them. Still, Lucy was fond of her and glad she'd agreed to Helen's pleas. Lucy yawned and inspected the small travel alarm on the bedside table. Three o'clock.

Her first feeling of something having woken her persisted. Perhaps someone in the adjoining room? Wide awake now, she stayed still and listened. Whatever it was, it wasn't repeated. Well, she may as well find something to read, or she'd lie there the rest of the night and be drowsy and irritable by morning. *And irritable is just what I must avoid on this trip*, she thought, looking at Dani again. Sighing, she fumbled for her dressing gown and slippers and headed for the sitting room.

Aided by the pale light coming through the window, she could just make out the travel folders piled on the small glass-topped table in front of the couch. Shivering, she fumbled with the lamp switch then closed the window drapes, shutting out the outside. She missed her comfortable sitting room at home, with its confused and cozy chintz.

This time, the sound was clear. A soft thump-bump, ending in a dragging scratch.

Someone was outside the door. Lucy's heart scudded across her chest. Her eyes riveted on the doorknob, she walked forward and put her hand against the door panel, peering through the small peephole. Nothing. For a moment she stood, then grasping the handle of the door, she turned the lock wincing at the small *snick* it made.

Taking a deep breath, she turned the knob and pulled the door inward, intending to open it only a crack and peer into the corridor. Her grip loosened from a solid counterbalance on the other side, forcing her back as the door flung open.

Miss Schmidt fell at her feet. Protruding from her chest was the metal-edged, black handle of a knife.

Three 3

LUCY STARED DOWN AT THE BODY of Miss Schmidt with horror and disbelief. Her mind fixated on the small amount of blood around the knife. A spasmodic movement from Miss Schmidt jolted her out of her paralysis. Lucy knelt by her side.

"Don't move, don't move," she said, touching the German woman's arm. "It's okay, I'm here. I'll get help—a doctor, the police."

"Nein." Miss Schmidt struggled with her words. "No police." Her eyes full of terror, she gave a ragged gasp. "The door—lock the door!"

Lucy scrambled to obey then returned to Miss Schmidt. "We have to call a doctor . . ."

Miss Schmidt shoved a piece of stiff paper into Lucy's hand. "You take . . . the name . . . I wrote it—you go there . . . find *Martin* . . . give him your . . . *tagebuch*."

"Tags? Oh God, I-I don't understand. What man? Who did this?" Lucy stuffed the paper into her dressing gown pocket, sobbing in her urgency, her hands fluttering around Miss Schmidt's head.

Miss Schmidt gripped Lucy's hand and closed her eyes, silent now. Lucy started to rise, but the woman's grip tightened, and her eyes opened again. She coughed, choking with pain. "Oxford town . . . you go tour. Find Martin . . . give paper. Important don't lose . . . *tagebuch* . . . you trust nobody." Her eyes held Lucy's with desperate pleading. "They kill . . . *gefährlich* . . . dangerous. You understand?" Her hand on Lucy's arm relaxed.

"Aunt Lucy?" Dani's inquiring voice came from behind, then by a strangled gasp. "That's Miss Schmidt! What happened?"

"Hurry, Dani. Phone the desk for the doctor. And the police!" Lucy turned toward Miss Schmidt again. She lay relaxed, pale eyes still staring at Lucy, their desperation replaced by puzzlement. Miss Schmidt was quite dead.

"Her name was Ida Schiller, according to her passport. You say you knew her as Schmidt?"

When Superintendent Proudlove of the London Police Force arrived, he took control of the room like a man with a foot solidly wedged against an open door. His tone was apologetic as he spoke to Lucy, but his eyes were persistent.

Dani sat on the couch beside her aunt in their hotel room. She had told Superintendent Proudlove her part, then watched as he questioned Lucy, who stared apprehensively at him. The remains of a tea tray were on the low table in front of them. Dani glanced at her watch; her eyes widened—only nine o'clock. It seemed days had passed instead of mere hours since they had taken Miss Schmidt . . . Schiller's body away. Was it yesterday she'd decided there was no chance of adventure on this trip? The thought switched to one of guilt when she remembered her pleasant conversation in Miss Schiller's room. Now, though, it was better to feel sympathy for her aunt. Her spine tingled at the thought of Lucy opening the door. She had shown a remarkable presence. One up for her. *Mother won't be able to dismiss this one.* Five years ago, at the funeral of Uncle Markham, Lucy's vague manner had worried the rest of the family. Only Dani's mother had pooh-poohed the suggestion that Lucy would be in desperate need without him, revealing that Lucy had been the drive behind Markham's fortune. *I wish she thought I was as competent.* Dani caught herself before her resentment of her mother climbed up for another feast. She rubbed her eyes and returned her focus to the room.

"I keep telling you, I didn't know the woman at all, Superintendent," Lucy was saying. "We only met when we shared a taxi from the airport. She told us she was from Stuttgart, and that's about it."

"She left no impression with you?" persisted Superintendent Proudlove.

Lucy moved her shoulders. "She was just . . . a tired traveler." Her eyes darted up to stab at the man's face. "Like the rest of us."

"You didn't think it strange that she came to *your* door last night?"

Lucy put her fingers over her mouth and shook her head. Her bewildered expression increased in intensity, her words spaced to illustrate her confusion. "I don't understand *any* of it, Inspector." Her arms spread wide to encompass the entire space. "But she'd at least *spoken* to us, so we were the first people she thought of. It really wasn't as if she asked a *stranger* for help, is it, Superintendent?"

Dani winced.

"Yes, well, perhaps," he said, blinking.

Lucy went on, her tone pitiful, "Nobody should have to die like that. In another country, among strangers."

Superintendent Proudlove contemplated Lucy. Dani couldn't tell from his expression what his thoughts might be. "Right then, Mrs. Trumble. I'll just read back your statement. If there are no errors or omissions, we'll have it typed, and I'll send it around for your signature." He held out his notebook at arm's length, reminding Dani of one of her students about to read an essay to the class.

Once again, Lucy's story of awakening, going to the door and finding Miss Schiller, was retold. "The woman fell into the room, and you saw the knife protruding from her chest. This one, in fact." Proudlove took a plastic bag off the table and held it up in front of Lucy, watching her closely.

Lucy shuddered and closed her eyes. Dani stared, fascinated. "At that point, your niece"—he nodded to Dani—"rang the desk for a doctor. Miss Schiller died without speaking." The superintendent's voice rose, suspicious, questioning.

Lucy beamed at him as though congratulating him. "That's accurate, Superintendent." In a dramatic twist, a flash of anger appeared in her eyes, her fists clenched in her lap. "That wretched coward, stabbing a defenseless woman like that! I hope you catch him soon!"

"You can count on it, Mrs. Trumble. It's fortunate he thought she was already dead. No one might have discovered her for hours."

Lucy paled. "You mean, it's fortunate I didn't see his face?"

Proudlove's expression showed appreciation, as if he knew she'd understand his meaning. "I'll send someone around with the statement later today. In the meantime, here's my card. If you think of anything, you can ring me at that number."

Dani opened her mouth, then shut it.

"You wanted to say something, Miss Morden?"

Dani shook her head, and mumbled, "It's all too frightening."

As Proudlove opened the door, Lucy called out, "Superintendent. Would it be all right if we changed hotels?" She gazed around, then shivered. "I don't like this one." Her hazel eyes pleaded up at him. "I'll let you know when we're settled."

The man glanced back at the two women with a harsh eye that softened more with each passing second. Eventually, he nodded before ducking out of the room, leaving Dani and Lucy in abrupt silence after the clunk of the heavy door.

Lucy sank against the cushions of the couch. Sighing, she closed her eyes, then opened them to confront Dani's stare. She ignored her niece's critical judgment, rose, and crossed the room toward the telephone. "Pack our bags. I'll get on the telephone and find rooms elsewhere. We should hurry."

Dani stayed where she was. "What's going down, Aunt Lucy? I want to know what you're hiding from the police."

Lucy bunched her fists, irritation plain. "Don't imagine things. My nerves are bad enough. I've never had a murder at my door before. I'm upset and not in any mood to pretend otherwise."

"Nuh-uh. I agree this is a terrible situation, but you've never had bad nerves in your life. Something is wrong here. And I think that policeman knows it. Are we in danger? Why didn't you mention the man at the airport and that she seemed frightened? And what about the freckled man in the lobby? Why would Miss what's-her-face try to reach *our* room? We were on different floors. How did she know our room number? I didn't tell her. You're hiding something, and I'm not moving until I know what it is!" Dani finished her inquisition gasping for air.

"For heaven's sake, Dani!" Lucy cried out, and sank down in the chair by the desk. Fingers shaking, she thumbed the pages of the telephone book. Her eyes became puffed like she'd been crying, but they were dry. "I've no time for explanations. We have to get out of here!"

Giving up on the fat phone book, Lucy rose and pushed Dani

into the bedroom to pack. "We will ask the cabby to recommend a hotel."

Fifteen minutes later they were standing in front of their old accommodations, the doorman hailing a taxi. The hotel manager had been as happy to see them depart as he was to see the back of the police with their cameras and evidence bags.

"Aunt Lucy. You can't keep this from Superintendent Proudlove," Dani said again, her voice clear and certain.

"I've thought it all out, Dani, and I've decided." A fixed set to her round chin, Lucy surveyed their new room at the Park Lane Hotel. "They will take our passports—keep us in London for weeks." Her tone turned wistful. "If only we had come here first. I hope the lock's secure."

Her own remarks must've put a fear in her because with a determined speed she went to the door and tested the latch.

Dani wasn't sidetracked. "But why us? Why should we take chances? Whatever it is, it's responsible for that woman's death. There may be more that we don't even know about."

"No." Her aunt returned to her chair by the window. She put her hand to her forehead as though to stifle a headache. "You see, it's that man you met in the lobby with red hair. He's the one I saw at the airport, and again in front of Holly Tours. Don't you see, Dani?" Lucy's voice sounded bleak. She put a forefinger against her lips and closed her eyes. "I could have warned her. It would have only taken a minute." She paused a moment, opened her eyes and gazed straight at Dani. "But I didn't think it was anything serious. She didn't have to die. Instead of saving her life, I took a nap—" Voice choking on the last word, Lucy dropped her face into her hands in self-accusation.

"You can't blame yourself for that," whispered Dani then, as Lucy's words sunk in, her mouth opened in horror. "You saw him following us?" Her voice rose. "This just gets worse. Maybe it was *him!* He thinks we knew her. He'll come after us too!"

Lucy shook her head, her face pale. "No, he won't. You told him we'd just met."

Eyes wide, Dani stared at Lucy and tried to think back. Surprised at first, then sarcastic, ridiculing his clumsy attempts to pick her up, she tried to bring a picture of the man's freckled face to mind. He had looked her over, feigning surprise to see her there—pretending he knew her; then, at her open laughter, he was apologetic, embarrassed almost. He backed away, his face acknowledging his clumsy pickup attempt. Surely, he was convinced of her innocence . . . ?

"I can't even go on an errand without doing the wrong thing," Dani moaned. "I shouldn't have spoken to him in the lobby. I'm getting scared." She felt her arms tingle, and she folded them around herself.

"Me too," admitted her aunt. Her chin grew hard again. "It's no matter. You didn't see her. That poor woman was so desperate. She came to us for help. She trusted me—us. How can I ignore that?"

Lucy continued, her tone reasonable, "The mention of getting the police terrified her. She must have had good reason for not wanting them involved. Furthermore, she was my age, a woman alone, and I don't like what someone did to her!"

Just like Lucy. Dodge the real issue, and pick some obscure reason like that to get involved. Dani wanted to debate further, but her throat closed up, and her jaw was so tight the words wouldn't come out. It occurred to her that she'd come bang on against Lucy's secret determination seen only by her mother. Or her dead uncle, perhaps.

"You can go home if you like," Lucy said, her tone cool, "if you think you don't want to continue."

Shocked, Dani stared at her aunt. Then shock turned to shame that for a moment, she had considered the option herself.

She held out her hand. "Let me see that paper."

At that, Lucy rolled her shoulders, straightened her back and leaned forward to pass Dani a dying woman's last wish. Dani wasn't sure, but she thought she saw a hint of a victory on her aunt's face. She took from Lucy a torn picture postcard of Christ Church in Oxford. At first glance, the tear looked haphazard, but closer inspection revealed the edges formed an irregular set pattern of curves. A curious excitement took over Dani's objections.

"The Oxford address on the back," said Dani, flipping it over again. "But how will we know this Mr. Martin?"

"He'll have the other half," replied Lucy.

Dani examined the address written there. "Like a spy novel?" She relaxed, releasing a long breath she hadn't realized she was holding. "Wouldn't a photograph be more effective?"

"Spy novels must be based on some reality. If a picture fell in the wrong hands, it would point right to the man she was to meet. But with a piece of postcard for identification, he can stay hidden. It's crude, even melodramatic, but it works."

Dani looked up from the postcard to find Lucy with the smug smile of someone pleased with herself.

Lucy registered Dani's angry flush. "It's all right, dear. I'm glad you're with me. It shouldn't be all that difficult. After all, we booked this tour months ago. What is more natural than visiting friends along the way? Besides, who would suspect us? Do we look like shady people? We'll deliver the card and settle

Miss Schiller's ghost."

Dani's mouth turned down in doubt. "Are you trying to convince me or yourself? So what about this Martin character? What happens after we give him the postcard? Is that all there is? It seems like a lot of trouble just to deliver a piece of postcard. Why not just mail it? Even you can't believe it's that simple, Aunt Lucy."

"Don't be rude." Lucy's rebuke was mild. She frowned at a point above Dani's head, looking like one of Dani's students puzzling over a date in history. "I've asked myself the same questions. But what difference would it make if we knew more? We'd still do it."

"Damn," said Dani, "I wish I felt better about this whole arrangement." She couldn't have told what feeling better meant, only that it shouldn't mean the deep but obscure unease twisting in her stomach.

I don't have the instincts of a person living with secrets. Are my fears realistic, or am I playing it safe as usual? Still, if Lucy is dumb enough to go off blind, ignoring that someone murdered Miss Schiller for the same reason, I suppose I have no choice. Dani sighed. She knew Lucy was right—they would do it.

"At least Oxford is in the first week of the tour," she said, breaking the silence. "Only five days. After that, who cares?" She took her notebook from her purse and copied the address written on the back of the postcard, before handing the piece over to Lucy.

"My thought exactly," replied Lucy, peering through the window at The Mall below. "Nothing difficult, is it? It will be a stroll in the park."

"People get mugged in parks," Dani muttered.

FOUR 4

THE MONDAY MORNING LONDON TRAFFIC moved briskly under a sunny, cloudless sky. Office workers and shopkeepers greeted each other and remarked on the unseasonably early June weather, with no rain in sight. Superintendent Proudlove hung his coat over the chair back, loosened his tie, and sat down to read his accumulated notes on the Schiller file. They were few.

The Trumble woman knew more. The signs were all apparent when he finally accepted her statement with no further comment. After twenty-five years interviewing witnesses and suspects he automatically registered the lowered eyes to hide the relief flickering there, the gentle drop of her shoulders in gratitude for relaxed neck muscles. Grunting softly, he mulled over Lucy's supposition that she had been the only person Schiller knew in the hotel. It's true, the telephone wire was yanked from its socket, but why not knock up the people next door? Why would anyone in extremity go down two floors? He could think of only one answer. To deliver a warning—or something else. He frowned, as a new thought struck him. He'd better request an interview with the commander. If his suspicions were correct, she could be in danger.

The telephone rang just as he reached for it. The voice of the deputy commander requested his presence in the commander's office.

"Now, if you will, Superintendent."

"Right." He put on his jacket, straightened his tie, and tucked the file beneath his arm before heading out the door. The deputy commander was about to retire, and Proudlove yearned to be his successor more than he had ever wanted anything else. This case could clinch his appointment, he could feel it in his gut.

At his superior's office, Proudlove knocked on the door and turned the knob at the same time. The commander was inspecting his stack of morning files and gave a nonchalant grunt of acknowledgement. While he waited, Proudlove rehearsed what he would say. The commander made several notations in a file before him then peered over his half-glasses at Proudlove.

"About that knifing, Superintendent," he said. "The German lady, Schiller."

"As a matter of fact, sir, I was just about to request an interview. Some items need approval before I proceed." Proudlove coughed into his cheeks, ducking his head toward his shoulder before continuing, "You might want to alert the commissioner if you agree with my suspicions."

The commander eyed his superintendent then removed his glasses and laid them down on his desk. "Sit down, Gordon."

Proudlove sat, sensing an atmosphere of bad news.

"The commissioner's office rang me up. Leave it alone, they said. And they'd like all the information you've got so far."

Proudlove shifted. "Leave it alone, sir? Whatever for?"

"The woman is the private secretary of a Herr Joseph Dittmahn. He's a big gun with Redstadt Electroniks, in Germany."

"You know that?" Proudlove's surprised expression cleared. "Oh. I see. The Home Office. Another matter, is it, sir? Can't we insist?"

"They've had their orders, Superintendent"—the commander's

tone was crisp—"and they have passed them along to us." He hesitated, eyeing the younger man, reading his mind and disappointment. He reached across his desk for a yellow file folder and extracted a news clipping from it. He handed it to Proudlove without comment. The item was dated July 1984.

West Restricts Computer Sales.

Fourteen NATO countries and Japan are tightening controls on the sale of computers to the Soviet Bloc, ending months of argument over which smaller computers should be embargoed. The U.S. Administration has pressed the West European governments for much tougher sanctions against the sale of militarily critical technology. Experts have maintained that desktop personal computers are just as valuable to the Soviets as big commercial models. A committee has been formed to improve the procedures for policing the abuses of embargo lists.

"That agreement establishes the authority for this." The commander handed Proudlove another file, this one with a red cover. The name printed on it read '*Schlafstrom.*' He searched his limited German for a near enough translation. *Sleeping river.*

"I needn't tell you to keep what you are about to read to yourself."

Proudlove read the two pages inside the folder then placed it back on his commander's desk. "Ingenious. How did they find them?"

"The usual way. By accident. A crate listed as containing tractor parts broke open." The commander turned his hands palm up. "Surprise, it didn't have tractor parts in it at all."

Proudlove rubbed the back of his neck, not ready to give up his case yet. "Can't we do something here, sir? Stop the shipments at their source, at least on our end, and let the Americans look after themselves."

The commander's expression chilled. After a long pause, he said, "And where would you start, Superintendent? If you wanted to find someone who was selling ordinary computer equipment to the Soviets?"

Proudlove flushed. Where would he start? He could think of several research centers right here in England. The Americans at Silicon Valley? Trade fairs? A computer retail outlet? It would be almost impossible to track a purchaser down, even more so with the embargo. What was it called? He glanced at the paper again. *Operation Exodus.* The man responsible would double efforts to maintain anonymity.

"Sorry, sir. It's just . . ." Proudlove shook his head, then pointed his finger at the red file. "They will use that agent, and those two Canadians, Mrs. Trumble, and her niece as well. She knows more than she revealed. She doesn't realize what she's letting herself and her niece in for. It's going to get sticky. They are the proverbial *sacrificial lambs.*" The thought nauseated him.

The commander nodded his head. "Nasty job, that line of work. But we can't upset their shark tank. Our job can get bad enough sometimes." He studied Proudlove's unhappy expression. "You must learn to trust them, Superintendent." He smiled, but it was an admonishment just the same.

Proudlove jerked back. "The man's a formidable opponent, sir. They will have to be right smart to catch him."

The commander leaned forward and picked up his glasses. "That's their trade after all, so they keep telling everyone. Add a personal footnote to your report, separate from the evidence. About your own suspicions on the case. Pack up the whole mess and bring it along to me." He handed Proudlove yet another file. "Here's a new suspected fraud case that I want you to sink your teeth into." He nodded and snapped his glasses over his nose in dismissal.

Proudlove returned to his desk feeling he had come out on the short end of a test. Well, it was nothing compared to what those two women would face. He hoped the man from Home Office, whoever he was, could meet the challenge.

At the office of Holly Tours, Inc., the dapper Mr. Holly, a fresh white rose in his lapel, finished up with two clients. He squired them through the door, then turned and smiled, rubbing his hands together in satisfaction.

"That's five more tourists since yesterday. It's the luxury that brings them in, Miss Drever, and people are willing to pay for it. Remodeling our buses in a train configuration, with tables and plush seats, is something nobody else thought of. Trains may be nice, but our tour buses can take you in style right to the door."

"Yes, Mr. Holly," Miss Drever replied mechanically, having heard it all before.

"There's plenty of money in the country in spite of what they say," continued Mr. Holly, jovially. "The tour industry needs new ideas to beat the competition. Just wait until every tour manager in town eats crow because they said we'd be out of business by the end of the year for taking out those extra seats." Mr. Holly almost hopped for joy.

"Those last two are a bit late," said Miss Drever. "That tour has already departed."

"They hired one of our private cars." Mr. Holly beamed full of self-congratulations. "Nice bit of work that."

"Odd, two men traveling together," said his clerk, smirking. "Not my idea of fun. One looks like he swallowed a lemon. Not someone to meet on a dark night."

Mr. Holly's smile turned into an authoritative glare. "That part is not our business, Miss Drever." He straightened the rose in his lapel, sniffed, and proceeded into his office.

Unconcerned, Miss Drever inspected a chipped fingernail and thought for a while. She took a slip of paper from her desk drawer, then after a look toward Mr. Holly's office, drew the phone closer.

"Hello, it's me. At Holly Tours," she said when she had connected. "You said you wanted any information on the tour those two women took." She listened then described the two men who rented the private car. "They particularly asked after that tour." She listened again, and said, "Yes, I will. . . . Yes, even if it's not important. It's your money, love."

At that moment, the luxury coach containing twelve passengers had just passed through the southeast suburbs of London, heading to Canterbury. Dani stared at the bus driver's head feeling something out of place. She grinned when she realized he sat on the right-hand side of the coach, instead of the familiar left.

She liked the fold down tables attached to the seat back in front of them. Someone had thought to include a cup holder and space underneath the lift top for small items like pens and maps. A bin for stowing handbags or parcels slid out from beneath the foot of each chair. "These seats are plushy. And lots of leg room." Dani had said to Lucy when they boarded, stretching her long legs out in front to demonstrate. "A good choice of tour, Auntie.

It's going to be comfy." Suddenly realizing Lucy was standing in the aisle waiting, she brought her legs in and said, "Do you want the window or aisle seat?"

Without replying, Lucy brushed past her feet to stake her claim in the seat beside the large picture window. "We'll alternate dear."

Now, bored with watching buildings as they cruised smoothly through the outskirts, Dani read the itinerary the driver had handed out, describing everything they would see and do over the next two weeks. Stapled to the back page was a list of passengers along with their nationalities. Six British, two German, one American, one Australian, two Canadians, and someone from Hong Kong. A few guesses, and she should be able to match the names with the people surrounding her. With luck one or two would be close to her age, and hopefully the rest not dull and boring. She bit the inside of her cheek at the prospect of traveling two weeks with a busload of tedious people, then felt a stab of guilt. Her eyes drifted sideways at Lucy in unspoken apology, then back to the list.

No problem guessing who owned the last name; the man now perched at the front of the bus in row two. He had arrived at the bus depot in a taxi just ahead of theirs. A tall, thin man, late thirties or early forties, she guessed. Attired in a three piece suit, vest and tie, he had the distinctive quality of a wealthy businessman on his way to an important meeting, even with the expensive camera he had slung over his shoulder. As he turned toward them, Dani saw he carried the same tour folder with the name *'Holly Tours'* across the top. He caught her looking at him and gave a wide grin with very white teeth which seemed too big for the space they occupied. Later, he had boarded the bus carrying a fat attaché case, which puzzled Dani. Why carry an expensive case which screamed out *VIP* on a tour? All it needed was a handcuff attached to his wrist. Nothing casual about the man himself, either, she thought, again studying his bespoke business get-up as he tucked the case into the seat beside him. For a second, the oddness made her uneasy, then she shrugged it off. Maybe it was the East Asian way, to dress up, not down.

She ticked off his name as likely dull, then darted discreet glances around the coach. Everybody else was examining their own itineraries. The two spinsters traveling together were easy to identify. In their eighties, Dani guessed, both sat directly across the aisle. The nearest was already asleep, white head resting against the seat back, upper plate of false teeth resting on the lower. Half turned in her seat was the other ancient, introducing herself to another silver-haired old dear behind her whose southern accent tagged her as the American lady. They seemed content to compare arthritic medication. The American woman was telling the other that she swore by a glass of brandy twice a day.

Dani ticked their names, writing a big "S" for sweet, adding an "NE" for not exciting.

Number one on the list, Andrew and Vera Brooker, had to be the couple sitting in the front seat. English. From behind, the woman looked tall and thin. Fluffy blonde hair. Her husband looked tall and thin too. As Dani watched, he pointed across the aisle through the opposite window and said something to his wife, who turned in the same direction. It was like looking at twin profiles. Their blunt noses and heavy eyes reminded her of two Staffordshire dog ornaments. He carried on talking, his words clipped and carrying a definite ring of authority. If the other half of the Staffordshire pair replied, it was inaudible. She put a tiny check beside their names, reserving judgement.

She also had no trouble recognizing the lone Australian. He had rushed up at the last minute, rumpled and breathing with a wheeze. Two cameras bounced over his spilling paunch.

"Hi, there. Wait up," he had shouted in a deep bass.

The man's pear-like figure waddled toward the back of the coach, favoring one leg. He stared straight at Dani and Lucy. For a moment, the light flashed off his glasses, turning his eyes into blank discs. It was like being confronted with a mask, and Dani instinctively flinched. In an instant, the man had passed them, sitting down near the back with a whooshing grunt.

"Now, there's someone who looks interesting," said Lucy.

Dani's eyebrows rose. "You've got to be kidding."

"Not him, dear. Number twelve. He's just arrived."

While she had her eyes on the Australian, another man had boarded the coach, smoothly taking a seat near the front. He placed a small bag next to the window and sat near the aisle.

The lone Englishman, thought Dani, guessing him at about Lucy's age. "An academic, if ever I saw one. Meritorious, nose in a book. And *borrring.*"

"Oh, I don't know," said Lucy. "He looks rather pleasant. Cherubic, with those pink cheeks. He pushes his shoulders back like he's had a military career. A civil servant now, I'd guess." She looked at her list. "His name is Weatherston."

As though aware of the scrutiny, Weatherston turned his head. Quizzical brown eyes regarded Dani, and she found herself readily answering his smile with her own. His eyes slid to Lucy, and Dani stifled an outright laugh at the familiar expression dawning over his face.

For the sheer fun of it, Dani put a checkmark in the interesting category beside his name. Grinning to herself, she turned her head to study the passengers sitting behind and gazed directly into a pair of mocking eyes. A tan from long hours in the sun emphasized the brilliant contrast between gray eyes and nearly black hair, giving his face a handsomeness unfamiliar to her. As her eyes met his, his full lower lip curved up at one corner in a half smile, emphasizing a deep cleft chin. She didn't need to guess who he was. Carl Hamel, from West Germany. Playboy type, she thought, like the rest of his kind; smooth, cynical, confident of his attractiveness. The girl beside him turned to say something and caught his inattention. She glanced around to Dani, wide china-blue eyes unreadable.

Dani flushed and gazed out the window, concentrating on the passing scenery. She had already decided Carl Hamel wasn't married to the girl beside him, even before she saw her name. Roberta Arndt. A pouty mouth and curly brown hair bunched up on one side with one of those oversized clips. Loose-fitting linen pants, baggy linen shirt tied around her slight waist. A girl bursting with healthy vitality, yet unaware of it.

Hey, watch it, you're starting to sound like Mother. Next, I'll be getting up and lecturing the girl on how to channel surplus energy for productive living. She grimaced at the thought, then stole another glance at Roberta Arndt. *At least she is independent enough to travel alone with her boyfriend. I bet she doesn't let anyone else choose her friends. She knows herself, that one.* The last made her sit up, stiffening at the unwanted thought, surprised and wondering where it came from.

"What is it?" asked Lucy, catching Dani's sudden shift in attention. Her eyes searched the space around them.

Dani leaned over the table, closer to Lucy. "Miss Schiller was booked to come on this tour," she whispered. "Suppose the killer knew? He might be here now . . . watching us."

Lucy didn't reply at once. She pointed out the window to a grand Georgian country house, willing Dani to turn and look.

She laughed as if Dani had said something amusing.

"I thought of it, dear," she murmured. "Because whoever killed Miss Schiller didn't get what he was after."

"You expected him?" said Dani, dismayed. "Just like that?" *I should have known.* For the first time in her life, Dani felt sympathy with her mother's interpretation of Lucy's character. "You sound as if being stalked by a killer is a natural side effect of travel. Like bad water and diarrhea."

"Not at all." There was no mistaking the sharp rebuke in Lucy's hazel eyes. "We must be very careful. Be tourists plain and simple. Never mention her name. For heaven's sake, Dani, stay calm!" Lucy's fluttery laugh sounded again.

Dani laughed too, hoping it didn't sound as unnatural as it felt. "Calm," she repeated under her breath. "Terrific."

"This Carl Hamel," whispered Dani, pointing to her list, "And his friend, the girl. They are both German. Do you think they might . . . ?" She left the rest unsaid and shivered.

Lucy raised her eyebrows at Dani. "German, yes. But you can't think they are involved with Miss Schiller just because they are German. I'm sure they would be worlds apart."

But Dani couldn't forget the sight of Miss Schiller lying on the floor with a knife sticking from her chest. Yesterday's doubts rose up. How close are a killer and his victim supposed to be, she wanted to ask. It sure wouldn't be engraved on his forehead. "But why should Germans choose this tour? Don't people of the same languages stick together?"

"Maybe they chose an English speaking tour on purpose, dear," said Lucy, eying Dani. "We can't go chasing after shadows, or we'll end up batty. Besides, wouldn't two Germans be a little obvious? If I were planning it, I'd pick an Englishman."

Or an Australian, thought Dani. Like the man with the

paunch and two cameras. She consulted her list. Stanley Palmer, it said. She stared at the names again, trying to see them in her original category of interesting or dull. She underlined the three names with a heavy pen; Palmer, Hamel and Arndt. Definitely interesting.

There was still one more passenger she hadn't sorted out. The English lady, traveling by herself. Her head started to ache. Forget it, she thought. Better to wait and see, meet each person with an open mind, liking them until actions decided otherwise. She was glad she wasn't on tour alone, forced to make decisions about people. Studying ten people, eleven if she included the bus driver with his customer-trained smile, was hard work. Lucy was right. She'd be paranoid soon if she let herself imagine a sinister interest in every glance.

Nervous now, she tugged the barrette free at the back of her neck, pulling at her hair with her fingers, then snapped it back in place. Keeping her face turned toward the passing countryside she concentrated on the view; at a curving river sparkling like bright crinkled tinfoil in the sun; the green meadow dotted with prancing lambs, at the rise of hills broken by tall clumps of chestnut trees, their mature leaves drooping in the humid air. The driver gave a short burst of recognition from his horn and pulled out to pass a car. Dani saw a limousine, smoked glass in its rear windows; '*Holly Tours*' stenciled on the door. Private tour, she thought and turned to tell Lucy, but her eyes were closed, head resting against the seat back. Dani returned to watching the scenery.

"Carl and I wonder if you would join us for eating . . . how you say, lunch?" Roberta Arndt spoke to Dani as they freshened up in the café washroom. They were at Hastings, where the coach had stopped for an afternoon break.

"Get acquainted," the driver had said and pointed to the small roadside café. The outside tables were placed to take advantage of the pleasant view of the coastline, complete with fishing boats. On the hill overlooking them, stood the ruins of the old Roman castle.

All that morning, at the stops along the way, the bus driver had given them plenty of time for exploring on their own. At Canterbury Cathedral, Dani's natural eagerness took over. She pulled an obedient Lucy behind her, popping off rapid-fire explanations of various tombs and treasures—"Here's where four armored knights did it to Becket"—until Lucy pleaded for mercy. She sank down on a bench in the sunny cloisters while Dani continued on. By the time the coach arrived at Hastings, Dani's tensions of the morning had turned into a contented immersion into history.

"We are the only young ones here," Roberta was saying now, as she attacked her hair with a wide tooth comb. "It is too bad. I hoped to meet other students like myself to improve my English."

Her English was already excellent, and she didn't look sad about being the only young one on the tour. Roberta Arndt wasn't the type to be sorry about anything, Dani decided. Her credulous face and round blue eyes told their own tale. Take life as it comes, they said; expect pleasure in everything.

Roberta finished dragging at her hair, and smeared her lips with a rosy gloss. "Oh well." She shrugged. "We'll find enjoyment here anyway. The country is beautiful, *nicht wahr?* And there is always something pleasant to experience in the evenings." She pouted at her image in the mirror, adjusted the yellow clip in her hair, and smiled at Dani.

"Shall we go now and have something to drink together?"

The group lingered in the sun. Conversation flowed, of nothing and everything, places and people, likes and dislikes, the earlier strangeness of the group already dissipating into single identities and personalities. At a separate table, Carl Hamel slumped in his chair, gulping a Coke. He lit a cigarette and pointed with it.

"That fellow Weatherston," he said. "He does not impress me as being compatible with the sea. What do you suppose he and that fellow from Hong Kong have in common?"

Dani gazed in the direction Carl had pointed. It was her academic and Lucy's civil servant. As usual, Lucy was right, she thought. He was typical English. The type one would always call Mister, never by his familiar name. A suit of good worsted material and excellent cut. He was standing with his back to them, facing the channel, the rolling motion of his hands highlighting his words. The breeze ruffled his salt and pepper hair, showing the larger pink area that was his bald spot.

The Chinese man with him put his head back and displayed his xylophone keys of white teeth. She could almost hear the *Log Jammer's Waltz* being hammered out.

"Now," said Carl, narrowing his eyes as he watched Weatherston through the smoke of his cigarette. "The Chinese man might just have something to do with boats, but Weatherston? His pink skin tells me he is not an outdoorsman, yet he strikes me as a person who has been around. But I ask myself, why is he on a tour such as this? He is not my idea of a typical coach tourist passenger. Do you know that Mr. Wong speaks French fluently? Weatherston as well. It is a puzzle is it not . . . Dani?" Carl sat straight and leaned his arms on the table while he smiled at her, teeth sparkling. "Dani. A pretty name. From where does it come?"

"Well, it's obvious that he has an interest in boats," said Dani, ignoring his question. She stopped herself from saying that Carl did not look like a typical tourist passenger himself. "Weatherston may stay out of the sun, but still be interested in boats." She knew she sounded stuffy, but Carl Hamel only smiled at her, his gray eyes catching his smirk and holding it even after it had faded. Her foot started to tap under the table, and she cracked the knuckles on one hand.

"And what is Dani Morden interested in?"

She told him. She referred to their itinerary, pointed to the castle on the hill, talking about Britain, explaining its magnetic attraction for a Canadian. "Canada is still an adolescent, compared to a thousand or more years of all this." She waved her arm around her. "To anyone interested in history and our personal connection to Britain's past, it can be heady stuff."

The amusement in Carl's eyes had changed to watchful concentration as he listened. Roberta looked from Carl to Dani, and back to Carl again, her expression unreadable.

"You care about your topic, don't you?" asked Carl. "When you speak of history, your eyes grow luminous. They light up your whole face. Very charming." His mouth curved upward again in his distinctive mocking smile. "Why do you live in the past? So young, and so intense. Easy to look at as well." His eyes raked over her modeled face, smooth skin with glowing undertones, and soft brown eyes.

Uncomfortable, she smoothed her skirt patterned with cool green palm leaves.

"I don't live in the past." Dani flushed. "The past helps us understand the present," she added, then cringed at her own cliché. *How I detest ignorant people. He's patronizing me, on purpose. Flirting in front of Roberta.*

"So philosophical. Never mind." He threw back his head and laughed out loud. "Anyway, there's still time."

"For what?"

"Getting to know each other." He didn't bother to turn his head as he added, "Isn't that right, Roberta?"

Roberta's eyes glinted with a brief flicker of anger directed at Carl before she nodded and smiled at Dani.

Dani returned the smile, dropping it as she turned to face Carl again. *I'll turn purple first.* She hated that she appeared old-fashioned to him—this lank, self-important brute, loose height sprawled in the chair, legs dominating all the space. "And what about you, Mr. Hamel?" she said. "Do your responsibilities encompass anything beyond pursuits of pleasure?"

"Of course," he replied, unperturbed. "I have interests in an export and import company. On this trip, we talk with the people along the way who import our products and find new products we can import to Germany for our customers there. So you see, I too expect to make this holiday useful."

"What products?"

"All various and diverse," he replied, waving his hand in the air.

"Carl's business is too complex to be speaking of it on a day like today," Roberta chimed in.

"Roberta has little patience for business." Carl reached out and patted Roberta's hand. Dani winced.

"That is so," agreed Roberta. "When my thoughts become too serious, I just lie down until they go away." Cheeks glowing, she laughed. "Not like Carl. His world is money and his work, and he says he still must make more money. He impresses many famous people in business. Why, only last week he . . ."

"Roberta," interrupted Carl under his breath. A level Dani didn't think he was capable of. "You wanted to buy postcards."

"Oh yes. I forgot." Roberta rose and went across the small

terrace into the café. Dani fiddled with the strap on her purse for a long moment, considering the girl. "And what about Roberta?"

"Roberta?" Carl said in surprise. He turned his head to search her out and found her sorting through the postcards. "She is still in university and does not work. Roberta will never work. She only attends the school to catch a rich husband. In return, she will make him a good wife, faithful, and a child every year." Carl stubbed out his cigarette and crushed the plastic can with one hand. He shrugged. "For now, she is a pleasant companion."

"Does Roberta realize that?"

Carl raised his eyebrows. "Are you now the little mother? Protecting the innocent virgin from Count Dracula?" He was no longer smiling; his eyes reflected his temper. "I suspect, Dani, you wouldn't always be a whole lot of fun to be with."

"You are telling me it's none of my business . . . and you're right." She stood, smiling at him, taunting his anger, then gathered her scarf and shoulder bag and headed to the other table and Lucy.

"Did you hear the one about the Russian who won a political joke contest?" Palmer was asking Lucy and Andrew Brooker, "First prize was twenty years." He laughed loud and long, while Lucy gazed at him with a puzzled expression. Palmer's laugh turned into a scowl as the three ancients, along with Weatherston and Wong strolled by the table.

"Did you hear that?" said Brooker. His protuberant eyes widened under his glasses. "The Chinese fellow speaks French."

"That's because he is from Mauritius." Palmer liked airing his information. "It's their second language, so he told me at lunch. Nice little bloke. Educated in Hong Kong. Not too particular about his friends though." He smirked.

That's the second person who has alluded to Weatherston, thought

Dani. "Do you know Mr. Weatherston?" she asked.

"Well, little lady, I might," said Palmer, his expression sly, "Though it isn't bloody likely he'll want to remember me."

"Long ago, then?" asked Dani. Odd, though. He was Australian, and Weatherston was English.

"Not long enough," said Palmer. His knuckles rapped against his leg, making a dull sound.

Lucy leaned across the table. "Oh, do tell us, Mr. Palmer," she said in her best old gossipy pensioner voice.

"Ah, I can't go spoiling your holiday now can I, little lady?" His hand squeezed Lucy's and lingered there. "Much better that people don't know what kind of hero is driving around with them," he added, in the same tone which natural rumormongers use to imply the opposite.

Lucy withdrew her hand. She reached for her bag lying on the table and made as if to rise. "We'll be late if we sit here much longer."

"Right-o. Here, let me help, little lady." He fussed over her chair, heaving awkwardly up on her arm to help her rise. His hand gripped the strap of her bag, just as her own closed around it.

"Feels like bricks," he grunted.

He pulled, and as Lucy resisted, let it go, conceding to her protests. The bag dropped to the ground.

"Aw, blast!" said Palmer, "I'm a clumsy sod."

To prove it, he bent to pick up her bag, and his large hands managed to turn it upside down spilling the contents. First, a souvenir package of coasters from Canterbury dropped to the ground, followed by numerous other articles.

"Leave it, Mr. Palmer. I'll do it," said Lucy, bending in front of him. Palmer's hands fumbled amongst the contents. Dani didn't see the postcard, and she gave a thankful sigh of relief.

"Just a moment, here's something else." Palmer bent with some difficulty, reaching between the chair legs. "A book." He turned it over in his hand and grasped the cover. "What's the title?"

"If you don't mind," chided Lucy, snatching the book from his hand. "It's personal. A travel diary if you must know."

Palmer turned red and apologized again, mumbling, "Thought it was a story." He retreated, leaving Lucy to sort out her handbag.

"You should keep your bag zipped up, Aunt Lucy," said Dani as they headed back to the bus. "I'm sure that was deliberate."

"Awful man. And he keeps telling the ladies he can read palms. It's just an excuse to hold hands." Lucy sighed. "Rather pathetic really. I think he's just very clumsy."

"He could be after the postcard."

Lucy only glanced sideways at Dani and smiled.

"What did you do with it, Auntie?"

"Later, dear. I think the bus driver wants us."

He was waiting at the rear of the coach. Everyone else had climbed aboard.

"Mrs. Trumble?" he said, grinning as they came near. "Enjoying the tour, then? If you need anything special, just ask. Our manager, Mr. Holly, insisted that I look out for you and your niece."

Dani stifled the urge to laugh. Remembering the manager's fussy anxiety, and she could only just imagine his instructions. He expected Lucy would get lost, and their late return to the bus no doubt reinforced this warning in the driver's mind.

Dani examined the driver's open, friendly expression. It would be a decided advantage to have a friend in case something went wrong. The feeling that she could depend on him relaxed her, and she took an easy breath.

Still basking in her self-assured calm, Dani looked forward to their next stop near Lewes to inspect a fifteenth century original Tudor house.

It happened in the parking lot after Dani and Lucy had gone through the noble private house. Impressed, Dani lingered over each one of the Old Masters collection, an early Gainsborough pastoral. Lucy went on ahead, in search of a Boulle marquetry cabinet listed in the guide.

Outside, Dani searched for their tour bus among the many parked in the lot. She spotted its wide red band and Lucy standing at the far end waiting. Another group of tourists, led by a guide, straggled across in front of her.

A small boy detached himself from the group and ran toward Lucy. As he passed, he reached up and snatched at her handbag. Lucy screamed, and held on to the strap. Dani leaped forwards, at the same time raising her own voice in a determined yell to attract attention. Suddenly, she felt a tug on the shoulder strap of her own bag. Before she could react, the strap slipped from her grasp, and another young boy sped off in the opposite direction.

"Stop that boy!"

Chasing him, a series of impressions flickered over her mind—the frozen postures of curious people, Lucy now laying on the ground, skirt up, wrestling in a determined tug of war with the boy over the strap of her bag.

"My purse," Dani yelled again, still sprinting.

The boy dodged around coaches, between and around people. *Why isn't anybody doing something? My God, people are actually making way for him.* The boy increased his pace, and so did Dani. The thought of her passport added a needed spurt of adrenaline, and she gained on him. The boy scrambled behind a bus but reappeared, struggling in the impressive grip of a tall, broad-shouldered man.

"Thank goodness," panted Dani.

Pressing her hand to her ribcage, she leaned against the side of the bus. "I've heard of disinterested bystanders, but until now, I've never believed it."

The man handed over her bag then peered at the boy, still trying to pull free. "Alright kid, take it easy. You aren't going anywhere."

American, thought Dani.

Dani patted her bag, hugging it to her, then straightened up. She had forgotten Lucy.

"He's got a partner. He's after my aunt's purse. Over there." She turned back just as Lucy, followed by an interested group of people appeared, an anxious bus driver, Palmer, and the Brookers among them.

Other than a torn stocking, Lucy looked none the worse. At the sight of Dani, she smiled in relief. Holding up her purse, she waved the broken strap. "He gave up and ran off." She regarded the boy, who had started to sniffle.

"Shut up, kid," said the American, his tone casual. "Somebody had better call the police."

At that, the boy struggled harder. "Let go of me! It was a joke. He said it was a joke!"

Dani studied the boy with renewed interest. He was about twelve. She tried to decide if his frightened eyes were innocent.

The boy hit upon Lucy's maternal expression, and his voice took on a whine. "Honest, lady, we didn't mean any harm. I've never done anything like this before."

"Are you going to fall for that old story and let the brat go?" said a man's disgusted voice from the crowd.

"He's just a lad, having a bit of a lark," said another.

Brooker's authoritative voice spoke up. "Catch them while they're young, I always say. Teach them what's what, or they will graduate to murder before you know it."

The American took a firmer grip on the boy's arm, turning him around to face him.

"Now, kid," he said, giving the boy a shake. "Who said it was a joke? Is he here? Can you point him out?"

The boy searched the crowd. "He gave us a quid."

"Which man? English? A tourist?"

"Dunno. Not an American like you, sir." The boy talked fast, lest he worsen his predicament. "He had red hair. He isn't here now, sir."

Dani's grip tightened on her handbag. She threw a shocked glance at Lucy. Lucy showed no sign she'd heard.

"He said he wanted to have a trick on them. He told me they would laugh when he explained everything to them." The boy's mouth trembled, then he squared his shoulders. "It's the truth, sir. We was to meet right behind this bus. Only, there was you instead."

"Who brought you here, son? Have you come off a bus?"

The boy's fright increased. "Me Mom, sir. She's in the hall, *Pleeeease* don't tell her. She'll tan my hide, she will."

The American stared hard at the boy, pondering. Then he looked up at Dani as if for a verdict. "I think he's telling the truth. I've got one like him at home, and I can always tell when he's lying. You got any weird friends that would pull a stunt like this?"

Lucy moved closer and put her hand on the boy's shoulder, looking over his head at the American.

"It has been some dreadful mistake. It's obvious he got us mixed up with someone else." She peered around in a distracted manner and smiled, bringing sympathetic murmurs from the men in the crowd. "There is no real harm done. Shall we just forget it?"

The American loosened his grip on the boy, but not until he gave a strong word of caution and a promise. Walking away slowly, the boy reached the crowd before he gave up and dashed off to freedom. Dani and Lucy stayed behind while the people dispersed.

"You should not have let the boy go," sniffed Andrew Brooker. Vera Brooker's protuberant eyes stared, seconding his statement.

"Don't whinge, Brooker," put in Stanley Palmer. "The little lady is right. We can't stay here all day, jawing with the coppers." He and the Brookers moved away.

Lucy examined the torn strap of her handbag. "I'll have to buy a new one."

"Did you hear? It was our red-headed friend."

"There is an inordinate amount of interest in this handbag," continued Lucy serenely. "A coincidence once, maybe. But not twice, I'll agree."

"Aren't you listening? The man with the red hair—"

"Yes, I heard, dear." She gave an exasperated cluck. "He is following us. I expected he would, you know. But this is all too silly. Why this parking lot of all places? The boy couldn't escape. There isn't any place to run."

"Another fright tactic, you mean? To keep us off balance and warn us he's serious." Dani's mouth turned down. "They aren't going to give up, are they?"

"Neither are we," replied Lucy.

"If I were after someone, I'd keep out of my opponent's way until she let her guard down, then grab the postcard."

Lucy smiled up at Dani, her expression agreeable. "On the

other hand," she replied, "I'd have someone frighten my opponent to distraction and offer my assistance at a crucial moment when it couldn't be refused."

FIVE 5

"WHAT ARE YOU HAVING?" Mavis Griffin asked Dani. She peered at her menu, a frown creasing her forehead. "Beef?"

With difficulty, Dani brought her attention back to the dinner table and fellow diners, away from the view of the Brighton seafront, superb in the evening sunset. The last rays of sun glinted off the stalagmitic domes of the Royal Pavilion.

Mavis Griffin was the lone English passenger. A middle-aged, straight up-and-down figure of a woman. Nervous lips gave the impression she just *knew* that sometime during the day she'd be called upon to explain herself.

Dani remembered her standing on the platform with the Staffordshire twins, Andrew and Vera Brooker, and then taking the bus seat directly across from them. Deciding that she and her nervous behavior wouldn't survive any casual acquaintance for long, Dani and Lucy had concluded that Mavis Griffin must be a relative of the Brookers. Now, seeing Vera Brooker's bulging eyes staring coldly at the woman, Dani deduced Mavis was Andrew's relative and not his wife's.

Mavis stroked at her short hair as if to keep the pieces down and scanned her menu again. "Oh dear, I don't know." She decided on lamb, smiled apologetically at the waiter, changed her mind to chicken, then back to lamb. The waiter skipped away as Mavis began to look doubtful again.

Stanley Palmer came into the dining room, looked around the room and spotted the group. He approached their table and stood for a moment, staring down arrogantly at Weatherston, who paid him no attention. Palmer muttered something under his breath and headed for a small table at the opposite end of the dining room. The implication was obvious. He ordered a beer in a loud bass voice.

That should be great good for his gut, thought Dani. *But, at least he's changed his wrinkled shirt and left the cameras behind for once.*

Wong went past the dining room door then backed up and came inside, looking around.

"Hey, Philippe," shouted Palmer, waving his hand. Wong looked uncertainly at the group and then joined Palmer, shooting an apologetic glance over his shoulder. Weatherston lifted one shoulder an inch and gave him a sympathetic smile. The last three were the spinsters traveling together and their new companion, the Southern American lady. They smiled greetings at everyone, seated themselves primly at the far end of the table and immediately started discussing the menu vis a vis their medical conditions. Carl Hamel and Roberta Arndt were nowhere to be seen. *We aren't exciting enough for them,* thought Dani, lifting her glass to her mouth, using it to hide her sour expression.

"The Australian," whispered Mavis, "What's his name, again?"

"Stanley Palmer," said Dani.

"Yes, well, the poor man has a wooden leg, you know. His voice was most peculiar when he told me about it. As if it were my fault."

Dani blinked. "If I lost my leg, I'd be peculiar about it too."

"I suppose so . . ." Mavis Griffin's voice trailed off. She put her hand up to her hair again then changed her mind and straightened the tableware instead.

"I was so worried I would have to share a room," she continued. "I didn't pay the single supplement. It is so often unnecessary, and I thought I'd take a chance another woman wouldn't be traveling alone. It's such a worrisome nuisance. My husband used to take care of all these things." She blinked rapidly.

Oh horrors, thought Dani. *She's going to cry.*

"Now, now, Mavis," said Andrew Brooker. He spoke as though he were used to offering comfort.

"Oh dear, I feel another headache coming on," apologized Mavis. "Do you have an aspirin, Miss Morden? I usually carry sufficient medication. In case someone needs it, you know, but I've left them in my other handbag." She laughed; a light flutter which trailed off at the end just as her speech did, and Dani had to strain to catch the last of her words. Lucy handed an aspirin over to Mavis, who choked out a thank you.

She had a twist of accent that Dani couldn't place. English, but with a slight variation of the syllables. Northern or Welsh, perhaps? Altogether, Mavis was the sort to rely on a spouse for everything. Her kind talked forever about their dead husbands as if they had only died yesterday. The waiter charged down on them, bearing the food, and Dani put Mavis out of her mind.

"More wine?" Weatherston lifted the bottle above the table, eyebrows raised in a question.

He had changed to a dark dinner jacket and bow tie. His cheeks were apple-red, his face benign above a crisp white shirt.

"I'll have one, please, Mr. Weatherson." Lucy, smiling, held out her wine glass. Weatherston obligingly filled her glass to the half mark then emptied the remainder of the bottle into his own.

I wonder when he disappears under the table, thought Dani. She looked expectantly at Weatherston, but he showed no effects from his second full bottle of wine. She glanced at Lucy, who was watching the man with a soft expression in her eyes. Dani looked from her to Weatherson and found him smiling back.

Uh-oh. Is she doing what I think she's doing? Is it real, or is she after something?

"This is your first visit to Britain, Miss Morden?" asked Brooker. He searched his pockets until he found a package of cigarettes. At a sound from Vera, he reluctantly put them away.

Vera Brooker's mouth settled itself into a prim smile. So far, she contributed nothing to the general conversation, evidently preferring to give her full attention to the buzz around her. Her heavy gaze rested on everyone in turn, making Dani feel as though she were on the wrong side of the fence at a game farm.

"Your aunt tells me you are interested in rubbings," Brooker continued. "There are still ancient tombstones in the country in decent condition. And there are some particularly splendid monumental brasses at Cobham, in Kent." Brooker took off on another round of statistics about the number and whereabouts of monumental brasses in England.

"You're remarkably well-informed," said Dani, not so much from interest, but because she felt he expected it.

The waiter appeared at her elbow with the vegetables, and she turned her attention to the food. The lamb had been rubbed with salt and spices, so the outside was crispy while the meat was juicy and tender. Completing the meal, were buttery new potatoes topped with cress and a salad of roast beetroot, radish, and orange.

After a dessert of gateaux, Brooker patted his stomach. "I read a great deal," he said directly to Dani, who after a bewildered second, realized he was still on the topic of rubbings. His eyes blinked myopically as he peered through his glasses at her. "It's gratifying to see a young person with more on her mind than designer trousers and funny cigarettes. They puff away, and all we hear are high sounding expostulations to explain a new order."

Dani opened her mouth but caught Lucy's cautioning eye. "Really?" She forced out a smile.

"You're behind the times, Andrew," interrupted Mavis Griffin. "It's a new computer age." At the puzzled glances, she waved her hands about in nervous impatience.

Andrew Brooker gave her his full attention. "Well, yes, someone would have to be deaf and blind not to notice all the attention on computers lately." He took out his cigarettes again, shook one from the pack, then at a look from his wife he rolled it between his fingers. "But what good will they be to everyday people like you and me, Mavis? One has to input to get output. Not in plain English mind you, but some other unintelligible method. If they are to be of any use, why not communicate in English for goodness sake?" In his agitation, the cigarette was beginning to crumble into flakes of tobacco.

"English is a very imperfect language," replied Dani. "Depending on the subject, the nuance of a sentence can have several meanings. I am not so familiar with computers, but I know that to get the correct result, the instruction has to be precise. And universal. So it follows that a common computer language is necessary. A language of numbers. A computer is binary, which means answers are either a yes or a no, and from there . . ." Dani saw all the faces around the table staring at her, eyes turning glassy. The three old dears at the end looked suddenly dyspeptic, as though she had stowed away on the spaceship returning from the moon. "Seems simple, really," she limped to a close.

Andrew Brooker's cigarette was now nothing but tobacco bits. He whirled them around on the tablecloth with his forefinger.

"Exactly. Just as I said," Mavis broke the silence. "Making the majority of us ripe for the picking. Haven't you noticed? A whole new culture of men obsessed with electronic wizardry and the money they can make. Stealing. They don't realize what they're doing." Her voice trailed off.

"Masterminds plotting against mankind?" Weatherston smiled at her, an odd expression on his face. He gazed into the bottom of his glass, as though surprised to find it empty.

"You may laugh, but my late husband . . ." Mavis bit her lip. The frown between her eyes deepened, and she fussed with the tableware. "I do think you are making fun of me, Mr. Weatherston."

"Not at all, Mrs. . . . ah, Griffin." Weatherston tilted his head to one side and gazed at Mavis, the expression in his brown eyes unreadable. "I just don't believe the machine age is the answer to everything, in spite of the popular vote. But, you are correct in one thing. Innocence about the application of electronics can be exceedingly dangerous."

Mavis paled and shrank back against her chair. "What do you mean?" Her voice quavered again, and her fingers plucked nervously at the buttons on her cardigan.

"They are called hackers, Mavis," interrupted Brooker. He spoke with satisfied authority. "*Wizards* who poke a few numbers into a computer and before you know it, all hell breaks loose. Or, what about new weapons? Like the war, Germany was making electronic guided bombs. Imagine. Suppose a dam were controlled by computers? These people could open the floodgates. They think it's all very amusing. Should be jailed. All of them." He turned to Weatherston. "Don't you agree?"

"A fair idea, Brooker," said Weatherston. He smiled faintly. "But it might be too costly to keep them inside. And what happens when our prisons become computerized, and your hackers only find a way of breaking out?" As though weary of the subject, he rose. "Think I'll take a turn around the block. Goodnight all." He strolled slowly out of the dining room.

Dani's eyes stayed on Mavis, who looked after him, an uncertain expression on her face. As though on signal, everybody rose and headed for the lounge, Dani shook her head at Lucy's suggestion they do the same.

"I'm going for a walk. Are you up for it?" she said.

Lucy pleaded off. "It's been a long day, dear. I'll sit in the lounge and write some postcards, then off to my bed."

Lucy walked as far as the front entrance with her. "You have your key?" She stood close to Dani, as though reluctant to see her go. "Don't be long, will you?"

"Phooey." Dani's wave of dismissal reduced Lucy's concern to the status of a pesky fly. "I refuse to let myself become a prisoner just because some lady had the bad grace to die in our hotel room. Besides, you told me to act natural."

She went through the revolving door then glanced back over her shoulder at Lucy still watching her. Grinning, she whirled in a playful half pirouette. Her heel caught on an uneven flagstone, causing her to stumble against a large, barrel-chested man. He glowered stolidly at her startled apology before rudely shoving her aside and continuing into the hotel.

"Charming," Dani mouthed to Lucy, pointing after his solid shape and rolling her eyes.

Lucy shook her head reprovingly but couldn't help but smile. She turned and marched with purpose to the elevator and pushed the up button. While she waited, she rifled through her handbag until she found a card. In her room, she went directly to the telephone and dialed the number on it.

"Superintendent Proudlove, please," she said to the voice on the other end, hoping he was still at work. Do policemen ever go home, she wondered. A long moment, and then another voice spoke. Ten minutes later, she collected a number of postcards and her travel diary and returned to the lounge downstairs, deliberately choosing a large wingback chair in the corner with its back to the room. A waiter appeared at her side, and she ordered tea.

She sipped the hot drink, wrote a few lines on each postcard and addressed them. After that, she opened her diary. The spine made a cracking sound. Lucy flexed the covers back and forth, and the sound stopped.

Gradually, the lounge emptied of people and became quiet. Lucy relaxed in the comfortable chair, alternately thinking and writing, and half-dozing until a voice intruded into her consciousness.

"A large Glenfiddich, please. What about you, Mr. Wong?"

"I would prefer tea, Mr. Weatherston. If it is all the same to you."

She heard the rustle of the waiter's feet as he disappeared.

"So, Philippe—it is Philippe, isn't it? How have you enjoyed the first day of the tour?"

"Not what I expected. Britain is a small island and many people. But the countryside is immense. So at odds, I think. I expected a crowded country. Like Hong Kong Island, yes?"

"Yes, I suppose . . ." She heard a shuffle, then Weatherston continued. "Stanley Palmer, isn't it?"

Lucy disappeared into the chair back.

"So you do remember me, *Captain*," Palmer's voice said.

"North Africa, wasn't it?" replied Weatherston, his voice mild. "And it's just been plain Mister for many years, now."

Palmer snorted. "I'm not surprised. Not since February 1943,

I bet. Round about the Kasserine Pass."

Lucy heard Weatherston's breath hiss, as though he had smelled something bad. "Facts have a way of becoming embroidered with time, Palmer."

"Facts, is it?" Palmer laughed. "That's really good." A hollow thunk sound. "This won't let me forget the facts."

There was a long silence. She wondered if Weatherston would reply at all. At last, he spoke, his voice low and calm, "In my experience, it isn't the facts; it's the interpretation that befuddles."

"You . . ." Palmer started.

The rest was lost as a party of people came into the lounge, giggling voices loud. Lucy strained to catch Palmer's words.

". . . treason doesn't befuddle," he said, his voice full of repressed rage.

"You will please excuse me," Wong's voice came next. Lucy heard the scrape of a chair. "I will come back for my tea when you have finished your conversation."

"Pick your friends carefully, Philippe," said Palmer. "Never mind, stay as you are mate. I've said what I had to say."

The waiter returned, and both men were silent for a long moment. "I apologize for that bit of unpleasantness, Wong. Something a long time ago, best forgotten."

"As you say, Mr. Weatherston. Best forgotten. We still have days ahead of us, and time to arrange to keep separate from each other. Yes?"

"Now that he's said what he wanted to say, I doubt whether we shall have any more words, Wong. Now. I have a few chores to take care of. Good night." Lucy heard a loud gulp as Weatherston drank his whiskey and then silence.

"May I sit with you please?"

Lucy looked up to see Wong standing before her, holding his

cup and saucer.

"Yes, of course. I was rather hoping I hadn't been noticed, Mr. Wong. It would have been embarrassing for me to get up and announce my presence, so I just hid like an eavesdropper." She smiled at him, shuffling her postcards and looking a tad confused.

Wong sat down and grinned happily at her. "You were very discreet. I only saw a flash of movement and knew someone was there. Only later I saw your hand and one of your cards and guessed it was you."

Lucy smiled back and maintained a relaxed manner. Most people in that situation between Weatherston and Palmer would have been glued to Palmer's statements and Weatherston's reactions. Perhaps even probing for an explanation from Weatherston. But Wong had not.

"What parts of the tour are you most excited about, Mr. Wong?" Lucy asked, sounding him out.

Wong sat back and thought. "The cathedrals, of course, are interesting, but too many takes away appetite, yes? One must be polite, but none of them are much different from the last one." Wong laughed again as if to apologize. "But I am waiting for when we will go to Oxford. There, I will have many opportunities to photograph buildings."

Lucy's throat tightened. Strange, she thought, how one's senses are heightened to hear warnings when everything is merely normal.

"You have a particular interest in Oxford?" Her heart sped up an extra beat.

"A famous university town," replied Wong, taking a sip of his tea. "With famous colleges. One library is rich in Eastern manuscripts, I am told. I always am jealous of those who go to the University. I am a poor orphan, born on Mauritius. I work hard on boat and then move to Hong Kong. There it is more hard work, but better prospects, and I become businessman." In his eagerness to explain himself, his English had taken on a kind of sing-song. "But Hong Kong returns to China soon, so I must prepare and spread out business interests before it is too late. I take a look to Oxford. Perhaps I will send my most favored nephew there. I have no wife, and I look upon him as son. . . ." Wong stopped abruptly about his nephew, and smiled an apology as if speaking of his family were impolite. His cup made a faint clink as he replaced it in the saucer. They sat in silence for a moment, his eyes still on her face. "Your niece—she is also intelligent, I think."

Lucy paused to find her bearings at the sudden change in subject before answering, "Hideously clever." She opened her bag and looked inside, taking a moment to collect herself. "Perhaps too much so. It has always put her on the defensive with her peers. But she is an excellent teacher."

Now why am I telling Wong something like that, she asked herself. She studied his cheerful face, handsome really, brown eyes assessing her in return. Guessing his age at about forty-five, she wondered what life had done to him in his rise from poverty. She remembered the feel of hard calluses when he shook hands with her. Yet, he spoke in a way which indicated more education than a poor orphan raised on a fishing boat would seem to have. She frowned at the enigma he presented.

"She stays in the home with her parents?"

Lucy nodded, a bit bewildered at his question. Surely he could see that Dani was not a child. "With her mother."

"That is good," he said nodding to himself. "Even in Hong Kong, young girls dare to live on their own before they marry.

They name it freedom, but truly they wish to escape the responsibility of family life." He shook his head, expression sad. "There is a proverb which say, *'That which is escaped now, is pain to come.'*" He turned to her, his black eyes somber, impenetrable. "To ensure a safe future, it is not wise to take a tiger by the tail." His teeth flashed again. "But I am disrespectful. You are older and wiser, and you have already learned that."

His words hung in the air like a warning. Her amusement disappeared and a chill enveloped her. Dani was right. If only they knew why Miss Schiller was murdered, the motive might point the way to a suspect. And they knew *squat* about Miss Schiller, as Dani would say. She gazed thoughtfully at Wong who was beaming at her, respectfully waiting for her to speak. Could his business interest possibly be connected to Miss Schiller? She tried to keep her expression bland as she struggled to read his face for hidden meaning.

"It is difficult to know about children, Mr. Wong. In the extreme, being sheltered from the world can hinder. Especially in our culture. When it comes time to leave home, she—the child, is suddenly expected to act with an experience and astuteness that has never been allowed to develop, you see."

Wong made a steeple of his fingers and regarded them meditatively. "Culture could make life difficult, I agree. But fortunately, I am Chinese. We are taught to face life as it is, I think. Of course, we have the advantage, as we are a civilized people."

"Well, China has had umpteen thousands of years to accumulate a thorough knowledge of life." She gave no returning smile but gazed at him with intent. If he had any connection with Miss Schiller, he would know she was aware of his warning.

He smiled, acknowledging her statement. "You are most

generous and kind, Mrs. Trumble," was all he said, leaving her unsure if he were only being polite. "We have had a pleasant conversation, and I hope we have many more opportunities to talk in the days to come." He stood and bowed formally, then put his hand out to help her rise. "And now may I escort you to your room?"

"Just to the front lobby, please. I must see if Dani has returned from her walk."

At the porter's desk, she dropped her postcards in the mailbox, trying to make sense of their conversation, then made for the front entrance. So far, things were progressing smoothly. She decided she needn't tell Dani just yet about her telephone call to Superintendent Proudlove.

Six 6

DANI WALKED BRISKLY ALONG the seafront, thinking about Mavis Griffin. A fussy person, timid and insecure, Mavis's attack on the computer generation had had an uncharacteristic ring. Though she didn't know enough about her to say for sure. Had she detected an undercurrent there? Had Weatherston really been referring to computer hackers when he had spoken? Application of computers can be dangerous. But how? Whatever he meant, it had frightened Mavis. Dani tried to remember what she had said, specifically.

Head down, hands thrust deep in the pockets of her sweater, Dani walked on. She passed few people—a middle-aged couple strolling arm in arm; a young man carrying a throwing stick for his Doberman. The Doberman started for Dani, curiosity in his trotting run. The man called him back and passed her with only a quick glance. She rounded a bend in the sea wall, deep in her thoughts, trying to make sense out of the jumbled information that had come their way so far, and the attempt to steal the handbags.

She sensed rather than saw the darkening sky. Turning her head, her eyes searched for the lights of the hotel. The hunching shapes of grassy knolls on her left, and the black swell of the sea on her right told her she had come too far. A gust of moist wind whipped her hair across her face, and she turned back the way she came; toward the bend in the sea wall. There it was quiet; the only sound was the sea lapping gently against the rocks below the concrete wall. Even her own footsteps were muted by the sponge soles on her shoes.

She hadn't gone far when she began to feel uneasy. Rounding her shoulders to make herself smaller, she gave sidelong glances at her surroundings, but her anxiety remained. There was no reason, she told herself. She was quite safe. To prove it, she gazed out to the sea and stopped to take a calming gulp of the salty air.

But she wasn't mistaken. When footsteps sounded from the direction she had come, she held her breath and waited. Whoever it was had stopped too.

I'm imaging things. She turned and began to walk with cautious steps toward the bend in the footpath, head turned to the sea, listening.

There. A scrape of a shoe against a loose stone. The man with his dog? She stopped and peered into the darkness behind her then over to the grassy knoll on her left. No, not that way. The grass would muffle the footsteps. But where could he be? She narrowed her eyes looking behind. Where had he come from? Had she been so unaware that he had passed her unseen, waiting for dark to make his move?

"Hello?" she said.

The footsteps stopped. She waited for a reply but heard only the sound of the surf rolling against the beach, now behind her. Fear gripped her chest. She turned and walked faster. The tempo of the steps from behind increased with hers. The bend in the walk was coming nearer. She broke and ran, mouth open, frantic, imagining a black form closing in, hand reaching out for her.

She turned the corner, eyes searching out the lights of the pier in the distance. She would never make it. Two paths stretched ahead of her, one going to the pier, another down toward a glass covered bus shelter, a shorter distance. Farther on, the road led to a row of houses. Dani chose the conspicuous path. At the bus shelter, she deliberately kicked her foot against the metal paneling covering the bottom third of the glass then dashed back the way she'd come, across the walk to the water. She leaped off the five-foot wall and crouched down in the sand below, flattening herself against the concrete. The surf rolled in, lapping gently at her shoes.

She felt his presence before she heard the footsteps, moving quietly now, stopping every now and again to listen.

Dani hugged the wall and bent her head, breathing softly into her folded arms. She heard him walk away from her and toward the bus shelter; she imagined him stepping inside. Her mind searched the corners with him. Suddenly, she knew he was above her, listening. Lifting her head, she looked up and almost sobbed aloud with relief when no face peered back at her over the wall.

His shoe scraped against the edge as he came closer.

Go toward the road where the houses are. Please. Go toward the houses.

Then suddenly, he was gone.

Dani stayed where she was, crouched in a heap, knees wobbling with released tension. Bit by bit, sensation drifted back into her body with the moving tide. Finally, she crept along the sand, still hugging the wall until she came to a rock that she used to scramble up to the walk again. Once there, she started to run, not bothering to brush herself free of sand. A figure loomed up at her out of the darkness, and she skidded to a halt.

Carl.

"Trailing around after me, Mr. Hamel?" she said, her voice sharp as she intended.

He nodded agreeably. “I had nothing better to do. Besides, it isn’t a good idea that you walk around in a strange city by yourself.”

“I managed quite well,” she retorted. Was he baiting her? Sweat-sodden hair stuck to her face and she flicked her head to the side to remove it. She realized how she must look and took off at a fast pace down the walk.

“Hey, don’t fling your hair at me that way,” he said, starting after her. “Why are you always so angry? Every time we meet, I feel as though something is dangling over me like the sword of what’s-his-name.” He grasped her arm and pulled her to a stop. “Do you have to walk so fast? I’m not such a bad guy if you give me half a chance.” He stood there, grinning boyishly at her. “Let’s start over, okay?”

Dani slowed. “I’m being rude,” she admitted. “Lately, I somehow do that to people.”

Carl’s expression turned to concern. “Hey, the world can’t be treating you as bad as all that, can it?” He hung on to her arm and stared at her. “What’s wrong? You look frightened. And you’ve got sand on your sleeve. Did you have an accident?”

“It’s nothing. I tripped and fell, that’s all.” She brushed at the sand clinging to her arms, then bent and did the same to her legs. “Did you meet anyone?” she coolly asked as she straightened up. “Before I came along, I mean?”

“Why?” He sounded more than curious.

Now who’s the defensive one, she thought. She dropped her eyes before his stare, not wanting him to see the panic in them. “No reason,” she said lamely, grasping for something to say. “Just making conversation.”

“No,” he said. “Something has frightened you.” Carl relaxed, and his familiar mocking cynicism returned.

"You are frightened because you thought someone was chasing you, is that it?" He put his hand on her arm and twisted his head, trying to see her face.

Oh rats. He thinks I'm being coy, that I imagined it. She pushed on ahead, hating his assessment and hating her emotions for rising to the bait. Defiant, she managed to deliver a flash of scorn at him over her shoulder. They were coming upon a busy road now, the shadows dispersed by the traffic and lights, and the faces of people milling about. Within the bustle, her fear seemed almost ridiculous.

"Come with me for a drink, and we'll talk about it."

Dani shook her head, disengaged her arm and shoved her hands back into her pockets. "I promised Lucy I'd be back soon. I don't want to worry her." Not quite a lie. But she really didn't want to be alone with him, although she couldn't think of a reason why not.

"Suit yourself." Casually, Carl took her arm and tucked it under his, forcing her to dawdle along with him. She felt the warmth of his body through his jacket, and her arm tingled with a new sensation. She felt safe—small beside him, even though his head reached above hers by only a couple of inches. The tightness in her chest released, and she forgot she wanted to get away.

For a time, they walked in silence. She became aware of the night air, the warm, gentle breeze caressing her face. They passed two young lovers pressed close to each other, suddenly breaking away and moving on, laughing, when Dani and Carl walked by. She wondered where Roberta was.

"Roberta has gone off to spend some time alone," he said, as though reading her thoughts. "She thinks if she ignores me, I'll worry that she is angry and come after her." He laughed then shrugged, his manner offhand. "I won't, of course. But it doesn't do any harm to spend time alone. Too much togetherness is not so hot."

Dani said nothing.

"You wouldn't play those games, would you, Dani?" he said, twisting his head to read her face. "No, I don't think so. You wouldn't know how."

"What's that supposed to mean?" she asked, half indignant, half serious, wanting to know.

"You are unaware of the world. You don't know the way it operates. You have never had to live by your wits to get what you want. I don't mean you are not intelligent. But I can tell by your manner, you have led a sheltered existence." He sounded almost bitter; his voice harsh. "You make people uncomfortable."

They were coming into the hotel area; the streets were well lighted now.

A sheltered existence? Next, he'll be telling me I'm still a virgin. She withdrew her arm from his. "Why should I make anyone uncomfortable?"

"Because you remind them of their own beginnings, which makes them feel vulnerable. They worry that in your innocence, you will see through them."

Dani considered his words, then rejected them. "Nuts."

Carl threw her a startled glance then burst into delighted laughter. It softened his serious face, transforming him into something warm and amiable, instead of the cynical amusement she associated him with.

As they continued down the street, she began to laugh with him, making no effort to stop the flow. All her repressed anxieties and tensions bubbled up and dissipated into the night. Several people smiled at them; perhaps remembering their own youth and a walk along a seaside in spring, when they also laughed at nothing and everything.

"That's exactly what I mean," said Carl finally. His face sobered. He pulled at her arm, turning her to face him. "Just remember Dani. The world has no mercy for innocents."

"What are you talking about?" said Dani, her first uneasiness returning. Was he warning her?

His gray eyes continued studying her face. The breeze ruffled his hair. He seemed about to speak then glanced over her shoulder at the hotel entrance.

"Your aunt is watching for you, I think."

Dani turned. Lucy was standing at the entrance to the hotel, looking her way. When she turned to Carl again, he was gone, walking quickly back toward the sea.

"What happened to you?" said Lucy. She brushed at Dani's sweater.

"I walked along the beach," Dani began, still aware of Carl's mocking eyes. "Actually, I hid on the beach. I thought someone was following me."

Lucy halted, sudden alarm leaping onto her face.

Dani hesitated. "I'm very tired. Perhaps I imagined it." She kept her voice light, so as not to stir up Lucy's anxiety, or perhaps to appease her own, she thought wryly. "I met Carl, and he walked me back to the hotel."

Maybe the whole thing had been Carl, playing games. *I might have seen him if I'd looked over the wall. Instead, I crouched in the sand. Like a coward. If it was him, I must have looked like a fool.*

Lucy seemed to accept it. "Never mind dear, after what has happened the last few days, it's understandable if your imagination fires up." They continued upstairs. "I sent off a postcard to Helen, and three more to my bridge partners."

"You didn't tell Mother anything about—?"

Lucy shook her head and opened the door of their room. She stopped so abruptly that Dani, following, bumped up against her. Her eyes squeezed shut, and she was about to erupt, but when she opened them, she found herself looking past Lucy and into the mess that was their hotel room.

Stepping gingerly, they went inside. Dani gazed at the willful vandalism—at the vicious slashing across the lining of Lucy's suitcase. An image of the hand wielding the knife popped into her mind.

Dani threw her handbag on the bed. "Okay, I'm ready to admit it. If this is another of his let's-deliberately-frighten-them acts, then he's done a good job. Do you hear?" she shouted at the wall, not caring that she sounded out of control. "I admit, I'm scared!"

"That's a good idea, dear," said Lucy. "For the benefit of anyone listening."

Lucy's encouragement, obviously unnatural in the circumstances, was enough to bring Dani up short. She gulped and gave a nervous giggle. "Aunt Lucy, you're an inspiration sometimes. Now, what are we going to do?"

"We'll do what people always do when they've been burglarized." Lucy's own voice became shrill, as though already speaking to the police. "Why, it's an outrage!"

The desk clerk telephoned the manager of the hotel, who came immediately upon the heels of a local constable. He took one glance at Lucy and began to hum soothing phrases then sent for the hotel maintenance man, who promised to have Lucy's suitcase repaired and back by early morning.

The constable asked the usual routine questions, and upon learning nothing valuable had been stolen, relaxed his attentiveness. Finding no visible evidence of forced entry, he and the manager held a murmured conference by the door. They threw Lucy a furtive look. The constable nodded to the manager and closed his notebook. After making more consoling noises, he and the manager departed together, as if on cue.

"Did you leave the door open?" asked Dani. "It's obvious they both think you did."

"I won't even answer that," said Lucy indignantly.

Still looking doubtful, Dani began to gather their scattered clothing and other belongings, piling them on the bed for sorting. Lucy began to do the same, paused, then turned on the TV, upping the volume. At Dani's questioning eyes, Lucy put her fingers to her lips in a shushing motion. Dani's shocked face, asked the question for her. Had they put a listening device in their room? A bug?

Lucy resumed piling their belongings on the bed, looking decidedly pleased. "Well, at least he didn't get the postcard," she said, voice soft.

That brought Dani upright again. She spread her hands apart in a silent question. Lucy smoothed the wrinkles from her blouse. "Oh dear, I wish I hadn't forgotten the adaptor for my iron." She avoided Dani's sharp gaze.

"You've lost the card!" Dani sat down heavily on the bed, leaned on her elbows and threw back her head. "Why me?" she asked to the air at large.

"Don't be so dramatic," said Lucy. She bent close to Dani and whispered, "I mailed it to myself. Before we left London. It's gone to our hotel in Bath."

Dani sat up and started to laugh. After a few seconds, it became uncontrollable. Lucy waited patiently for her to stop.

"Why didn't you tell me?" said Dani as soon as her fit allowed.

Lucy averted her eyes, face pink.

"I can't be trusted, is that it?"

"Not at all," said Lucy like a single mother assuring her child the divorce was not her fault. "I just wasn't sure what you'd say. You've been strained—not happy for some time, I think."

"Even so . . ." Dani began to move restlessly around the room, picking things up off the floor, setting a lamp upright.

"Would you like to talk about it?"

Dani turned to look at Lucy, opened her mouth and shut it tight again. *How do I begin to explain always feeling like I'm in the dark—like I'll never get there?* She shook her head. "I don't know what to say. Just that I'm so blasted angry all the time."

"I've noticed," replied Lucy, with an encouraging smile. "But at what?"

Dani tugged at her hair impatiently. "At everything. Mother mostly." She stared at Lucy, eyes wide and dark.

Intuitively, Lucy deduced what Dani wanted.

"No, I'll not agree with you, Dani," she said, suddenly weary. "Helen may understand more than you think. Why, she even . . ." Too late, she stopped short of what she wanted to say.

Dani's eyes narrowed. "Oh, God. This trip was her idea."

She stared down at her hands, to the dress she was savagely bunching. It was blue, form-fitting with polished beads sewn across the bodice, held up by slender shoulder straps. A type she had never owned before. About to pass it by, she'd decided to try it on. In the mirrored dressing room of the boutique, looking beyond the glass, a host of expectations welled up. But when she modeled it for Edward, he had smiled at her saying it wasn't in her nature to chase excitement. *He expects I'll come home and say it was just a trip, nothing exciting, ho-hum.*

"You see us as just a comfortable old couple, not about to

change, is that it?" she had asked, and he had laughed, saying, "I love us the way we are. You can share your adventures when you come home."

"I should have realized. I *really* should have." She laughed harshly now, aware she might not only be speaking of her mother. "Couldn't she at least have let me make one decision on my own?"

"You did, my dear. You're here, aren't you?"

"I let her talk me into it, you mean." Dani's mouth turned down. "So how did she convince you?"

"If I hadn't wanted you with me on this trip, I would have said so," replied Lucy firmly. "It's insulting to tell me I'm not happy with the idea. I am." Lucy smiled, trying to ease the strain between them. "Dani, just think for a moment. I've known you since you were a baby. If you had not wanted to come on this trip, nothing on earth could have dragged you here. You remind me of a two-year-old who insists on tying her own shoelaces, and when it doesn't work, she blames someone else because she hasn't learned yet. All of us need a push at one time or another."

"More shove than push," Dani said. "I want to follow my own instincts. So why can't I do that?"

"Because you're intelligent, and intelligent people hate to be wrong?"

"I don't want to talk about it anymore." Face averted, Dani went back to sorting out toiletries. "What have we let ourselves in for?" she mumbled, expression bleak.

Only half believing that Dani was referring to Miss Schiller, Lucy said, "In our case, ignorance is definitely not bliss." She paused gazing around the room, her small figure looking somehow vulnerable. "Tomorrow morning, I'll ask the bus driver if there were any passengers who registered late for the tour.

Then perhaps I'll phone Mr. Holly for a complete rundown on each and every one of them. That's what the police would do."

But early the next morning, when they boarded their coach, they were greeted by a new driver.

"Good morning, everyone," His voice rang with hearty cheerfulness.

Young, his blue company uniform pants fitted tight to his thighs. He had a slight accent, which Dani couldn't identify. He ran his hand over his short-cropped brown hair and held the microphone as though he were about to sing a show tune.

"My name is Gerald Jeffries. I'm your new driver, replacing Nigel who is ill." Jeffries laughed and held up a hand, palm out. "Don't worry. He'll be okay in a few days. It's the old flu bug, that's all. So you'll have to put up with me—your guide and friend of last resort. With God's help, we won't get lost." He paused, eyebrows raised, inviting laughter. It didn't come.

Lucy glanced around. All faces showed only curiosity.

Except Carl's. He scowled, fury displayed all over his rigid posture.

As the coach started on its way, Lucy stared at Gerald Jeffries's back, wondering if Nigel's sudden sickness was the real thing. But then, why wouldn't it be? Her eyes lifted to the driver's mirror and met Jeffries's own. They locked on each other for an instant before he turned his attention back to the road.

Lucy's plan to call Holly Tours rose in priority.

SEVEN 7

IN BERLIN, A CESSNA CITATION II/SP CORPORATE JET bearing a black Gothic 𝔅 logo circled overhead and lined up with the runway of Tegel Airport located in the French sector. The lone passenger gazed down at the city, his eyes mechanically following the line of the Berlin Wall, dividing the city. Shadows fueled by scudding clouds, flickered over the cracks and crevices of the wall as though searching for an escape route to freedom in the West. Not for the first time, the man's mouth twisted in silent ridicule. A tribute to Hitler's thousand year Reich. Leaving half a world hostage under the Russian flag, and the once-great city divided into four administrations. If the people of Berlin banded together and pulled down the wall stone by stone, would the American, British, French and Soviet foreigners leave Germany? Would the Russians care enough about that hideous symbol to start a war over it? He grimaced, dismissing futile thoughts as the plane descended.

The jet taxied past a row of hangars and halted not far from a building with the name *Bennig* displayed in large letters across the front. The door of the plane opened, and the folding steps smoothly dropped. First, the pilot emerged, followed by the man carrying a briefcase. As he hurried across the tarmac toward a waiting limousine, the wind whipped a shock of brown hair back from his head, etching his cadaver-like face. The pilot watched the limousine driver say a few words to the man before handing him a package, touch his hat brim, and open the rear door. The pilot made his way to a white Audi displaying the same black logo and drove off toward the airport operations building.

Inside the limousine, the thin man spoke briefly into a telephone. "I suggest we meet. I will come directly to the house." He hung up and gave the waiting driver directions.

"Choose a quiet route please Hans, where the traffic will be scarce. I need time to examine these papers before we arrive at Grunewald. Perhaps the Havelchaussee road?"

"With pleasure, Herr Hoeffner."

Hoeffner waited until they had left the airport and crossed the bridge over the river then opened the envelope and drew out several pages. He sifted through them and started to read, making notes in the margins. After a time, he lifted his head from his papers and stared blankly at the scenery for a long moment. They traveled west along the valley following the Spree River on his right. Far to the left, he noted the outline of the Bell Tower of the old Olympic Stadium. Satisfied, he returned to the papers on his lap. The valley gave way to trees and parkland, and as the late afternoon shadows deepened, they had left the French zone and entered the British. Just as the limousine came upon a long private road in the Grunewald vicinity, he returned the papers to the envelope and stuffed it into his briefcase. At a set of tall wrought iron gates, the driver inserted a card into a box, and the gates slid open on an electronic track, disappearing long enough for the limousine to proceed through before they came back together with a faint *swick*.

The limousine continued along a curved driveway, between double rows of beech trees, to a house of gray weathered stone and stopped under the portico. The driver got out and held open the limousine door. The passenger exited the car without so much as a word or nod to the driver and hurried up the wide steps. In the entry hall, he nodded unsmilingly to the butler who took his topcoat and continued up the broad, curving staircase.

The study on the second floor of the house smelled of cigars, polishing wax, and leather. The thin man strode directly to an enormous black walnut desk and laid his briefcase on the top. He shrugged his shoulders as though to dispel tiredness then turned to face a wing-backed leather armchair at the far side of the room and greeted the man sitting there.

"Hello, Paul," said the man. His finger in his place, he closed the book he was reading. "You had a good trip?"

"Yes, Friedrich, thank you." Paul Hoeffner stood straight against the desk. His face showed no expression. "The flight was uneventful."

"You had no trouble in Vienna?"

"Dittmahn's death has raised much . . . curiosity," said Paul. "There was a visit from a customs official, and a policeman named Mueller."

"Mueller," nodded Friedrich Bennig. "Ah yes, the fat man from Stuttgart. He was here, as well."

He smiled when Paul's taut eyelids momentarily flickered.

"You are surprised I granted him an interview." Friedrich dismissed Mueller with a wave of his hand. "It is of no matter. He can do nothing. A mere peasant, on a fishing expedition. How did our man in Vienna react?"

"Unfortunately, he has begun his own search for the microfiche. Of that I am sure. What I am not sure of is whether he knows who killed Dittmahn. And the Schiller woman for that matter. He hides information well. But if he is involved he must believe we are vulnerable."

Paul went behind the desk and sat down. His hands moved restlessly over his briefcase. "Friedrich," he began but stopped as the other man held up his hand, commanding silence.

Bennig rose at last and walked across the room, taking his time. He placed his book neatly in one of the two bookcases flanking the marble fireplace. A tall man, with hair still dark and combed straight back from a widow's peak, he held himself with a military bearing that created an air of elegance. His body had that carriage as though it resented anything but the most expensive clothes.

He turned to face Hoeffner. "So. Chetkov doesn't like our chess game, and now he will begin his own, hoping to leave us with a checkmate. It is too bad we cannot just cut him out. His hasty action trying to track the stolen equipment made Dittmahn suspicious in the first place. However, we must save his neck if we are to save our own. . . . At least, for now. You have the dossiers?"

Paul reached into his case and took out a slim folder. He opened the folder and extracted a sheet of typewritten paper.

"Mrs. Lucinda Trumble, nee Manley. Born Calgary, Canada," he read aloud. "Age fifty-eight, five feet three inches tall. Widow, now living in Montreal. Generally, she is considered a helpless woman; flighty and absent-minded. Finances; stable. Married Markham Trumble in 1946, after the war. He was a squadron leader in the Royal Canadian Air Force. He built up a successful paint manufacturing business from nothing. Died five years ago. No children. The woman has one older brother, Louis Manley who lives in Toronto. He is in the insurance business. Her father, Thomas Manley, English. The mother, Lucinda Marie Dressler, German.

"Ah," said Bennig. "Does the woman speak German also?"

"There is no indication."

"Is it possible she knew Ida Schiller?"

"Negative."

"And yet, the Schiller woman died in the woman's hotel room. And she was booked to travel on the same Holly Tours excursion. . . . Coincidence, Paul?"

The slit that was Paul's mouth widened. "It does happen from time to time. However, I am inclined to agree that Schiller slipped the documents to the woman or her niece."

Hands clasped behind his back, Bennig paced in front of the desk. "Since the microfiche was not found with the Schiller woman, we must assume she handed it to someone. It is logical to assume that these two women possess it. Mueller's visit tells me the police do not have it. What of the girl?"

Paul chose another sheet of paper. His flat monotone continued. "Danielle Morden. Commonly known as Dani. She calls the woman aunt, but in reality is a second cousin. Her mother, Helen Morden, is Mrs. Trumble's cousin. Their fathers were brothers. The girl is twenty-five years of age, five feet nine inches tall, lectures in Canadian and English history at a local college. Does moderately well, but teaching seems a stopgap until she moves on to something else." He shrugged at the other man's raised eyebrows.

"An opinion my source says is reliable." Paul scanned his report again and continued. "Her intelligence is superior. She is fluent in French, German, and speaks Russian passably. She is studious and has few close friends. Possibly because she is considered immature in spite of her intelligence. She lives with her mother and is seen frequently with a young man named Edward Pierce. He runs an accounting and consulting practice. We were unable to conclude if this is a serious relationship. If it is, she might confide in him, but . . ."

Bennig waved his hand. "Enough, Paul. Let's concentrate on the girl for now, since she speaks German. It is possible she does not trust the aunt and is hiding the document without the aunt's knowledge. I am troubled that the girl speaks Russian. There are too many coincidences. A girl with a '*superior intelligence*' might collect the missing pieces and fool us into thinking she is innocent. What did the search reveal?"

"Nothing. It was thorough and purposely destructive to force a reaction. Our agent says the girl shows signs of resenting the aunt. He believes fear will increase their dissention, and they will panic and show their hand."

"Ah, we shall see. If one of them has the microfiche, they will suspect the arrival of their new bus driver. They will phone Holly Tours to make sure he isn't a plant."

"I'll take care of it, Friedrich. There is one more thing." Paul drew a slow breath then continued, "The new bus driver. I believe he serves two masters."

Bennig stopped pacing, stared hard at Paul, then sat in the armchair. "You are worried the situation is becoming uncontrolled." It was a statement, needing no answer.

Paul's expression did not change. The tight skin around his eyes gave them a curiously flat appearance.

Bennig rested his head against the back of the chair and with a small sigh of impatience, closed his eyes. "You and I have faced worse crises than this, Paul. You must not blame yourself. We were both aware of what Chetkov was when we began this project." He opened his eyes, then pursed his lips before adding, "However, the risk stirs up the blood, does it not? And pays well?"

"But the new embargo," insisted Paul. "Our enemies will be

after us now with a vengeance. They must know that Chetkov is Russian Intelligence. GRU."

Friedrich Bennig shrugged, rose to his feet once more and went toward the door. His hand on the knob, he turned to Paul. "Issue instructions. If the microfiche cannot be found, your agent must seek out and eliminate every possibility of anyone else finding it. If he lives up to your belief in him, he will be able to make it look as though the Russian is to blame. I'll allow two days, no more. By then, the police will have their eyes on the women as well and close in on them. In the meantime, step up the shipments to Vienna." He turned and opened the door.

Alarm flickered in and out of Paul's eyes. "Do you think that's wise?"

His employer paused then softly closed the half open door. He turned, expression calm, but the rebuke in his eyes was clear. "Relax Paul. Two things you should consider. They will expect a guilty man to stop or slow the shipments immediately. Increasing them will catch them off guard. They can do nothing without proof. Also, the group of countries who imposed these sanctions did so at the request of the Americans. Soon they will realize the agreement cannot logically continue. They will halt the embargo, and the venture will no longer be profitable for us." His voice remained casual. "As for Chetkov, kill him. And whether our agents find the microfiche or not, we cannot take the chance that these women know too much." Bennig shrugged again, a slight lift of his shoulders, indicating he had all he needed and no further interest in a discussion.

"I'll leave you to it, then. You'll stay for dinner? We will have a game of chess later." Bennig left the room, leaving Hoeffner staring dead-eyed at the closed door.

EIGHT 8

THE MORNING PASSED UNEVENTFULLY. Chasing white clouds flying across the blue sky, the bus continued on toward Chichester, turning inland after passing through the old walled city, across the South Downs toward Winchester. The coach straggled through villages, their stone walls dressed with old-fashioned flowers—foxglove and harebells. Rounding a curve in the road, the bus suddenly emerged into the open, displaying fields bordered with yellow gorse.

At various stops, they mixed with plodding tourists, every shape and size, rubbernecking with glazed eyes at cathedrals and castles. Bored guides held up umbrellas, drawing their charges along like iron filings to a magnet.

"Come on," said Dani at last, as they got off the bus at Winchester. "There's lots to see here." She eagerly linked arms with Lucy. "Winchester was the capital of England when . . ."

"Can't we just look, dear?" interrupted a tired Lucy. "You're beginning to sound like Andrew Brooker."

Dani let out a strangled sound and shuddered. She had been about to start on a discourse of Saxons, Danes, and Normans. "Sorry, Auntie. Sound a bit like a school field trip, do I?"

They hung back from the rest of the group in the Great Hall of Winchester Castle.

"Let's eat lunch today by ourselves," Lucy whispered while

pointing to a hanging of King Arthur's legendary Round Table fixed in the wall. "We are supposed to see King Alfred's statue then. We can break away, and I can telephone Holly Tours."

"Ask him what happened to the other bus driver while you're at it."

Twice during the day, Lucy had recognized the solid figure of the man Dani had bumped into the night before in front of the hotel. He appeared to be traveling alone, for he stayed separate from any group. She spotted him again as they went for lunch.

He was standing in front of King Alfred's statue, hands behind his back, staring at the bronze figure with studied persistence as if it were a duty. In spite of the warm day, he wore a top coat. It did little to hide his massive build or powerful shoulders.

Dani snickered. "I bet he makes bombs in his spare time," she said, losing interest and turning away.

Before Lucy could follow, she noticed their new bus driver stroll up and begin to speak. The big man wasn't pleased with the encounter. Startled, he glanced at Jeffries then around the street. Lucy had time to turn to a shop window, still watching through the reflection in the glass. The man shook his head and stabbed his finger against Jeffries's chest, punctuating his sentences. Jeffries shrank back, then replied. Abruptly, the man turned hard and stomped off.

Lucy searched for Dani, saw her turning the corner and bustled to catch up. They spotted a small cafeteria along the street and right in front was a telephone booth. Dani went inside the cafeteria to find a table and order lunch, while Lucy stepped into the booth. She sorted out some coins and dialed a number from her address book. "Mr. Holly's been called away on a business trip," said the girl who answered. "He's arranging a special tour for a large group, and the organizer demanded his personal attention."

"Then I don't suppose, dear, *you* can tell me anything about our *new* driver?" Lucy said, keeping her voice small and curious, like a proper little old granny.

"No, ma'am, I'm afraid I can't be of any assistance in that respect. Mr. Holly always assigns the drivers himself, but I'm sure he won't be a problem." The woman added an assuring, high pitched "Alright, love?"

Lucy hung up the phone and walked into the cafeteria to join her niece.

"I've quit believing in coincidences, Aunt Lucy. Every time we raise a new balloon, somebody pricks it." Dani leaned across the lunch table, her voice tight. "We should leave. Make excuses, and take the train direct to Bath. We can pick up the postcard, then start for Oxford."

"No, Dani," said Lucy, almost in a whisper. "We're safer in a group. If we run, it will be the same as saying we have the postcard. They know who we are, but we'll run blind. We won't have a chance."

"So what do we do instead? Sit around and grow feathers?"

"You do pick up picturesque language, dear." Lucy sipped her tea and took a bite from her cheese sandwich then speared a pickled onion with her fork. "These pickles are very nice. My father always had a jar of English pickled onions kept in the house. Eat your lunch dear. You can't think if your mind is sagging with hunger."

Dani threw her aunt a glare that could have shot a songbird out of the sky. Her feathers unruffled, Lucy took another bite of her sandwich, chewing it thoroughly. "I think we are overlooking an important item."

"Only one?" asked Dani, her mood sour now.

"Let's be logical and review what is new. First, we now know that Miss Schiller's enemies are aware she was booked on this tour. Second, we know she was going to Oxford to meet someone who was her friend. Her enemies may or may not realize her ultimate destination, but I'd guess they don't. Conclusion? If Miss Schiller's enemies know about this tour, then we can assume Mr. Martin does too."

That drew Dani's attention; she straightened. "Yes, of course. One of them has to be on our side!"

"It's possible, dear."

Dani slouched back in her chair again. "But how do we find which one it is? We could approach the wrong person."

"Yes, Dani, I know." Lucy's eyes were penetrating. "I don't have any illusions about how dangerous this is. Miss Schiller's murder is enough proof for me. We're safe only as long as they aren't sure whether we have the postcard or not."

"Well, then," said Dani, her own eyes bright, "we can only wait and watch." She stabbed a fork into a tomato wedge. "Who are the prime suspects?" Dani counted on her fingers by jabbing the fork at each in turn, "Mr. Wong is Chinese—his name can't be Martin, can it? Anyway, I don't think he's involved." She saw Lucy's expression change and stopped.

"You don't agree? Something that I should know?"

"Yes, and no. I don't think he is involved, but we spoke while you were out having a walk. He is very interested in Oxford. And you."

"Me?" Dani raised one eyebrow and lowered the other. "Whatever for?"

"I'm not sure. It may be just curiosity about North American women. He says he's looking for someplace to live when China takes over Hong Kong. Any businessman would be wary with

China on the horizon." Lucy couldn't stop a delighted grin. "Or maybe he's wondering if you are single."

"Stop it, Auntie. He is a little on the old side for me, don't you think? What is he? Forty? Fifty? Whatever. I hope you told him I am not on the market?"

"Don't worry, Dani. We can only hope his interest in Oxford is confined to buildings and museums. Who's next on our list of suspects?"

Dani took a minute to think. "How about the Brookers? She is a woman who says nothing, while her husband thinks he knows everything. Mrs. Brooker only stares with her buggy eyes as if we were the main attraction at a zoo. We have Mavis Griffin, a fussy insecure woman. Then there is the Englishman who likes to knock back his drinks." Lucy cocked her head at her, so Dani added, "Weatherston, in case you haven't noticed. Oh yes. There is also Palmer the Australian. He has something against the Englishman who drinks too much. I wasn't aware such weird people existed until now."

"I knew an alcoholic," said Lucy, unaccountably. "But it was a sham. People always ignored him. Acted like he wasn't there. Markham said the man—I can't remember his name—picked up business secrets that way. It appeared unproductive to me at the time. Fooling people, I mean. Now I'm not so sure." Lucy wiped her fingers on her napkin.

"You think Weatherston only pretends to drink?"

Lucy sighed. "I'm only suggesting that things are not always as we see them." A smile played around her mouth. "You haven't mentioned Carl and Roberta."

Dani frowned. "He was with me when our room was trashed." She thought for a moment, then added, "Maybe it was to keep me away from the hotel? Or am I barking at shadows, thinking everything people do has a sinister purpose."

"He's good-looking, don't you think?" persisted Lucy.

Dani shrugged. "He's smooth alright, but he uses Roberta. It is a contemptible thing to do. Maybe she likes the virile chauvinistic type."

Dani thought of Roberta with her pleasure-seeking manner and bright blue eyes, and then she remembered the flicker of anger in them before Carl sent her off to look at postcards.

"Good Lord, Dani, what are you suggesting? Treating a girl as a convenience doesn't necessarily paint him a murderer."

"I don't . . . know what to think," replied Dani. She shook her head. They needed a clue. An image of the killer. "If only we knew why Miss Schiller was murdered."

"Undoubtedly because her employer gave her something just before *he* was killed," said Lucy, fiddling with her teaspoon.

"Agh, no." Dani's mouth dropped open, leaving her gaping at Lucy. "Was he murdered too?"

"I thought it might be plans for secret electronic equipment. The company Miss Schiller worked for deals in electronics. Computers mostly."

Dani made an incoherent sound, crumpled her napkin and threw it on her plate. "Isn't it time you trusted me, Aunt Lucy? Are we a team or not? I can't just keep blundering around like a half-wit, you know."

Lucy made a vague wave of her hand. "In the muddle over our room, I forgot to tell you. I telephoned Superintendent Proudlove. Miss Schiller worked for a company called Redstadt Electonics in Stuttgart. They deal in computers."

"Computers again?" said Dani. "Did he say her murder is connected to her work?"

In the midst of swallowing the last of her sandwich, Lucy

could only wave her hand. "Either he doesn't know, or wouldn't say." He had cautioned Lucy not to play games and withhold information; warning her it might be too late. She had declared her innocence. It was only that Miss Schiller had mentioned a sister in Canada, and if she contacted the employer, she might learn the sister's address. "He did give me information on her employer, though."

"Oh sod it," said Dani, mouth turning down in disgust. "This is becoming nothing but a guessing game."

Lucy began in a rush, "It was obvious Superintendent Proudlove was telling me that Ida Schiller's employer was murdered for something the killer didn't get. And that Miss Schiller had it with her when she arrived in London."

"Where she was stabbed to death," finished Dani rudely. "And are we next in line?"

She rose abruptly, her meal only picked at. "I'm starting to speak of murder in the same casual way I talk of blowing my nose or something. Come with me to the museum. It might confuse the enemy if we behave like ordinary tourists. And I really am interested in looking at their collection of medieval and prehistoric pottery."

"I think I'll just roam around a bit, dear. I'll meet you back at the coach."

On the street, Lucy watched as Dani disappeared around the corner toward the museum then turned and meandered in an ambiguous direction, crossing the street when it suited her and peering into various shop windows. She stopped to watch a young girl with odd-cut hair richly colored in strips of magenta and green, window-dressing a dummy. The girl was having trouble attaching one of the mannequin's arms. Rolling her eyes and smirking at Lucy through the glass, she finally left the arm at an unnatural angle. Lucy laughed, gave her a thumbs up then continued along the street, relaxed and enjoying her moment alone.

She passed a computer shop, and curious, backed up to examine the layout in the window. There was a sign advertising the Sinclair ZX80 up against a small white box with blue keys. To Lucy, it looked like a boxed-in typewriter. A brand new Commodore something or other promised the user *'only a day to gain a new friend,'* and essentially the best thing since pockets.

Lucy peered through the window at the customers ambling around inside, gawking and handling the various displays, clerks beside them pointing out the features. Were they really the best thing since pockets or were they just a fad item, truly useful only in certain occupations? Maybe in a business organization, but would only gather dust in a house after the novelty wore off. She was about to move on when she recognized Wong. He was speaking to another Chinese man, this one much younger. The nephew he'd spoken of? Both of them moved off to one side as if wanting to remain unnoticed. She just stood there, in full view of anyone inside and watched. Wong said a few words, waiting for a reply, then traded his briefcase with one that looked exactly the same. Any second now, he would look up and spot her watching him.

Gasping, she hunched over and moved on, speeding around the corner, confused thoughts twirling in her head. Another computer connection. Or was it just chance? What was Wong's real purpose on this tour? What was in the briefcase he never seemed to let out of his sight? Clearly, he wasn't keen on anyone in the group seeing him with the other man, or what he passed over to him. The whole scene was out of the ordinary.

She stood at a street corner amongst the crowd until the traffic light changed then crossed the street and walked aimlessly along. She finally hesitated by the window of a camera shop. Entering, she asked the clerk for film and turned and smiled at Mavis Griffin who was biting the insides of her cheek, utterly lost.

"It doesn't take long to run out of film, does it?" Lucy said as she accepted her change from the clerk.

"I buy postcards, mostly," said Mavis. She ducked her head nervously, frowned, clutched her package, and headed for the door.

"I always waste film," Lucy continued, following her. "Are you going back to the coach?"

"Oh." Mavis peered at her OMEGA digital watch, gold with black face. Not new, but very pricey; just another thing out of place on Mavis Griffin. "Are we late?" she asked. Her anxious frown implied that if Lucy were contemplating a return to the coach, they must be late.

Lucy shook her head. "No, no, there's really lots of time. How about you and I get a cup of tea while we wait?"

Mavis reached up and stroked the short pieces of her hair, looking doubtful.

"There's a tea room right here," said Lucy, indicating a shop, whose cozy red checkered tablecloths peeked invitingly at them through the window. "I didn't have much lunch," she hinted, gamely willing to swill in a bit more tea. She put a light touch on Mavis's arm, gently persuading her through the door.

"The start of a tour is the worst," she continued once they had given their order. "I'm always afraid I'll miss something, so I take pictures of everything, just in case."

She reached across the table, patted Mavis's hand and giggled, poking fun at herself. "One English meadow after another. Who can I show them to when I get home? The fields don't look any different from our own country fields."

"Yet you are organized," said Mavis. "Each time you take a picture, you make a note in your travel diary."

"My late husband taught me that trick." Surprised by Mavis's observation, Lucy put up a hand to her ear and pretended to tighten the post on her earring then leaned easily into her chair looking relaxed and ready to chat. "My travel diary is the only link to my memory of England. When one gets old, heaven forbid, there's not much else to do except dust off our old memories."

At that, Mavis visibly relaxed. Her forehead smoothed out. "Memories are what's left when everything is gone," she agreed. "The time I was a girl in school was the best time of my life. I didn't realize it then, of course. How could I? I could hardly wait to be out of school." She frowned at Lucy then laughed self-consciously. "Eager to begin a new adventure."

Lucy stared at Mavis, mentally trying to bridge the gap between a young woman on the brink of carefree adolescence, and the image presented now—anxious adulthood in an unbecoming shade of green. Mavis's bleak eyes didn't mirror any consciousness of Lucy. The hand holding the tea cup was frozen in mid-air, her blank expression a mirror of someone locked inside a shadowy back view of time. A moment later it was gone, and she took a sip of her tea. "It's a pity, isn't it? I married late in life. We had no children. Then happiness snatched away." She put down her cup and blinked rapidly several times. Her eyes gradually refocused on Lucy. "It's a mistake to trust life—or even people. I confess I'm angry, don't you see? It wasn't fair."

This conversation is turning into incomprehensible madness, thought Lucy. "I know what you mean. We, the ones left behind, never do think it's fair," she said, gently patting Mavis's hand again. "It's not all bad, though. Relatives can be a comfort. It's obvious that Andrew and Vera Brooker care for you."

"You don't understand." Impatience and annoyance flickered across Mavis's eyes.

Lucy opened her mouth to ask what profession Mavis's husband had worked in, but before she could ask, Mavis tapped the crystal of her OMEGA. "Blast. It's one thirty. And now we *are* late." She fumbled for her handbag and hurried from the tea shop.

Lucy paid the bill and ran after her, but Mavis had disappeared. She searched the length of the street, then the other side.

Directly across the road, in front of a news magazine shop, two men stood talking. One man slashed his hand through the air in short, emphatic jabs to capture his companion's attention. Lucy forgot about Mavis, not wanting to believe the sight before her. As it always happens, when someone is watching, Weatherston glanced up and spotted her. Aware he had lost Weatherston's attention, the other man turned, and Lucy's breath caught in her chest. Unable to hide her shock, she stared directly into the eyes of a man with red hair and freckles; the man who had watched Miss Schiller at the airport.

NINE 9

THEY REACHED BOURNEMOUTH by late Tuesday afternoon. Lucy, tired and pale, stood by the window, looking down at the street. Dani watched, worry creasing her forehead. Her aunt had been uncharacteristically subdued all afternoon. Ever since lunch, Dani realized. On impulse, she apologized for her abruptness during their meal, but got no reaction.

"Aunt Lucy?" she prompted. Still receiving no reply, she said it louder, adding, "are you deaf?"

Lucy sighed and turned her head. "Yes, I suppose I might be getting that way. Some days are worse than others."

"What?" Dani said. "I never noticed." Was deafness one of those things she put on when it suited her? Like being helpless, or pathetic? She opened her mouth to challenge her.

"Do you think Wong has anything to do with the computer industry?" Lucy's voice told Dani she wasn't really interested, only curious.

"Who knows?" her shrug indicated an unspoken *'who cares.'*

"Nothing really." Lucy stayed looking out the window. "I saw him in a computer store this afternoon with someone else. I wondered, that's all."

"So what? It's a growing business. Everyone wants one." Lucy didn't look at her but stared fixedly through the window. "What are you looking at?" Dani came up beside her and peered through the glass. Finding nothing unusual, she turned back to Lucy who had one hand on the curtain; her eyes were blank, looking inward.

Dani leaned a shoulder against the wall, examining Lucy's face and reflecting on the information about Wong. He seemed so insignificant, uninteresting, but was it really that simple? This morning at Salisbury Cathedral, Wong had surprised her. They could see the cathedral spire on the Plain far before they reached it, and they were all remarking on the view from the windows. Jeffries pulled into a siding and stopped the bus. Everybody piled out with their cameras.

"The tower is leaning over, is it not?" Wong remarked.

Everybody looked at Wong and then back to the spire again. Weatherston positioned his thumb in front of his face and inspected it, one eye closed.

"I do believe you are correct," he said, and looked again. "About four degrees I'd say. Very observant, Wong."

Now, Dani said to Lucy, "Wong is surprising, isn't he? He notices things other people don't."

"He traded his briefcase with the other man and told him to guard it with his life, and their future depended on it." Lucy muttered from the window. "It could matter."

"You were close enough to hear what he said? Did he see you?"

"I don't think so. I saw them from outside."

Dani blinked, wrinkling her forehead in confusion. The conversation was rapidly becoming unintelligible.

"Okay," her tone was patient. "But you heard what Wong said." *Right*; she bit her tongue.

"I read his lips."

"Is there no end to your talents, Auntie?" Dani didn't disguise the mixture of surprise, disbelief, and sarcasm in her voice. "Too bad you can't read minds as well. It would come in handy."

"It's not that I'm proficient at it, Dani. But because I am getting deaf, I've tried to overcome it by watching people's lips."

Lucy switched her position from one side of the window to the other, her back to Dani, and sighed heavily.

What is wrong with her? What I said about reading minds was rude and should have provoked a response. Lucy was behaving like a pet dog tied to a post waiting for his master to come out of the store, and Dani opened her mouth to say so.

"Palmer accused Weatherston of treason," said Lucy, her voice listless, eyes looking at nothing in the street. "A man who has faced a charge of treason can become bitter. And a bitter man makes me wonder what else he might become involved in." She paused, face pale, absently winding and unwinding the blind cord around her finger.

"What are you getting at?"

"Motive. Why he might be involved with Miss Schiller." Lucy smiled weakly. "Not that it matters now, but I thought he was, well, nice. I thought both of them were nice. Wong and Weatherston."

"Aunt Lucy," whispered Dani savagely, "I feel like I'm pushing water uphill with a broom. I swear I'll shake you in a minute."

Lucy dropped the blind cord and turned to look at Dani, misery written all over her face. "I saw Weatherston with the freckled man today at Winchester."

"Oh rats!" Dani grasped the reason for Lucy's frame of mind. She reached out, seeing an unexpected side of her aunt. *Why, she's really crushed,* Dani thought. *It isn't only that she has always thought her judgement infallible, either.* Dani stared at Lucy, seeing her in a new light. Her heart sank. Did she have romantic ideas about

Weatherston?

"Maybe it's about time we admitted that we've no idea what we are doing," said Lucy now. She shivered and crossed her arms, hugging her chest.

"Come on, Auntie," Dani whispered, regretting her earlier sarcasm. She should have realized. "In London you were so resolute."

"It's different now. He knows we've realized who he is."

"It works two ways. Knowing our enemy is the same thing as knowing who to avoid. The important thing is that it also makes it much easier to find the person who is on our side."

"Look." Dani led Lucy to the couch, gently pushing her to sit. "Let's give things a shove. Carl and Roberta asked me to go with them and Jeffries to a cabaret tonight. Maybe I can find out something useful."

At the mention of Jeffries, Lucy sat up straighter and told Dani about seeing Jeffries and the big man in front of King Alfred's statue. "I think that man is following us in the Holly Tours limousine."

Dani pulled at her earlobe, expression doubtful. "Now who's chasing at shadows? Sounds perfectly ordinary to me."

"He's followed our exact route. And I don't trust Gerald Jeffries. Carl was also upset when Jeffries turned up." Lucy paused, remembering Carl's unconcealed anger at the sight of their new bus driver. "I'm sure that Carl knew Jeffries before this trip. It's the only explanation for his reaction."

Dani nodded, and pressed her lips together while she thought. "Well, they will both be at the dance tonight. I think it's important that I go. Everybody is bound to be relaxed, and I just might learn something interesting."

Dani's lightened tone—eager to get on with planning their

next move—finally cracked Lucy's mood. Her aunt darted a penetrating stare at her, alarm beginning to dawn. At the same moment, Dani realized that in the past day, the personal dynamics between them had shifted. "What's gotten into you Dani? I imagined you'd be the first one to agree with me we might be in too deep. A few days ago you wanted to go home."

Dani had the grace to blush. "Truthfully? A few days ago, I thought I'd rather be at the dentist having my all my teeth drilled than be here. But now?" She shook her head. "Now you share your thoughts and ideas with me, which means you accept that we are in this together. Besides, isn't it a bit late to back out?"

Lucy only tugged the sleeves of her sweater down and pursed her mouth.

"I'm right, and you know it."

Reluctant to give in, vexation crossed Lucy's face. "Young people think they are immortal, and there's the rub."

The music was quadraphonic, frenetic, and pounding. The walls were plastered with space age fantasy posters. Mirrors were strategically placed to reflect colored lights that whirled across the room and bounced off the bobbing heads on the three meter square dance floor. Someone in a silver pantsuit, his face painted dead white, in stark contrast to his brilliantly colored punk hair style, appeared through the smoky haze. He passed Dani and disappeared into a similar crush of bodies pushed up against the bar, all looking like a bunch of groupies from the bar scene in Star Wars.

Dani sniffed the sweet smoke and wondered if she had made a mistake after all then laughed out loud at the idea of what Lucy would think, or if she would even know what the odor was.

Carl caught her eye and grinned. Jeffries opened his mouth and shouted something. She pointed to her ear and spread her hands helplessly, shaking her head and shrugging. He gestured toward the back where Roberta was already headed, hips happily undulating to the beat as she went. Dani followed and sat beside Roberta at a small table.

Carl moved in close and put his mouth to her ear. "Are you sure you want to stay?"

"Of course. What else?" Dani shouted and flapped the back of her hand at him, as if waving away a pesky mosquito.

Carl's lips formed a reply, but Dani turned away, laughed and raised her arms over her head, moving her shoulders and snapping her fingers. Carl shrugged and went off to the bar, returning with drinks for her and Roberta, ignoring Jeffries. They drank for some time, deafened by the music and watching the antics on the crowded dance floor under shifting strobe lights.

Jeffries waved his arms at her, caught her attention, and lifted his eyebrows inquiringly, pointing to the dance floor. She grinned her approval, and took his outstretched hand. They joined the bump and grind for a time, then broke with the crowd to form a ring around the small floor while an exhibition of break dancing started. The throbbing music went on, more beat than music. One dancer, his sleeveless T-shirt setting off knotted biceps, balanced horizontally over his hand, testing the theory of gravity to its last degree. He whirled off center and fell to the floor, drunkenly trying to find a fixed spot to focus his glazed eyes. The other dancer reached out a helping hand amid the laughing cheers of onlookers.

The sudden halt to the music made the silence more deafening than the noise.

"Drink?" said Jeffries, his voice booming out. He shot an embarrassed glance around then pulled her toward an empty space at one end of the bar. The rumble of conversation in the room increased in volume.

Jeffries ordered two pints of bitters from the bartender, then turned to Dani and leaned one elbow on the stained oak countertop and came closer. "Enjoying yourself?"

Dani nodded, examining him curiously. It was the first time she had paid any real attention to him. It struck her that nobody would ever pay Jeffries a whole lot of attention, or else would quickly forget him the moment he left. Their drinks came, and she turned her back to the bar, facing outward at the people around them. She looked away while Jeffries paid.

"Have you worked for Holly Tours long?" She accepted the thick tumbler from him and stared to the bottom of the glass while she nervously took a long drink. It had an odd after taste, bitter like the name. The second mouthful was better.

Jeffries shook his head. "My summer job. It's only a temporary situation until I get enough money to finish school."

School? She studied him again. His face looked mature. His chin line had already begun to blur. A bit old for school.

"What's the name of the university? Where you go?" She took another gulping swallow.

He named a school. "It isn't a university. High tech. Computers, that sort of thing. I'm aiming for a post at Silicon Valley in America."

"Is everybody I meet involved with computers?" Dani rolled her eyes, asking the whole area at large.

"It's the future, Dani. You, me, Carl. Anyone who wants to get ahead. We're all competitors."

"Leave me out of it. But why Carl?"

"Sure, didn't you know? You just mentioned him."

"I did?" asked Dani. Somewhere in her brain, a dim caution reminded her she wasn't used to drinking so much.

"The one who is involved with computers." He smiled at her confusion, patient, sociable. "You just said everyone you meet is involved with computers. I assumed you meant Carl." He touched her elbow. "Come on, bottoms up, love."

She drained her glass while he signaled the bartender for another round.

Unable to stop herself, Dani said, "I didn't actually mean Carl. Somebody mentioned a company called Red something-or-other. They make computers too." She frowned, puzzled. "Or do they? Or are they only agents or something? Know it?"

"No, but then I'm not likely to, am I? Who told you?"

Dani opened her mouth, and let it hang there then closed it. She felt giddy. "One of the people at dinner last night I think, or was it two nights ago? Hackers. They were talking about hackers." She spoke too emphatically trying to cover her slip.

Surprise, then doubt, showed in his eyes. He raised both brows but dropped one along with his smile, clearing his throat.

He whisked her glass away from her, half finished, and gripped her arm. "Come on. You need some air."

The rest of his words were lost as the music started to shrill again. His hand on her arm, he was pressing her along through the crush of bodies. The noise was a confusing mixture of music and voices, pounding in and around her head. Her body didn't seem to want to do what her brain told it to. She felt like laughing. She did, a high giggle. He pulled her through a doorway; a cool breeze tickled her face, but in a vague, unreal sort of way. She stumbled down some steps, and Jeffries stopped to help her up, pressing himself against her.

His voice breathed into her ear. "Just a little farther, love. The car. We'll rest a bit."

She pushed at him, protesting but with no strength. His grip tightened. He pushed her up against the car, holding her there while he opened the back door. Then she was being forced. Too late, her brain registered a warning. She half fell onto the seat.

Suddenly Carl was there—*where did he come from?*—wedging between her and Jeffries. "You're a fool," he shouted at her. He dragged her to her feet. Dani giggled.

Angrily, he pulled her close. "You talk too much."

"For crying out loud, give me a break, Carl." She pushed him away, twisting her arm against his grip. "Let me go."

Jeffries came up behind Carl and jumped on his back. Carl shook him off, lifted his arm and connected with Jeffries's cheekbone, forcing him into Dani, who fell with him.

That was *very* funny. She giggled so much her stomach cramped, then she managed to get to her feet. Rid of Carl's hold, she stumbled around the cars toward the stairs and back into the club. She looked around, spotted a door marked with the glittering figure of a woman and headed for it. Inside, she bathed her face, letting the cold water run over her wrists.

Feeling better, she gazed at herself through the mirror and straightened her mussed hair. She needed lipstick and automatically reached for her small purse which wasn't there. What had she done with it? She had it at the bar, so she must have dropped it when Jeffries tried to stuff her into the back seat of the car.

At the door of the washroom, she stopped and looked around for someone she knew and spotted Roberta on the dance floor, laughing at a man Dani didn't recognize. Carl and Jeffries were nowhere to be seen. Dani imagined them still rolling around in the dirt, and she giggled aloud just as a young Chinese man peered into her face.

"Care to dance, Miss?" He bowed politely and held out his hand. Dani stared at him for a moment, thinking at first it was Wong, but this man was much younger. The bow did it. "Sure, why not? I'm Dani," she said as he led her to the dance floor.

Unrealistically, the music had changed tempos. The gyrating beat of disco drifted into a fast jazzed up Tango. The crowd cheered, grabbed partners, and the next minutes were taken up with an interpretive mix of Latin and nightclub dance. Anybody's choice and everybody's game. This was new. Dani shivered in delight. She felt herself being clasped into a close hold, right arm held out stiffly in the air, his arm around her waist so tight, her body tilted backward, and she found a pair of brown eyes smoldering into hers. Her feet followed his automatically, her body moving as though it weren't hers, like her feet were somewhere in space with her toes hovering just above the ground. The next minute, he had whirled her away in a dizzying spin, his arm acting like a tether keeping her from sweeping away. He was a magnificent dancer, and for the first time in her life she happily let someone lead her into a hypnotic pulse down the magic rabbit hole.

When the music stopped, she obediently let him take her to a small table, and still in a trance, agreed to wait while he brought her a drink.

The man who brought back her drink had aged. She peered at him, dizzy and still half woozy. "Mr. Wong? It is you, isn't it?" Blinking, she lifted the glass and took an unladylike gulp.

"I have never seen a more beautiful partner," he said. "All eyes were on you."

"What are you doing here?" Dani tried to focus on his face. Was it Wong or the Chinese dancing boy?

"You are an innocent girl. I saw the bus driver take you out of this place, and I asked Mr. . . . Carl . . . to go after you. I think that someone must always be looking after you, Dani."

She tried to look at him closely and saw only a blur. The music had started again, and the lights danced around the room in a kaleidoscope of colors in time to the crazed beat. She had the impression time lapsed while she watched from another dimension.

"How dare you pre-shume . . . how dare you watch me," Dani finally slurred. She put her glass down. How many different drinks had she been downing tonight? Then she giggled. "If you were watching me, then maybe you can lead me to my pursh . . . puurrrse. It's outshide in the car, I think. Ask Jeffries. You can fight him for it." She laughed again then felt sick. She rose, and without saying another word, weaved her way to the ladies room where she leaned up against the sink wondering where everybody was. Had they left her here all alone? Panic rose.

The door opened and Roberta came in. Her short dress, gathered loosely below the waist, sloped carelessly off one rounded shoulder. Dani almost threw her arms around her and kissed her.

"You spent a long time with that Chinese man." Roberta gave her a curious look. "That was a very, how you say, unrestrained dance? Carl was furious that you were gone so long. He sent me to find you. He is worried. Here is your bag. Carl found it outside somewhere."

"He needn't be." Dani took the purse, her words slurring over each other. Her lips felt like rubber bands slapping together, twisting this way and that. "Chinese man? Just someone I picked up. I was overcome when the heat got to me, that's all. And I left Carl and Jeffries having a free for all in the parking lot. First time anyone fought over me." She giggled again, blinking with the effort to focus on Roberta's image in the mirror.

Roberta returned her grin. Her candid blue eyes held nothing that shouldn't be there.

"Speaking of fights. Roberta, what has Carl got against Jeffries?"

Roberta shrugged and moved farther along the counter to gaze into the mirror. "They are competitors. I think it has something to do with Jeffries's boss."

"Who? Holly Tours?"

"No, somebody else. Carl says Jeffries burns too many candles." Roberta examined herself in the mirror then picked at her curly hair. "Carl is so protective. I think he is afraid I will also be burnt by Jeffries." She studied Dani's image alongside her, her face thoughtful. Roberta took a deep breath.

"Dani, don't pay too much attention to Carl," she said softly.

"You can rest ashured . . . rest asher . . . rest easy, Roberta. I don't chase men who belong to someone else."

"No, no," Roberta protested sharply and stood aside to let two girls by. "For me, I am not worried. But you don't know him. He can be charming, yes, but underneath . . . he is hard."

"Why did you come on this trip?" Dani asked, curious. "He doesn't appreciate it."

Roberta shrugged again. "I am having a good time. When he invited me, I took advantage of it, even though I know he only asks me at the last minute because another girl refused. Carl can hurt my feelings, but I am careful just the same. He can be ruthless when he wants something. I do not trust him too much." She smiled at Dani, but her eyes held a warning.

"No, I wouldn't either if I were you." Dani's head began to ache. A cold perspiration broke out on her forehead. "Tell me

Roberta, does Carl do business with Redstadt Electronics? In Stuttgart?"

"I can find out if you wish."

Dani hurriedly said no, condemning herself for asking. Roberta would mention it to Carl. "Forget I asked, will you?"

Roberta nodded, her face showing it was already forgotten. Dani pitied her suddenly. *How can Carl take advantage of her? She seems so anxious to please.* Dani's head started to pound in earnest now. A queer taste rose in the back of her throat.

"Oh," said Roberta, taking a step back. "I think you are not well. The drinks . . ."

Dani made a dash for one of the stalls.

"Here, drink this."

She heard the plop and fizz of a bromide. Dani opened her eyes and contemplated the glass that Lucy held out.

"How do you feel, dear?" asked Lucy. Somewhat cruelly, thought Dani.

She lifted her head and groaned.

"Who poisoned me?" she said. She drank down the contents of the glass, considered the results and decided she would live.

"Was it worth it?" Lucy stared at the blank expression on Dani's face. "Don't you remember anything?"

"Certainly." Dani's tone didn't sound as indignant as she wanted. "Just because I tossed my biscuits doesn't mean I was exactly swacked, you know. . . . It just needs sorting out first."

Lucy pointedly inspected her watch. "You have exactly forty minutes before the coach leaves. I'm going down for breakfast. Take your umbrella out of your case. It looks like rain." She frowned at Dani. "Do you have to take such risks?"

"*Pleeeease*, Aunt Lucy. Not now."

Dani heard mumbling that sounded like *'young'* and *'immortal,'* then the door slammed. She cringed and put her hand to her head.

When the rain came, it hung above the ground more like mist and accumulated against the coach windows in fine streams. As the coach continued east toward Exeter, Lucy thought about the torrents of rain on the prairie, washing the air clean then disappearing almost as fast as they arrived, leaving huge arcing rainbows against the far background of dark sky.

Most of those on the coach were huddled quietly into their own moods, gazing at the gray landscape with a depressing lack of enthusiasm. She could hear Carl and Roberta murmuring in German. Listening, Lucy frowned, a fleeting sense of something forgotten about Miss Schiller's words flickered across her mind. About danger? About Martin? She tried to concentrate. No, it was gone again. Her thoughts turned to Weatherston. He had stayed behind in Bournemouth. Too embarrassed to face her, she supposed, or else he had decided there was no need to pretend anymore.

"He isn't feeling well, poor dear man," cooed the smaller of the two unmarried ancients.

"Couldn't have planned it better myself," leered Palmer.

Lucy almost wished he were back on the bus with them. Better the evil you see.

"Care to share?" asked Dani, giving her a gentle poke.

"Two more days until we reach Bath." Lucy smiled at Dani's face, noting the circles under her eyes, revealing the effects of the night before. Wong had given Dani a dazzling white display when she boarded the bus. Lucy had been dismayed at Dani's lack of manners when she ignored him and took her seat. Wong looked disappointed.

"Was Wong at the dance last night?"

Dani's forehead creased. "No, why do you ask?"

"Just that he . . . oh never mind. Feeling better, dear?" Lucy teased.

"Last night," Dani said, her voice low, she was propped up by her elbows and resting on the small table in front of them. "Roberta said this trip was last minute. Carl told her another girl had turned him down. Does that sound characteristic? To be turned down, I mean?"

"No. He is too confident of his seductive powers, dear."

"Exactly," whispered Dani, sounding excited as she warmed to the idea. "And even if he'd been refused, he'd never admit it. Not Carl. I think he came on this trip at the last minute and is using Roberta as a cover."

Lucy studied Dani's face. "You think Carl is involved. On whose side?"

"He's Martin, Aunt Lucy. I'm sure of it. Last night, he saved me from Jeffries. And he conveniently showed up at Brighton, two days ago."

"Saved you? From *what*?" Lucy's eyes darted storm warnings at Dani.

Dani shrugged aside the lightning flashes. "Jeffries questioned me too closely. I made a slip. I let him know I knew about Redstadt Electronics. Right afterwards, he got me outside; Carl punched him and tried to warn me." For a moment, the memory of two grown men fighting over her replaced a small tremor of fear with self-serving vanity. She grinned at Lucy.

"What about Weatherston? He must be involved somehow."

"Weatherston and Jeffries are partners. It's the only thing that fits. And that big man in the limousine you saw talking to Jeffries? He could be the one giving the orders."

"I was thinking about him last night," replied Lucy. "It's possible there is another factor that we haven't counted on. Someone entirely separate. And he may be after the postcard."

Dani considered the theory. "Three people? Okay, let's call them A, B, and C. If A is Miss Schiller's enemy and B is Miss Schiller's friend, then B is also A's enemy. Who, then, is C?"

"Perhaps an enemy of both?" Lucy suggested.

She got a disbelieving but sympathetic smile in return.

"Good try, Auntie, but no dice. You're trying to put Weatherston back in his own niche, sitting on the fence. Neither good nor bad."

Lucy bristled at the idea, but she knew Dani wasn't altogether wrong. She sighed in reply and turned to peer out the foggy window at the rain.

"Your theory makes it all the more complex," Dani added. "I vote we go with what we know until something different shows up."

"I suppose so." Lucy didn't say what she had been thinking since last night. The third man could be waiting to see which one was successful before he made his move on the winner. Which targeted Dani and herself as pawns in any event. "Still, it doesn't explain Carl's dislike for Jeffries."

Dani pressed her advantage. "Right. What's more, Roberta told me that Carl told her Jeffries burns too many candles. Roberta thinks Carl is jealous and warning her to stay away from him, but Carl isn't the jealous type. I should have paid more attention to Roberta's answers, but . . ." She broke off, looking guilty.

"All a blur was it?" Lucy chuckled.

"I had to upchuck."

Lucy grinned then grew serious again. "But why doesn't Carl show us the other half of the postcard?"

Dani slumped against the back of the seat and after a few moments sat back up, face animated. "I know why." She put her head closer to Lucy's and whispered. "If you were Miss Schiller, how would you go about delivering half a postcard?"

Lucy leveled her brows and blinked, waiting.

Dani gave up. "Mail it! Just like you did. That's why Carl can't prove he's Martin. He doesn't have the postcard! He has to wait until we reach Oxford. And he wants to keep us in full view, to make sure we stay safe." Triumphant, she waited for Lucy's confirmation. "It feels right, Aunt Lucy. That has to be it."

Lucy brought the diary out of her handbag and gazed vaguely at the cover, still looking unsatisfied. "Puzzles are always so simple once they have been solved, aren't they?"

Dani's triumphant expression faltered. "Do you have a better theory?"

Lucy sighed softly. "No dear. Only, I just wonder if it isn't a bit *too* simple." She opened her diary to a clean page and gazed at Dani, face sober. "Promise you won't force Carl's hand just yet. At least until we reach Oxford."

TEN 10

THE RAIN HAD DISAPPEARED, and so had the coach carrying Dani and the rest of the group for Thursday's excursion. Lucy waited until the last moment before telling Dani she wasn't going on the day trip across Dartmoor and points north.

Now, arms full of parcels, Lucy strolled serenely out of the Guildhall Shopping Centre and turned onto High Street.

"Exeter, by myself," she had told Dani. "Shopping. I especially want to visit an art gallery." Separating might also throw their followers off guard, perhaps confusing them, while giving Lucy and Dani a time bonus.

"And also have a cream tea?" suggested Dani.

"If I remember rightly, there is a place called the Chapter Tea House," Lucy admitted.

"Silly me for asking."

"You'll take care?" asked Lucy, with a guilty qualm. "Promise that you'll stay with the group and not wander off by yourself?"

Dani had put her hand to her chest, almost affronted. "I can give a mean punch, yell my lungs out, and run fast. All at the same time, if necessary. Don't worry, Auntie, I'll be careful. Will you do the same?"

"I promise to stay in crowded areas at all times and to always be aware of what is going on around me," Lucy replied. She held up the two-finger Girl Scout salute.

A satisfying day, thought Lucy now. At first, she had mingled her shopping with cautious glances behind her, searching carefully for the man with the freckles or any other face she was seeing too often. As the day wore on, she relaxed her vigil and went on with her strolling about the shopping area.

She found a pair of shoes exactly the color of a tan purse she owned. Her short hair gleamed in a freshly shampooed and bouncy new style. After lunching in a small café with a pleasant overview of the River Exe, she visited an art gallery. Upon due consideration and advice, she arranged with the manager to have a painting shipped to Montreal. The painting, a pastoral scene done with plenty of detail; billows of green elms and an English sky, suited her mood at the moment.

At last, she decided it was tea time and headed for the tea room opposite St. Peter's, already salivating at the idea of tea with scones and thick Devon cream, topped with strawberry jam. Telling herself that her pleasant day had done wonders for her peace of mind, she turned down a narrow side street. An electrical shop across the way made her immediately think of an adapter for her iron. Lucy stood about thirty paces from the crosswalk, but the road wasn't very busy. A foot off the curb, she looked in both directions. The only vehicle in sight was a dark green saloon car parked further down. Through a tinted windshield she saw the driver, his head turned toward the front door of a shop. She decided to chance it.

She stepped off the curb and started briskly across the street. There was an awful sound of screaming tires, and a powerful roar drawing nearer.

He's going to run me down! The world around her slowed, voices blurred—a film in slow motion. Frozen in place, she could only watch the green saloon car hurtling toward her. She closed her eyes and waited. A terrific push from behind; someone screamed. Was it her scream? Her parcels scattered, and she fell into the arms of two startled men at the curb. Dazed, unsure, the fading sound of the motor still roaring in her ears, Lucy held tight to the two men and stared back to the crowd gathering in a small circle on the street.

Lucy heard soft murmurs and excited gasps as people gave their versions of what happened. A police constable appeared, and the crowd parted before his quiet authority. He sent a young man hurrying to a telephone and bent over the body lying in the road. Sickened, Lucy couldn't avert her stare.

The constable straightened and shook his head. Someone pointed to Lucy. He took his notebook from his pocket and started toward her.

With great effort, Lucy pulled her eyes away from the body and up to the blue uniformed constable. He spoke to her, but she wasn't listening. She stared at a point behind his shoulder. Her eyes eventually focused down to where the car had vanished with a final fearful screech of its tires.

Weatherston was there looking at the scene, taking in the details and Lucy.

Of their own volition, her eyes sought the body of the man who had pushed her out of the path of the oncoming car, saving her life. Someone had placed a handkerchief over his face, covering the blood now forming a crimson pool under his head. Her fingertips made their way to her mouth, and she closed her eyes. Air escaped her like a serpent's hiss. When she opened her eyes again, Weatherston was gone.

A rush of blood, and a loud roar filled her ears. Black waves skidded around her, and she gratefully submitted to the seductive pull of darkness. Her last thought was that she never need worry again about the man with the red hair and freckles.

The coach skirted the edge of Dartmoor, traveling west on a route which would eventually turn north along the coast to Lynton before returning through Exmoor to Exeter.

As soon as Dani boarded the coach, Palmer had slipped from his seat to hers, his bulk taking up most of it. His arm, sure to be uncomfortable across his personal beer basket, lay in the small space between them, forcing her to push closer to the window. Anticipating what he was about to do next, she moved the foot nearest him farther away. Sure enough, the movement of his leg gave away the alternating heel and toe of his big shoe slyly creeping closer to where he calculated her foot lay. All the while he gazed guilelessly past her through the glass until he could not shift his foot any more without becoming obvious. Dani bit her lip at his look of surprise when it reached its calculated point and found nothing.

She wasn't the only one on the bus who disliked him. When the coach had stopped for sightseeing sessions, Palmer snapped pictures incessantly, and the group often had to wait while he strayed off about the countryside. In a foul mood after his run-in with Carl at the disco, Jeffries threatened to leave him behind if he kept them all waiting past the appointed time again. As Palmer appeared, Jeffries stepped up onto the bus without waiting for Palmer to enter first.

"We have a schedule to keep, Mr. Palmer," Jeffries said sharply as he took his place behind the wheel. His dark glasses didn't hide the large bruise coloring his cheekbone.

"Hear, hear. Quite Right too. There are other people on the tour, Palmer." Brooker began. "Why should—" Palmer shot him a piercing glance, cutting him off mid-sentence.

The Australian had heaved up the steps of the bus and sulked to his seat.

Now, he took off his glasses and started to polish them, all the while blinking at Dani. The sight of his eyes without the shelter of his glasses disturbed her. Poor eyesight didn't altogether account for their impermanence, as though a certain chaos resided there. What went on behind those blinking eyelids, she wondered again.

Watching Jeffries, Dani wasn't too thrilled with him either, remembering his attention at the club. She couldn't make up her mind whether he had been after a groping session in the car or something more sinister. His apologetic smile that morning when she boarded the bus seemed to her like a smile the wolf might give to Red Riding Hood. "You never gave me the chance to apologize last night."

"I don't believe in being pals with some guy who tried to get me drunk and into the back seat of his car. Your bruise suits you by the way. Too bad I didn't get to give you one too."

"You should talk," Jeffries shot back. "You ditched us all and kept company with that Chinese bloke for hours, while we all sat waiting for you like servants to a princess. Didn't anyone ever tell you to stay with the people who brought you?"

"What Chinese guy?"

"That Mr. Wong. The one you talked to all night."

He had looked at his watch and then behind her. "Your aunt not coming with us today?"

"No," she answered sweeping past him. She turned at the top of the bus steps and glanced back at him, catching him staring at the hotel door, an uncertain look on his face.

Chinese guy? Wong? Great balls of fire. After the episode in the parking lot, she went into the restroom to wash her face and clean up. A dance with someone was a dim memory. Who? Later, much later than her round with Jeffries, Roberta had joined her in the washroom. She pulled a face remembering her inelegant rush to the toilet. Should she ask Roberta what happened in between? No, better not. Roberta would just tell Carl. Dani wasn't likely to give Carl an excuse to laugh at her expense.

Now, Jeffries pushed his foot down on the gas pedal making up for lost time, swinging the coach around winding valleys and rugged coastlines toward Lynton and across Exmoor. *Whatever else he may be, he's certainly a competent driver,* Dani conceded, but her resentment flared just the same. She hadn't told Lucy, reluctant to confess that she suspected Jeffries had drugged her drink. Revulsion nagged at her, as she remembered the careless way she had permitted him to steer her out to the parking lot. What if he was the killer? Or was it sex in what amounted to rape? Dani stifled a gag and stared at the back of his head with a new loathing, some of which she directed at herself, realizing she had no idea whether she could have fought him off. Before this new reality began to conflict with prior beliefs of her capability, she transferred her vision to the world passing by outside the bus, and forced herself to think of the day ahead.

The scenery was one of the most magnificent she had ever seen. An impression of windswept trees, bashed into odd shapes by the coastal winds, flashed by her window. They drove through villages where color washed cottages either clung to the sides of the valleys, or butted against narrow roads. Their shapes appeared deliberately molded in a jigsaw pattern to fit the available space.

At Tiverton, Jeffries stopped the coach for the afternoon break.

"Two hours here," he announced, turning around in his seat to face them. "I've laid on a walking tour." He grinned at the tired faces staring back at him. "For those who wish to remain behind, we'll meet here"—he glanced at his watch—"say, five o'clock? Now, who is coming on the walk?"

Everybody raised a hand except Dani and the Brookers.

Jeffries stood by the coach door as Dani got out, and held on to her arm. "You didn't raise your hand. Are you staying with the Brookers?"

Out of the corner of her eye, Dani saw Carl move closer. "I'd like to know too," he said. "It isn't a good idea to roam around by yourself." There were a few questioning murmurs from the group at this piece of news about safety.

"I've got to know where all my charges are going to be, in case someone gets lost," added Jeffries, his voice brittle, and he shot Carl a dirty look.

"I'm not a child, and I do know directions. You know, East, West, North, South?" Dani waved her arms in the four directions. She was in an impossible position now. If she backed off, they would all think she was frightened to be alone. "I am going to search out a cemetery." At the circle of curious faces, she added, "To do a rubbing?"

"I say," said Brooker. His face lit up. "That does sound interesting. Mind if I come along? I know the place well. After all, Tiverton goes back to King Alfred. It was called *Tuyford* then." He turned to his wife. "You wouldn't mind, would you, Vera? You can have tea with Mavis." So eager for something new, Brooker paid no attention to his wife's horrified expression.

"Andrew," she muttered through tight lips.

"Miss Morden shouldn't go traipsing about by herself." Brooker said. "We shan't be long." Turning quickly to Dani, he said, "Come on, off we go." He took her arm and fairly hustled her off down the street.

"Really, Mr. Brooker," protested Dani. "If your wife . . ."

"Nonsense." He seemed pleased with himself. "I'll have to listen to it tonight, but experience teaches one to turn it off. She seems so quiet, doesn't she? But you should just hear her when we are alone. Drone, drone, drone. On and on. She saves it up all day and talks all night." Brooker grinned sheepishly.

He struck her so much like a truant from school that she had to smile in return. Somehow he didn't seem quite like the crushing bore who'd quoted statistics nonstop.

She had to admit she welcomed his company if only to keep her promise to Lucy. She was determined to find a brass rubbing on this trip, regardless.

Lucy sat in the small hospital lounge drinking a cup of hot sweet tea given to her by a crisply starched nurse with a no nonsense look in her eye.

The door opened, and Weatherston walked in.

Lucy sat up and frowned at him. "Who let you in here?"

He sat down across from her. He spoke in a conversational voice, as though he'd just encountered her on the street. "The police said I could see you back to your hotel." His expression was benign, his pink cheeks shining in the light.

At a loss of how to express her emotions, Lucy shrank back from him, afraid he might touch her. The attempt on her life aroused ambivalent feelings in the knowledge that she was only alive because another was not. Both allowed silence to dictate the path of conversation.

"The police have been more than kind," she said finally. The after-effects of shock showed in her quivering voice. "I'm sure they think it is my fault for not crossing at the proper crosswalk.

They were polite, but severe."

Her eyes landed on Weatherston, the outrage in them unmasked. "I suppose I should have told them the truth. That I was the target of an attempted murder. But I'd never be able to explain why." She sank back in her seat. "I don't know why. Not really."

Weatherston kept his eyes on her, not saying anything, letting her speak. "*You* could tell them." Lucy said, with more hope than conviction that he would. She lapsed back into silence.

This time, Weatherston bridged it. "How are you feeling? Still a bit unsteady?"

"How do you feel?" replied Lucy coldly. "He was your colleague."

"My friend as well as colleague," he replied simply. The lines about his mouth deepened. "A good man. With a wife and daughter."

"Why did he do it? Save my life? I saw him at the airport. He followed her to the hotel." Lucy felt the temperature of her blood rising. She bunched up her fists, wanting to hit him. "Why did he kill her?"

"Charlie didn't kill Ida Schiller. He followed her to protect her. He failed. . . . He didn't want to fail with you."

"Oh my God." Lucy closed her eyes against a wave of nausea, and shivered. "Who are you?"

"Edgar Weatherston. More generally known as Martin Weatherston."

Careful. She was so vulnerable right now. "Martin?"

"Yes, the same one who had arranged to meet Ida Schiller." Weatherston paused, then said, "Where is it, Mrs. Trumble?"

"Lucy," she corrected absently. *What should I do? Have we both been wrong?* She couldn't be certain. *How do I know he wasn't driving the car that killed this Charlie? Maybe he murdered his own partner to gain my trust.* Thoughts played continuously through her head, and the whole time she didn't blink once. Her terror returned in a wave.

She took a deep breath. "Why did you leave the tour?"

"The man following in the limousine. He knows me. You know who I mean?"

"Yes, Jeffries is in with him." *And possibly you too*, she finished in her mind.

Weatherston tilted his head and looked at her from under half-closed lids. "You've learned about Jeffries?"

"We figured it out. He talked to the big man, and he tried to get Dani alone in Bournemouth."

"Rather flimsy evidence, isn't it?"

"Don't patronize me! He doesn't know about—other things."

"The identification item which ensures you are dealing with the right person." A casual statement, but insistent.

She knew she needed to tread lightly, *Watch it. Let him mention the postcard first.* Something niggled in the back of her head. Triumphant, she grasped at it. Of course! The real reason nobody has come forward.

"You have no idea what it is!"

Weatherston smiled at her, admiration in his eyes. "I underestimated you, Lucy."

"You don't know, do you?"

Weatherston sighed. "No. Miss Schiller neglected to tell me. She was altogether too competent, you see." He smiled, and the cherubic expression came back. He resembled a schoolboy caught doing mischief. "She told me she mailed it to my shop in Oxford, and I'd know it as soon as I saw it. I was to show it to her when we met. Once I identified myself, she would give me the microfiche. . . . I repeat, Lucy, where is it?"

"A microfiche?" Lucy didn't fake her astonishment. "I have no idea what you're talking about."

Weatherston rose and faced her, his eyes harsh and piercing. "But she must have given it to you. Along with the identification item." In spite of the emphasis in his words, she detected puzzlement. She held on to it.

"Identification item? She didn't have time to give me anything else before she died." Dismay flooded through her. She couldn't believe the words coming out of her own mouth.

My God, she thought. *Here I am, talking about one murder right on top of witnessing another. Almost my own.*

Weatherston shook his head gently, "They would have given up by now if it had been found with her belongings. Where is the identification item? Show it to me."

"I don't have it." She lifted her head at his open hostility. "Never mind looking at me like I have spinach in my teeth," snapped Lucy. "It is safe. I just can't lay my hands on it until tomorrow." Her thoughts scattered. She'd been wrong to brush aside Dani's insistence that there had to be something else. They wanted a microfiche. She only had a piece of a postcard. Lucy bit at her thumbnail. Had it all been for nothing?

"You didn't find a microfiche when you broke into our room at Brighton, so why should I have it now?"

"Jeffries searched your room the night before he took over the bus driver's duties."

"What's the difference which one of you did it?" she asked irritably.

"He paid the driver a nice sum of money as an incentive to book off, by the way."

Lucy flipped up her hand at him with a who cares attitude, condemning his catty remark. "What's on the microfiche?" she asked abruptly. "Plans for classified electronic equipment?"

"No." Weatherston smiled faintly. He gazed at her, brushing the side of his jaw, as though missing an absent beard.

"Let me see you back to the hotel," he said finally. "After dinner, I'll come along to your room, and we'll talk more. Your niece should be present."

At the mention of Dani, a new worry asserted itself. If Weatherston was Martin, then Dani was at the mercy of Jeffries. But Dani had promised she wouldn't go off by herself. As long as she stayed with the group she'd be safe.

Weatherston saw the concern in her eyes. "You can trust me," he said, misinterpreting.

The starched nurse came in to ask her if she wanted more tea. Lucy made a point of mentioning Weatherston's name and said he'd take her back to the hotel.

"If I disappear," added Lucy lightly, "you can tell the police."

The nurse glowered at Weatherston, who only smiled, his eyes twinkling.

Dani tacked her proof paper over the tombstone with masking tape and proceeded to rub briskly with a heelball stick. She worked quickly but attentively, dragging her fingers along the outlines and rubbing. A few minutes later she straightened, transferring the action of rubbing on paper to rubbing her cramped back muscles and gazed around her. The blue of the sky had faded to a dull gray. A mist was forming, drifting in slowly and turning the ground into a swirling haze. Headstones leaned sleepily forward. She peered at her watch. Four forty-five. *Where on Earth has Brooker run off to?*

The fog was looming closer in unbroken drifts now. She could barely make out the outlines of the church. Bending to roll up the tracing and gather her supplies, she heard a footstep crunch on the gravel path behind her. With a surge of relief, she began to turn. Two arms tightly locked around her; she struggled and opened her mouth to cry out. The cry was stifled in her throat as a hand roughly covered her mouth.

"Shut her up," a voice grated harshly.

She felt a hard pressure in the area behind and below her ear, then nothing.

ELEVEN 11

SOUNDS PENETRATED THROUGH A HAZE and into her consciousness. "Dani! Miss Morden!" She opened her eyes and saw nothing but cold, damp fog. Sweat soaked her back. Heart racing, she screamed.

"Easy, easy," said Carl. She shuddered and focused her eyes and mind toward the soothing voice. Roberta, Brooker, and Carl were huddled around her, their expressions alternating between relief and concern, except Roberta's eyes which held more curiosity. She smiled down at Dani.

"Thank God." Brooker let out a chest full of air. "She's coming out of it. I should never forgive myself if she had been hurt." His voice rose. "Disgusting, filthy rotters, picking on a defenseless girl."

"Oh Carl." Dani held on to him, burying her face in his coat. "Am I alive? Someone came at me from behind. I thought it was Mr. Brooker coming back for me."

Brooker contorted his face in horrified injustice. "I was in the shed hoping to find old tools, and they locked me in. I shouted, but you didn't hear." He hopped from one foot to the other in his frustration. "I was right about leaving you by yourself. Cowards! Dani, you should have let me stay."

"Them?" Carl said. "You saw more than one?"

"Well . . ." said Brooker grudgingly, "not exactly." He dropped his head and clasped his fingers together behind him. “I had my back turned when I heard the door slam shut.”

“He’s right,” said Dani, “there was more than one. Whoever it was told someone to”—her voice broke and she swallowed—“to shut me up.”

Brooker looked at Carl and Roberta, suspicion in his eyes. “Odd that you came by so conveniently, Hamel.”

“Relax, Brooker. Be glad that we did. You’d still be locked in the shed. When we expected you to arrive back at the coach, and you were nowhere to be seen, Roberta and I volunteered to look for you. Check it out if you want.”

They helped Dani to her feet and collected her tracing and supplies. The contents of her bag were strewn over the ground, the bag itself turned inside out. Brooker suggested the police.

“No.” Dani’s tone was sharp. “Please. Just take me to the bus. Nothing is missing. Maybe something frightened them off. Maybe they thought I was dead.” Though shaken, she attempted a laugh and brushed ineffectually at her clothes.

“It’s all so very stupid,” said Brooker. “What could they want if not money?” He stopped and jerked his head to Dani, his eyes wide, lips almost quivering. “I say, Dani, they didn’t . . .” Brooker’s face turned crimson and his eyes fell hard on the ground. Carl and Roberta gave her speculative glares.

“No, Mr. Brooker.” Dani now wanted to laugh. “I haven’t been raped.”

Visibly relieved but still embarrassed, Brooker busied himself scrambling around to collect the last of her purse contents. Carl continued to stare at Dani, and she shook her head faintly.

On the coach, they sat in the last seat, removed from everyone else.

“I wish you had told me sooner that you were Martin,” said

Dani in German. "What a relief! I don't know how much longer I can take this business. It isn't much fun."

"You speak German very well."

"I have this flair," she apologized. "I need to know some things."

Carl raised his finger to his lips then pulled out a small cassette player from his pocket. She heard a whining noise like a mosquito. He adjusted the volume, and bending, tucked it underneath the small table.

"High frequency," he said. "For the bug underneath."

Well, that's a thing. She tried to keep her expression neutral. *I'm learning,* she thought, more dismayed than she let on. If Jeffries had wired them, then he'd heard all the discussions she and Lucy had while traveling on the bus. About the postcard—their assumptions about Carl and Weatherston. *Oh blast it!* "Tell me about Jeffries," she said.

Carl raised his eyebrows. "So you did take my warning seriously after all. Jeffries pretends to be a student, but he is employed by a high tech company in England. Their main concern is computer research. And even that is a cover. Jeffries's real specialty is industrial spying. Freelance, for whoever pays his rate. An Austrian company is his special customer. In turn, that company is a subsidiary of a larger conglomerate controlled by a man called Bennig." He paused. "Am I going too fast?"

She shook her head, tongue pinched between her teeth. She said nothing.

"Bennig's headquarters are in West Berlin. He also owns Redstadt Electroniks, the company who employed Schiller. An important document came into her possession, and the Austrian company sent Jeffries here to get it back."

"And that man in the limousine? I'm sure Jeffries told him

where I'd be this afternoon. He followed and searched my bag."

"You are quick, I'll say that for you," said Carl. "The limousine carries a telephone, so Jeffries can check in with him every few hours. It was difficult for me to follow you without him becoming suspicious, so I asked Roberta to insist she was bored. We were almost too late. They were still there when we freed Brooker." He grinned. "He shouted his wounded dignity all over the cemetery like a hound at bay, but it may have saved you further harm. We heard a car drive off just as we found you."

"Is Roberta involved too?"

Carl looked amused. "Hardly. Roberta can't keep secrets."

"But where do you come in? Does Jeffries know who you are?"

"I'm sure he doesn't. I let him think his flirtation with Roberta makes me jealous."

"I do know that Weatherston is involved."

Carl took a deep breath. He gripped her arm. "He is your enemy, Dani. He's clever and dangerous, the kind that can't be trifled with. He has been known to say he works for the British Security Service. Actually, he is very close to Bennig—a ruthless, powerful man whose interests extend around the world."

"How did you learn all this?" she asked, disturbed by his intensity. "And tell me where you fit in. Why are you so sure Weatherston doesn't work for the British?"

"Because I work for them." He searched the coach with his eyes, speaking casually as though discussing their next tour stop.

"Did Weatherston kill Miss Schiller?"

"Honestly?" Carl shook his head. "I'm not sure. They hire agents to do their dirty work." His hand clenched into a fist.

Miss Schiller's death upsets him, Dani thought, watching him. Did he also know her? She thought of the man with the freckles, and opened her mouth to tell Carl about him, but his next statement made the thought vanish.

"You see, we must retrieve the document before the man in Austria gets it. What you do not realize, is that he is a Russian military agent."

"A Russian?" *Lucy's third person after all.* "Is someone selling plans of electronic equipment to the Russians? Is that it?"

"No, not the plans. The equipment itself." All of the sudden, his sinewy fist gripped Dani's arm tighter. "That's enough. Already, you know too much. So far, your innocence has played in your favor. Forget the whole thing, Dani. For your own sake, and your aunt's safety, go home on the next plane. Hand it over, Dani. I can't protect you forever. Not if they are determined to kill you."

His grip loosened abruptly and he relaxed, smiling at her wistfully. "Get on with your life. I envy you."

Dani subsided into silence, studying him. Without his usual contemptuous smile, his manner revealed a soberness she hadn't thought he possessed. His bottom lip jutted out, pulling the corners of his mouth down.

"Why don't you give it up then? Tell your British bosses to go to hell and just quit."

She sat, waiting for him to reply. His features were blurred in the shadows. The sun had set, the after light already fading, the black line of the horizon nearly indistinguishable. Other conversations on the coach had scattered. People dozed or stared through the windows, engrossed in end of day meditations.

Carl ran his fingers through his black hair, his eyes bleak and cold as though staring into past moments.

All at once, he laughed quiet and deep from inside his chest and out through his nose.

Dani squirmed in her seat uneasily, her thoughts returning to the cabaret and Roberta's warning about Carl.

But Roberta can only speak about Carl from her own narrow frame of reference, she argued with herself. *A different Carl.* It was true, when you moved in the shadowy world of intrigue, you learned to be different. She could vouch for that. "Believe me, nothing would give me greater pleasure than to give you the postcard. If I could."

A momentary sense of something out of place in his manner struck her, then just as quickly, slipped away leaving her wondering if the shadows were playing tricks on her.

"What do you mean," he asked, his voice tight. "Don't you have it? Did they take it?"

"No. It's safe." Frowning, she considered her words before continuing; her unease solidified into caution. "But only I or Aunt Lucy can pick it up. We made sure of that. We can have it by tomorrow, but it had better match your half. Better yet, let me see it now. I can tell if it matches just by looking."

Carl was silent so long, she wondered if he had heard.

"I don't have it either. It's in Oxford." He watched her as if calculating her answer.

He's testing me, she thought. Her laughter sounded relieved, even to herself.

"So Miss Schiller did mail it to Oxford after all. Will you have it by tomorrow?"

"I can't fetch it myself. It would mean leaving you unprotected, I don't suppose you would give it to me without the identification?"

She shook her head, laughing at him sideways. "No. Ida Schiller thought it was important. By the way, the address in Oxford . . . is it a computer store?"

This time Carl didn't hide his surprise. He smiled broadly, like someone who had searched and finally found a long sought answer to a puzzle. "For once you did not guess correctly. It is not a computer shop. It is a bookshop." He snorted out loud at her expression.

"At least you are careful," he added. "You should be in the business full time."

"No thanks," she said dryly. "I'd rather criticize history from the armchair, if you don't mind."

"It's easy to be an armchair critic," he agreed, smiling now. "Dreamers don't worry about the lives of the little people, the true history makers."

They sat in silence. The coach bounced over a rough portion of road under repair. From her seat, Dani could see Jeffries. The light from the dashboard illuminated his face, reflecting in the mirror above his head. He was driving carefully, maneuvering around bad spots in the road, seemingly unconcerned that she and Carl were conversing so intensely. *Comfortable enough with the tape he gets from the bug,* she surmised. Likely, he thinks the pair found what they wanted that afternoon. Her eyes narrowed, as she thought about her purse contents.

"The address," she muttered to herself. "I had the Oxford address in my notebook."

Carl groaned. "But that changes everything! Don't you see Dani? The postcard is meaningless now. You must give it to me now. Even if they find the other half, you wouldn't be fooled into giving them the microfiche."

Shock hammered at her full force, and sinking despair quickly followed. *A microfiche? Why am I so stunned? I always knew there was something more.* Carl registered her floundering expression, and his lips pressed together in anger.

"Can't we just cut out the games, Dani? I want the microfiche Schiller passed on to you."

Oh Lucy, why didn't you tell me? Dani's lips moved numbly then repeated aloud, "Microfiche?"

Carl's nostrils pinched in fury. His eyes turned freezer cold. "Schiller had no time to dispose of it to anyone else."

"She gave us a postcard and said to take it to Martin in Oxford." Dani's own temper rose. "We thought it was a key or code. Oh hell," she whispered with a hoarseness to match Carl's expression. "Don't you think I'd tell you?"

"Nevertheless, you have it," he said stubbornly. His head turned, and his eyes penetrated hers with a seriousness that chilled her to the bone. "Your life depends on it."

"And now a little something to lower our spirits. Thanks bunches." The scene in the graveyard closed in vividly on her. Her heart thudded.

Outside, darkness was total now. Leaning back, Dani stared at her reflection against the black window. Lucy had kept information from her before, but did she know about the microfiche? She rubbed her forehead, trying to think, weighing the whole sequence of events, then gave up and closed her eyes. *My brain has gone missing.*

She opened her eyes again, thinking of Miss Schiller and Lucy's missing luggage. Dani smiled triumphantly and sat up. Across the aisle, Palmer groaned in his sleep and moved stiffly. Odd how things happen, she mused. It must have thrown Weatherston when he saw Palmer on the tour.

She turned to Carl. "I wish I knew what Palmer had against Weatherston," she said, desperate to avoid the subject of the microfiche, needing time to sort her thoughts. "He accused Weatherston of treason. Pretty heady stuff."

Carl glanced up to where Palmer lay softly snoring, his mouth open.

"Buy him a few drinks, and he'll tell you. It won't take much."

"Somehow, I think you could save me the trouble."

Carl grinned. "It was in 1943. On the last big push against Rommel. Palmer was in the British Army then, and Weatherston was in command of a small attack force. According to Palmer, Weatherston was inept; too young and a coward. Men under him died. Whispers circulated that to go on a mission with Weatherston meant certain death. The men suspected him of being an enemy agent. Weatherston was transferred out, but not before Palmer's leg got shot off during a raid. He was young, barely eighteen."

"That's ghastly." Dani felt a twinge of guilt about her earlier rejection of Palmer. "No wonder Palmer acts the way he does." At a sudden thought, she added, "How do you know his history?"

He darted a quizzical glance at her, eyebrows raised. "I followed my own advice. As I said before, with a few drinks inside him, Palmer isn't shy about revealing his whole history."

Dani nodded. She had never been anxious to give him the opportunity of sounding off. "But Weatherston," Dani started to say, then paused.

"What?"

"I was going to say Weatherston seems a bit old to be mixed up in murder, but then again if he is desperate enough . . ." Her voice trailed off.

"Weatherston hasn't changed much. He still works for the enemy." Carl sat straight as the coach pulled up in front of the hotel. Jeffries turned on the interior lights.

Squinting in the abrupt shift from dark to light, Dani rose from her seat. Spasms of pain radiated across her back and leg muscles. She could only think of food, a warm bath, and bed. Carl bent down to retrieve his electronic scrambler. She stopped him before they moved down the aisle. “Please don’t tell my Aunt Lucy about the cemetery. I told her I’d stay with the group.”

“Next time, listen to her,” Carl advised. “Tonight, do not leave your hotel room. Stay with the group all day tomorrow. By tomorrow night, I’ll have everything settled.” He smiled thinly. “Keep the microfiche safe.” He strutted quickly up the aisle and swung down the step, leaping to the pavement.

TWELVE 12

DANI'S NAGGING DOUBTS THAT LUCY KNEW about the microfiche disappeared when she learned of her aunt's near brush with death. But when Lucy told her about Weatherston's revelation, her skepticism returned full force.

"Carl warned me that Weatherston would claim he is working for the British."

"Weatherston knew all the correct answers too, Dani. He even volunteered information without prompting. Can you say the same about Carl?"

"He knew about the postcard." But had he really? Dani sat down on the edge of the bed mulling over their conversation on the coach. Lucy's unspoken thoughts hung in the air. *She thinks I want Carl to be Martin because he looks great, and he's the first man who isn't scared of my brains.* She forced herself to recall his exact words.

"You're right," she admitted reluctantly. "I let the scrape in the cemetery throw me off balance. I got so frightened, I babbled it all out. Damn. I did just what they wanted me to do."

"What scrape?" Lucy stiffened in alarm.

"But we need to trust someone, sometime," Dani added, sounding defensive. "I think it should be Carl."

"Dani! What scrape?"

Annoyed with her slip, Dani told her, keeping it short as if to emphasize its insignificance. When finished, she waited for the expected recriminations, but they never came.

"I understand now," Lucy sat down beside Dani, taking her hand. "You want to believe Carl saved your life. Just as this man, Charlie, saved mine."

"So, here we are, at another impasse." Dani shook off Lucy's hand and rose from the bed to pace across the room and back again. "What if they were in it together? Attack us both, then conveniently save us. Only Weatherston's plan backfired, and this Charlie person died. But the result is the same. We'd be ready and willing to trust that person. Either way they win."

"Sounds a bit thin, dear. Nobody could stage that car accident. The driver wanted to run me down. The person saving me would have known there was little chance of escaping harm, unless . . ." Her voice straggled to an end.

"Weatherston planned to kill his own partner," finished Dani.

Lucy waved the suggestion aside with an adorned hand. "No, the idea is too bizarre."

"Carl said Weatherston will stop at nothing to achieve his objective." Dani slammed the flat of her hand on the desk. "Carl was right about one thing. Our life depends on that microfiche. Our surprise at its existence may have bought us precious time."

Carl's warning and its deadly meaning echoed in her head. *Know too much, and you're dead.* She glanced at Lucy. No use adding to her fright; she's had enough today. But suppose they never found the microfiche? Could their enemies afford to let them go free? Dani pushed the answer from her mind.

"I wish this were like the old movies," said Lucy. "All the crooks wore black hats, and the heroes wore white. Up to now, we've been searching for someone who fits our image of the good guy so we can plunk a white hat on his head like a tag." Opening her mouth to continue, she stopped, lips slowly turning up into a smile. She then alternated between pinched face groans and half gasps of near triumph. Dani watched as Lucy began shaking her head and muttering to herself like someone possessed. Moments later, she shook her head again and muttered, "No, that's not it."

"Hey, are you okay?" Dani moved closer and touched Lucy's arm.

"What?" Lucy stopped muttering and smiled at her. "Something I said about the good guy, dear. It rang a bell. What Miss Schiller said when she gave me the postcard." She frowned again.

Dani waited for Lucy to continue, then unable to hold back her impatience any longer, prompted, "You said something about good guys and hanging tags—"

"That's it. *Tag,* she said *tag.*"

"Like *Guten Tag?* Good day?"

"Something like that, I'm sure."

"It's absurd. She's dying from a knife wound, but staggers down two floors just to say 'good day?' *Auf wiedersehen* would be more like it." Dani sniggered, close to hysterics. "Or how about *Wie gehts?*" She waved her hand in a semi-circle, palm outward.

"What's that mean?"

"A rough translation? *'How's things?'*"

Lucy made a sound of irritation. "I am only telling you what she said, Dani. If you can contain your macabre sense of humor, we might figure it out, and we could get on with it."

"Okay, okay," said Dani, struggling for calm. "Let's put the words together: *Important. Don't lose a day. Trust nobody. It is very dangerous.*" Dani shook her head, "*Day* doesn't fit. Are you sure that was all?"

"That's all I could remember, under the circumstances," snapped Lucy. She darted to her feet, and in a fit of feverish haste, threw her suitcase on the bed.

"She must have hidden it somewhere inside. I'll find it if I have to tear this case apart. When I think of that woman! She hatched her plan in the taxi and mixed up our luggage. It's unforgivable. Involving innocent people in her spy schemes." She punched her arm out to the side, palm up, fingers splayed. "Get my manicure scissors!"

Ten minutes later, they sat beside the mess of her suitcase. Lucy plucked at the contents. "Nothing. What's a blasted microfiche look like anyway? Like the ones in the library?"

"Either that, or a roll of film. They use a special camera with thirty-five or sixteen millimeter film, which reduces a lot of material to a small size."

"At this rate, everything I own won't be worth wearing." Lucy picked up a pile of clothes and threw them in a heap back into her case. "Blast it. I'm at the end of my patience. I'd just as soon thumb my nose at the lot of them and go home."

A soft knock sounded at the door, and she froze. Dani moved to answer. "Who is it?"

"Martin," a soft voice called from the other side.

She lifted her finger at Lucy and pointed toward the desk. Lucy grasped her manicure scissors as she moved to stand where Dani indicated, near the desk on the opposite side of the room. Dani opened the door and backed away. Weatherston slipped in, closed it, and stood for a moment, his hand still on the doorknob. He pushed an eye to the peephole before turning to face them. Quickly noting their careful stance away from each other on opposite sides of the room, he smirked.

His eyes sharpened on the suitcase. "What's happened?"

"Why did they kill her and not us?" babbled Dani, nervous now. "Whoever killed her didn't wait to make sure *she* had the microfiche. We've searched everything and we don't have it either."

"They tried to kill Lucy this afternoon," said Weatherston.

"To frighten me into giving up the fiche?" Dani stabbed her forefinger in the air. "It doesn't take Einstein to figure out that one."

Weatherston nodded. "Miss Schiller wasn't the first mistake they made. It's dawned on them that killing first and looking for the microfiche later is counterproductive."

"Like Mr. Dittmahn?"

"Among others." Weatherston put his head back and gazed at Dani as though assessing a painting he might purchase. "You seem to know a lot."

Hardly, thought Dani. She watched as he moved to an armchair. "Each time something happens to us, we learn a bit more. All the pieces are coming together. We'll have it all soon. If we last that long."

Weatherston's pink face and benign smile beamed at them. Against the chair's flowered chintz covering he resembled a vicar come for afternoon tea. His self-assured manner was convincing, Dani had to admit. How easy it would be to just believe him. She found herself relaxing at the thought. But less than twelve hours ago, Carl seemed believable too.

She watched him, looking for some slip of expression that signaled he was telling lies. Flickering eyes, a nervous twitch of his hands, sweating, smiling too much when he should be serious. Anything that didn't ring true. "We realize that she came to England to hand a document to someone," said Dani, reasonably. "I want you to tell us why we should believe that person would have been you, Mr. Weatherston."

Weatherston cleared his throat, tipped his head and stared at her.

"Why all this business and fuss about the postcard?" she continued, "Why didn't Miss Schiller just hand it over to you at the airport in London? It sure would have been easier and safer."

Weatherston looked disappointed. "A postcard? I wish it had been that simple." He pressed the heels of his hands against his eyes then looked at Lucy. "I say, have you eaten?"

"No," Lucy replied, looking pleased at the thought of food. Dani glowered at her for falling for the deliberate change of subject, giving him time to come up with excuses.

"I could do with a bit of tea and some food," said Lucy, smiling at Weatherston as if they had just exchanged Sunday after-church invitations. Like a belated afterthought, she turned to Dani. "It won't do any harm, will it? We could all think better after some nourishment."

Thinking better is not the goal I had in mind for Weatherston, was the silent message Dani sent across the room to her apathetic partner. About to challenge the idea of food, her stomach gave a traitorous rumble. Conceding their position of offense had weakened, she stomped toward the telephone and called room service, ordering a large pot of tea and a plate of sandwiches.

"For how many, miss?"

Dani hesitated. "Two people. Two *very* hungry people." One of them would have to use a water glass. Weatherston's eyes shone approval.

"Now," Dani said to him later, with pointed bluntness. "I don't know what or who you are, but you have answers, and we want to hear them." She wished Lucy would quit bustling around the tray, handing the last sliced beef sandwich to him and draining the pot into his glass.

"Aunt Lucy was almost killed," she continued. "I was mugged

and left unconscious, we had our luggage trashed, and someone has followed us. I think we've paid our dues, don't you?"

Weatherston's face remained closed, impassive. "The danger you have faced is nothing compared to facing certain death if you get any closer to the truth."

"The attempt on my life this afternoon wouldn't have ended in certain death?" said Lucy.

"They have done worse," said Weatherston. Lucy paled.

Dani rose and stood over him. She kept her voice low and steady, emphasizing every word. "We can force the issue. Either you agree, or I will telephone every newspaper, radio, and television station in England. I'll give them the facts as I see them. You have one minute, Mr. Weatherston." From the corner of her eyes, Dani saw Lucy fidget in her seat.

Weatherston's mouth went slack, then his features hardened. "Do that, and you won't be alive long enough to read it more than once." In the silence that followed he did a complete turnaround. He smiled.

"It seems once again that I underestimated this team." He looked almost delighted as his eyes twinkled at them from the chair. "Newspaper coverage at this point is out. Without proof, there would only be speculation, but reporters can make bloody nuisances of themselves. A hint to the media would only alert the wrong people. There is also the fact that the microfiche is in your belongings. May I?"

Weatherston's fingers explored the suitcase with expert ease. He straightened and faced Lucy, frowning. "Why were you searching your luggage in particular?"

"Your minute is up," Dani interrupted.

Shrugging like someone used to humoring ill-tempered people, Weatherston returned to the chair. He moved without noise like a cat.

"Joe Dittmahn and I met in Germany after the war," he said without further preamble. "While I was on assignment with the Foreign Office. Like every German, he denied being a Nazi, but we liked each other from the start. He led me to an extensive cache of Nazi records hidden behind a fake wall in an abandoned castle. They proved invaluable evidence at the Nuremberg Trials against high-ranking Nazi officials. After the trials, I stayed on with the Foreign Office, in the German section, dealing with postwar settlement. Dittmahn went to work for a company which later became part of a large conglomerate. We had kept in touch with each other until about ten years ago."

Weatherston leaned over the tea tray and lifted the lid off the teapot, frowning when he found it empty.

"Two weeks ago, he tried to get in touch with me. He asked for me but by a codename we'd used years ago. The chap who took the call decided on his own that Dittmahn was a crackpot." Weatherston made a wry face then took his glass to the bathroom and filled it with water from the sink faucet.

When he returned, he continued, his face suffused with real anger. "The boy is one of a new breed, full of energy and hustle. They think the older men—the ones with experience—take up rentable space instead of being put out to grass."

Lucy pouted for him, but Weatherston was gazing deep into his glass, turning it between his hands as if reading the water.

"Dittmahn didn't know I was one of the . . ." Weatherston sighed, "semi-retired. It was by pure accident that I got his message. I telephoned him, and he told me he had information about illegal deals with the Russians. He had compiled the proof, but he refused to give it to anyone but me. He said it went too deep. My people were reluctant; they wanted someone younger to pick it up. A week passed while they weighed their preference against the information they would get if they sent me. Dittmahn was on his way to Munich to meet me when a man called Bennig found him first."

"But not before Dittmahn sent Miss Schiller the microfiche." Dani put in.

"Yes. He feared someone had found him out. He was right."

"But why you? Why not the German police?"

"He wasn't sure how many organizations were involved or how many were penetrated. I was the only one he knew he could trust."

"How long were you there?" interrupted Dani. At his confusion she added, "In Germany after the war, I mean?"

"About four years. . . . Does it matter?"

"Go on please." Dani kept her eyes steadily on his.

"You know the rest. Dittmahn gave Ida Schiller a set of instructions. She got in touch with me."

"Why didn't you meet her at the airport?"

"I was unknown to her, and she needed proof of identification. She was also afraid, and with good reason. I'd get one of a pair of something at the place which I and Dittmahn had discussed. An unknown piece of identification sent to an address I hadn't repeated over the telephone. She must have taken an extra precaution and waited until she arrived in London to mail it. An English stamp would not flag the piece of mail for anyone hoping to spot it. But she lost valuable time. I assigned Charlie to the airport. When he telephoned me, I decided not to wait, but I was too late . . . again."

Lucy's head rose. "Why the tour, I wonder? It seems a roundabout way to Oxford."

"Tour?" Weatherston straightened up in the armchair. "What

gave you that idea?"

"She told me so," said Dani. Dismayed, she realized Ida Schiller had asked all the questions when Dani went to fetch Lucy's suitcase. She had given Ida Schiller all the information about Holly Tours she needed. A lesson learned. She wouldn't be so gullible again, to believe things just because someone else said so. She glowered at Weatherston with fresh determination.

"Miss Schiller mentioned the tour when she gave me the postcard," Lucy said. "Go find Martin, in Oxford, she said." Lucy wrinkled her forehead. There was more, she thought. Something else Miss Schiller had told her intruded into her memory. Lucy's mind reached for it, but it slipped away.

Weatherston digested their information then nodded. "The tour was a wise plan. She wanted to take attention away from herself, so she avoided doing anything of real interest, like going directly to Oxford. We expect tourists to look at everything. To anyone following her, she would appear an innocent on holiday." His eyes lit up, and he smiled. "Some women are too clever by half."

"Oh boy," muttered Dani, her derision clear. She took a breath and opened her mouth.

"How did you know about us?" Lucy interrupted before Dani started on a rant.

"Charlie saw you at the airport and get in the taxi to the hotel. At first, he suspected you killed her." He smiled at Lucy's shocked face. "The rest we got from Superintendent Proudlove."

Anyone could get that much information from the police, Dani told herself. "What kind of information is on the microfiche that makes it so important? What is so vital that they would kill for it?"

THIRTEEN 13

"MONEY," SAID WEATHERSTON. He glanced at his watch then pressed his eyelids with the heels of his palms and blinked a few times as if to bring them back to life.

"Thirty-five million dollars a year," he said. "That's a conservative estimate. People have killed for much less." He rose and went to the window, parted the heavy drapes a fraction, and gazed out at the street.

Lucy kneaded a painful swelling in her shoulder while she peered at her small travel alarm on the bedside table. Eleven o'clock. The hotel was becoming quiet, traffic in the hallway diminishing. A waiter pushed a cart down the hall, dishes rattling in tune with a squeaky wheel. Lucy placed a pillow behind her back and leaned against the headboard.

Weatherston returned to his chair and sat on the edge. His eyes swept over the room as if he might jump up again, given the right reason.

"There is a man in West Berlin by the name of Friedrich Bennig. His age would be close to seventy by now, I expect. He is the principal owner of a large industrial network called *Bennig*. The organization is complex. So complex it's anybody's guess as to the depth of it. Through it, he controls most of the industry of Western Europe. He also has extensive interests in the United States, Canada, and the Pacific Rim."

“What do you know about the man himself?” asked Dani. “What’s his connection to all this?”

“His background is as much a mystery as his companies. Our knowledge of him is part fact and largely conjecture. We know that his rise to power occurred after the war, though he never saw action during it. He always operated in the safe ministries; in administration and as the keeper of reports. He never rose above the rank of major. A picture emerges of a careful man who realized from the beginning Germany would lose and planned to come out of it intact.”

“While he waited for the end, he gathered information he could use. He collected papers which implicated high ranking officers, industry leaders, managers—all of them people who might prove to be of economic importance to Germany after the war. He retrieved and altered documents, and hid the originals. Sure enough, these same people were never charged with any crime.”

“For certain favors, no doubt,” Dani remarked.

Weatherston’s head bobbed in agreement. “He never pushed, or forced. Nor did his demands always involve money. He never asked for more than what the victim could pay. On the flip side, he was utterly ruthless if refused.”

“If he’s such a big man on campus, why isn’t his name a household word? Like the Rothschilds, for instance?”

“Old habits, Dani,” replied Weatherston. “He still prefers to remain in the background. The only man who gets anywhere near him is Paul Hoeffner, a man badly wounded in the war, his face damaged. Surgeries have left him with a zombie appearance, if you like. He altogether keeps Bennig unapproachable, and his loyalty is infinite.”

Lucy spoke up. “This man Bennig. A wealthy man with a

rational history. Why get mixed up in anything illegal? Business with the Russians leaves him open to blackmail. It can't be for the money."

Weatherston smiled. "It has been my experience that when the powerful rise from nothing, they become dazzled by themselves. A man called Seneca said something about avarice being so insatiable that abundance will not content it."

Lucy rose wincing at her painful spots and opened her travel bag. When she fished out the small bottle of brandy, Weatherston's eyes gleamed. He held out his glass. His first swallow brought him back to life. "Ah, that's better. Now, where were we?"

"The fiche?" Dani said, not hiding her impatience.

Weatherston sighed, voice partly annoyed and partly patronizing. "All in good time, Dani." He took another sip, rolling it around in his mouth before swallowing. "I'm trying to tell this as it came to light. Some time ago, crates of goods bound for West Germany became damaged while they were being loaded in Britain. The supporting export declaration stated that the shipment contained tractor parts. But customs agents found the damaged crates actually contained sophisticated computer hardware. Instead of confiscating the shipment, someone in their wisdom wondered what would happen if we loaded the cases with sand and sent them on their way. With us following along behind, of course. The cases bypassed West Germany and ended up at a company in Austria."

"But surely there are shipping procedures. Things like customs declarations of imports at the Austrian border?" Dani pulled at her bottom lip, leaning forward. "Even with the Common Market, is it possible to ship goods into a country without a piece of paper?"

"The president of the Austrian company declares the tractor

equipment won't leave the country. However, Austria is neutral, and the Russians have an easy time trading from there. Soon the equipment is on its way to Moscow, at three times the original price."

"And Bennig makes a huge profit. But why would the Russians pay so much money for something that becomes obsolete so fast? It really doesn't make a lot of economic sense to me."

"Ah! Ordinary business people would think so, wouldn't they? It isn't the computer hardware itself, Dani. The high technology making up domestic computers and other gadgets is more useful when used for items of military strategy."

Dani's comprehension sharpened. "But can't the police, or whoever, stop the shipments at the source?"

"If you think about it a moment, you'll see it's near impossible. That they are domestic goods works to Bennig's advantage."

"I'd have no problem buying computer equipment," Lucy broke in. "I would just attend one of those trade fairs, like Markham and I used to do with our own products, place an order and pay cash right then. I might even ask someone else off the street to do it." Lucy nodded at Dani. "Oh yes, I could. Nobody would ask questions, nor remember it afterward. Ordinary people like me don't know the difference between a microchip and a potato chip. If someone asked me to buy a piece of computer equipment by stock number, for instance, I wouldn't think I was doing anything wrong, because it is a domestic product. Public property really, isn't it?"

"Precisely right, Mrs. Trumble . . . er . . . Lucy." Weatherston's face turned pink, but it was apparent she had shaken his composure. He stared at her, eyes pensive.

"I could also purchase computer plans," Lucy continued. "Wouldn't China be interested in the same thing as the Russians?

Plans are easier to pass than parts."

"Ah!" Weatherston's grin was boyish, amused. "You are thinking of Wong? I don't believe he has any sympathy to Red China. Quite the opposite."

Lucy only shifted against her pillows.

"But where did Dittmahn come in?" Dani wasn't interested in switching the conversation to Red China.

"The president of the Austrian company opened the cases and saw nothing but sand. He assumed the West German connection was holding out for more money. They denied it, and the suspicion fell on the only man who had complete access to the cases. The person who arranged the transportation."

"Dittmahn?"

"No, but someone he was acquainted with. The man gave him a lot of information before they got to him. Dittmahn pieced the rest together from the paperwork." Weatherston's mouth turned up at the corners. "The Germans always were sticklers for paperwork. He came up with proof of transactions, chain of command, routes, alternates, methods of payments. It reached higher than even he had bargained for. And it even had a name; *Schlafstrom.*"

Weatherston shot an expectant stare at Dani; the type that teachers give their star pupils. She didn't disappoint.

"The river that sleeps," she said.

"With deadly undercurrents."

"Did he give you any names?"

Weatherston shook his head. "We know of only one. The man in Austria, by the name of Chetkov. He's Soviet Military Intelligence. The rest, according to Dittmahn, are government officials, high ranking people in electronic research in three countries. He said their names would cause great consternation in the political sense. And those names give the Russians unlimited blackmail opportunities."

"No wonder everybody wants to get their hands on the microfiche," Lucy said. "But knowing the extent doesn't make me feel any better. It not only involves loss of money, but loss of reputations, prestige and power. Fines. Maybe even prison."

He nodded. Again, his gaze was one of speculation, almost as if she were a bug under the microscope. Dani interpreted his stare. *He realizes she is no fool,* she thought. She started to rub her thumbs anxiously. *I rather wish he believed she was scatterbrained.*

"Just a minute," she said, holding up a finger. "How do we know you aren't working for this Bennig? You were in Germany after the war. Maybe he did a little favor for you too."

"Dani!" Lucy scolded.

"Come on, Aunt Lucy. This is no time to worry about good manners." Dani faced Weatherston again, defiant.

He let out an exasperated breath. "Palmer has been busy, I see."

"It doesn't matter how I know. Are the accusations true?"

"It is none of your business, Miss Morden. It is not relevant to this operation." Expression cold, he turned his back on her and said to Lucy, "We're tired. I advise that you let me help search for the microfiche. Once in my possession, I can get you out of the country to somewhere safe. Until the lid has blown."

"Wait." Dani wasn't ready to let him go just yet. "You mentioned the shop in Oxford. What sort of shop is it?"

Weatherston squared his shoulders and faced her. The lines of his face hardened, and Dani flinched. "A bookstore, by the name of *Martin's*. It's my shop. I left a man in charge. He'll take good care of the postcard when and if it arrives. But it isn't relevant now, is it?"

"It may help to identify you."

Weatherston's lips tightened and he made a show of looking at his watch. "It's late, but I can telephone. Let's put a stop to this here and now. My man stays in my apartment above the shop. You can ask him anything. My description, the picture on the postcard. If I've never seen it, I won't know what your half is, will I? Is that good enough?"

"Maybe," said Dani, uncertain. She chewed her lip. "What's the address of the store?"

"Becket Lane, Seventy-four."

It agreed with the address she'd written in her notebook.

She lifted the telephone and asked for information. Some moments later she heard the double ringing sound of the telephone on the other end. A man answered almost immediately. She handed the receiver over to Weatherston.

"Say only that he should answer my questions."

Weatherston nodded. "Hullo, Peter?" He listened, then, "Martin Weatherston here. And who are you, sir?" He glanced at Lucy then Dani as he listened. His expression became wooden. "I see. Thank you, Sergeant." He hung up then stared down at the desk, still and remote.

Dani arms tingled with goosebumps. Lucy moved closer to her.

Weatherston looked at them, blinking. "They found the shop. Earlier tonight they broke in. Peter may not live. The police sergeant said Peter kept saying he couldn't help it. He had to give them what they wanted."

Lucy sucked in her breath and stared at him. *Torture?* A suffocating sensation gripped Dani's throat, and she struggled for breath.

"You must let me search for the microfiche," said Weatherston, his manner the more deadly for his soft voice and cherubic expression.

"No." Dani sat on the bed hugging her arms to her chest, "Even if the fiche were here, we don't know that you weren't there today. Did . . . that. You have nothing to lose."

"If I wanted to kill you I could do it here tonight." Weatherston's eyes narrowed as he peered at Dani. "All this reluctance to trust me. Someone else has got to you first. Who is it? Someone claiming to be me?" He reached Dani's side in two strides. "It couldn't be Jeffries. You must know he's working for Bennig."

Dani said nothing and kept her expression neutral as she met his penetrating eyes.

"I should have guessed," he said, not hiding his contempt. "Chetkov knows the fiche exists. And if he had it, he'd have a hold over Bennig. The power that goes with the knowledge of what is on the fiche is enormous." He turned to Lucy again. "I was wrong. Your attack today was Chetkov's doing." He headed for the door. "I'll bring the proof you need. Tomorrow night at the hotel. Meanwhile stay with the group. The more, the merrier."

"The group? Who would you suggest?" replied Lucy, angry that he deemed it acceptable to issue her orders. "The three in their eighties? The Brookers? Mavis?"

Weatherston turned to her, interested again, his eyes curious. "Why are you certain of Mavis?"

"Perhaps because she's a widow like me." Lucy shrugged. "Well, as a relative of the Brookers, she's harmless."

"Mavis, yes, I'd forgotten about Mavis." He smiled broadly. "But you're wrong. Mavis Griffen had never met the Brookers before this trip."

He left as silently as he had come.

Lucy turned to Dani at once.

"Whatever it is, Auntie, save it." Dani threw her suitcase on the bed. "Get your things together. We're changing rooms again. Somebody may decide we have the microfiche and come after it tonight. We'll talk tomorrow and play guessing games of which story-teller has his pants on fire then." Her shoulders hunched with stiffness and pain from her encounter in the cemetery.

"But that man at the shop. Peter," continued Lucy. She followed Dani into the bathroom and waited while she collected her toiletries. "Dani, did you tell Carl the address in Oxford?"

Dani handed over Lucy's toothbrush. "No. Look, I know what you are getting at, but any of them could have attacked Peter in the shop. Those two in the limousine may have found the address when they searched my bag today. Weatherston may even have ordered his own men to do it."

She remembered Carl's smile of discovery when she mentioned Oxford. He knew it was a bookshop. Tears neared the surface as she looked around the bathroom to check if she had gathered everything.

Lucy wasn't finished. "Think about it, Dani. Make sure you aren't trying to convince me only for the sake of argument. They tortured that man, Peter. Enough so that he's in serious condition. If Weatherston took the postcard, he'd have presented it to us when he came here."

"Oh, forget the postcard." Dani threw things in the suitcase any which way. "Don't you realize it's become a red herring now? No matter who comes up with the blasted thing, we can't be sure they didn't steal it."

Lucy paused, not ready to give in. "That's true. But have you thought of the alternative? It might also mean the killer can claim someone stole the postcard to make his own case look more convincing."

"Oh rats!" said Dani. "Anything is possible, but at this moment, I don't care. We have absolute zilch to give them anyway." She picked up the telephone and spoke to the desk. When she hung up, she said, "We're moving two floors up."

She picked up her case and turned to face Lucy, triumphant with the last word. "Most English people say '*Nuremberg.*' Weatherston pronounces it the German way, '*Nurnberg.*' I think he lived there a lot longer than four years."

FOURTEEN 14

LUCY WOKE VERY EARLY AFTER A FITFUL SLEEP filled with dreams. Her eyes felt heavy with weariness. They had failed. Bennig's people would never believe they didn't have the microfiche. After yesterday, she had no illusions. Even if they returned home, they would not be safe from pursuit. It was a bitter lesson.

She punched at the uncomfortable pillow and thought about her dream. In it, Palmer had stolen her diary, teasing her with it, holding it up in the air just out of reach like her brother used to do with her treasures when she was a child. First angry, then frightened, she fought him, frantic that he might open the cover. She had finally grasped the edge of the diary, and as she pulled on it, the cover tore.

Sighing now, she mused about the silliness of dreams. Another idea followed on its heels, and she held her breath, hanging on to the image. She got out of bed and fetched the diary from the desktop.

In the bathroom, she softly closed the door and flipped on the light. She unclipped the pen tucked between the pages as a bookmark, then pushed it down through the space between the binding and the spine. Nothing. She examined the inside front and back covers and leafed through each page. *Wait a moment. When I bought this diary, didn't I admire the cloth binding on the inside covers? Not this usual white bond paper.* Heart racing, she ran her fingers over the cloth on the front cover then turned the book over and traced along the edge of the back. Still nothing. Feeling lower, about half an inch inside the edge, her fingers traced a small ridge about three by five inches. Slight, barely noticeable under the give of the cloth binding, but definitely there. It had to be the microfiche. Miss Schiller had replaced the lining with a piece of heavy white bond paper to hide the marks of tampering. She had even made an identical inside front cover.

Instead of the elation which usually follows discovery, Lucy was outraged. *Miss Schiller planned to be on the tour all along, carefree even, knowing we carried a time bomb for her. Well, good for Miss Schiller's devious mind. Too bad she isn't here so I could give her a piece of* my *mind. If I am playing Russian roulette, I want to be the one holding the revolver.*

Lucy contemplated the diary for a long time then rose, replaced it on the desk, and went back to bed. Before long, she fell into an exhausted sleep.

The next morning before Dani could bring up the events of the last night, Lucy said, "When we get to Bath today, we'll take a short break from the tour."

Dani shrugged without so much as looking in Lucy's direction. Feeling defeated and weary, she was irritable in consequence, not eager to begin a conversation. "Run away, you mean? Like rats deserting the ship? In spite of Weatherston's instructions? Well, why not?"

"I'm sick of doing what everyone else tells me to do," said Lucy. "We've got three free days. At the last moment, we'll say we're going on an excursion to Wales, through Snowdonia National Park, Then we'll disappear to a different hotel. After that, well, I have a plan."

Dani slumped in her chair, reluctance written all over her

face and posture. "I hope you're aware that Bennig's people know we plan to go to Oxford."

"Keep your doubts to yourself," said Lucy. "I have enough of my own." She closed her case with a determined thunk. "We are going, so no argument."

"You'd better pray they believe you."

"Sometimes the answer to a prayer lies in the one who prays."

At breakfast, Carl ignored Dani. He had stared at her from across the dining room, looking tired and angry. She was glad of the respite. Last night, she had lain awake, endless questions hammering away at her which she couldn't answer with any honesty. Lucy had moaned in her sleep, dreaming, she supposed. Dani had risen and gently pulled a blanket up around Lucy's shoulders and watched over her until she quietened. Back in her own bed, she plumped her pillow, resolving to put the microfiche out of her mind and was soon asleep.

Now, she unfolded her road map, searching out their route. Jeffries told them he was evading the M5 motorway for a more picturesque route leading to Taunton. It struck her that he could say whatever he liked, and nobody would know the difference, almost all of them unfamiliar with the road identities. He could say the alternate was more picturesque, and who'd know the difference? Well, maybe Andrew Brooker might. This view looked all the same to her, although the drivers seemed less frantic on this route. Turning to the map again, she plunked downs her finger at Taunton, then branched off through Axbridge and let it come to rest at Cheddar. If her forefinger had a little face on the tip, its mouth would open to a round O at the view of the magnificent Cheddar Gorge and the stalactite caverns. Stalactite and 'mite . . . which was growing up and which hanging down? Impatient and in a morning funk, she brushed the difference aside, telling herself she'd remember when they got there. From Cheddar there was a planned stop at Wells and another cathedral. *How many have I seen in four days?* She let out an exasperated sigh and watched her finger tripping along the route on the map. Her mouth pursed in a childish *zoom, zoom* sound as her finger cum bus continued its journey from Wells through the Mendip Hills toward Bath. Finally, her mood turned somber as the black print saying *Oxford* loomed up at her. She eyeballed the distance from Bath to Oxford. About sixty-five miles, she guessed.

She pushed the map away, angry again, hating the whole mess that had ensnared them. Even Lucy looked tired and pale. *Maybe I could convince her to go home.* Lucy would never go.

She'd give anything to be back in London on Saturday morning, just arriving at the airport. For one thing, there'd be no pulling her face at traveling with Lucy. She wished that Ida Schiller hadn't chosen their hotel to be murdered in. The malicious thought surprised her. The wait was getting her down, she decided. It was really the action she liked, having to think fast. In some queer way, it was the only time she felt in control. Dani made up her mind to join the afternoon walking tour of Bath and somehow make Lucy relax. Above all, she would avoid Carl. She had no patience for him or his problems today.

She need not have worried. Roberta appeared alone for the walking tour. "He will find us later," she said. "There are telephone calls he is expecting."

Carl caught up with them after an hour, while they were in the historic Roman Bath area. He came up on her as she stood on the fringes of the group, listening to the guide. She gave a violent start when his voice sounded behind her, low and urgent. "I must speak to you."

Dani turned, bracing herself when she saw his angry

expression.

"Someone broke into the shop last night," he said. "We were too late."

"Weatherston showed up at the hotel just now," continued Carl. "At least now we know his friends found the address when you were attacked. He went to the shop."

Dani frowned but felt a pang of curiosity. *So Weatherston was telling the truth about the break-in. But he was with Lucy and then took her to the hotel. Would he have had enough time to reach Oxford, search the book shop and return in time to meet us that night?*

The guide moved to the next room. They followed, Carl pointing up to the ceiling and muttering something about restoration. "Did you find the microfiche?"

Dani shook her head, irritable. "For goodness sakes, Carl. We don't have it, and I can't do anything more about it!" She shifted her body away from him, ready to tell him to take a flying leap into the water. "It might be too late anyway. Maybe they've found it."

"And maybe if you hadn't changed hotel rooms last night, you would also be dead by now," Carl put in.

"How did you know we changed our room?" A thrill ran through her. Oddly, she welcomed and encouraged it. Almost like she'd been craving the excitement this whole time.

"I had surveillance put on your room," said Carl. "The bookshop . . . they went there thinking to find your contact. Which tells me that so far they don't know it's me. When they found nothing, their next thought would be to come back for you. You can't pretend innocence, Dani. Just having that address on your person tells them you are involved." Carl ran his fingers through his hair. "You should have told me you changed rooms."

"Why? I surmised we could be in danger all by myself. I acted without your help."

"You little fool." Carl put up his hands as if he would shake her but became aware others had their eyes on him. He ground his teeth at her in a false smile. "These men are professionals. It's only your stupid luck you escaped. You are fortunate the night clerk didn't note down the change in rooms, or they would have found you soon enough."

Chagrined, Dani stared at him. Should she tell him about Lucy's escape from death yesterday? And Weatherston? She glanced toward Lucy and took a deep breath. Carl's powerful hand gripped Dani's arm as Lucy separated from the group and came over to them.

"I'm going back to the hotel," said Lucy. "The smell of sulphur in this place has given me a headache."

"I'll come too," said Dani.

"No, dear. I'll take a taxi." Her eyes lingered on Dani's for a moment, and she took her leave just as Roberta spotted them and started over.

"I'll meet you later," Carl said. "Together we'll find the microfiche."

Oh jollies, thought Dani, her own head starting to ache. *Let's all have a cozy treasure hunt. You, me, Weatherston, and Aunt Lucy. Whoever wins, loses.*

Following the tour, Dani returned to the hotel. After a short rest she and Lucy departed as if to go shopping. They left a note for Jeffries at the hotel desk saying they were taking an excursion to Wales and would meet up with the group in Oxford on Monday night. Lucy had used her excuse of a headache and already arranged for the removal of their luggage from the hotel.

They walked in and out of several small shops then into one larger department store, mingled amongst the throng of shoppers and tourists, and disappeared.

FIFTEEN 15

ONCE SETTLED IN THE PALACE GARDEN HOTEL far across Bath, they breathed easier.

"This is the first time in five days I haven't felt my every move being watched." Dani gave a satisfied sigh and threw herself across the nearest bed, stretching out on her back. "We have three whole days to decide what to do." After a long moment gazing at the ceiling, she sat up, turning her attention to Lucy. "So, what's this plan you dreamed up?"

Lucy waved her hand. "Later, dear. Now I've another idea. I saw a pool when we checked in. Fancy a swim?"

"Great!" Dani jumped off the bed. "Let's have a race. Loser pays for dinner."

"You don't exactly have the appetite of a bird do you?" grumbled Dani later when they came back to their room. "If I'd have known you had kept up with your swimming, I would have demanded a handicap."

"Just because you are out of shape doesn't mean I have reached the Geritol stage, dear." Laughing, Lucy wiggled her fingers through her hair then rummaged in her suitcase for her dressing gown.

Except for the one flash of wariness in her hazel eyes when they bumped into a man entering the pool area, she seemed revitalized; almost back to normal. "It serves you right. If you'd won, you would have ordered the most expensive item on the menu. I know you too well."

Dani laughed in agreement. She lounged in a tub chair and eyed the room, crowded with small tables and chairs placed to provide an atmosphere of Victorian clutter. Her gaze stopped at the wallpaper with alternating rows of stripes and cherry clusters.

"So then, time we got down to the cherry pits," she said, making a face at the wall. "What do we do now?"

But Lucy didn't reply. She stood beside her open suitcase, diary in hand, lost in reverie. Dani returned from the cherry pits to reality.

Expression intense, Lucy sat in the matching tub chair across from Dani.

"If you had the microfiche, who would you give it to?"

Perplexed, Dani jerked her head back and raised a brow. She waited a moment, then eyed the diary in Lucy's hand.

"I thought you had stopped playing these games." Her anger was close to the surface. "You knew you had it all along."

"No, I assure you I did not. I dreamed about my diary last night. It woke me up, and I realized it was always in my subconscious. Miss Schiller saw it packed in my suitcase when she organized the switch. When our tour began, I kept it in my handbag, and it was such a visible item I never gave it a second thought." She handed the diary to Dani, pointing out where she'd found the microfiche.

"A daily book," said Dani, at last. "Miss Schiller said *tagebuch*—diary. She was trying to tell you the diary was the key. But why didn't you tell me this morning?"

"Because we have to give the microfiche to Martin," Lucy said. "But which one is Martin?"

Dani had no reply, knowing Lucy hadn't trusted her to keep it from Carl. She didn't know whether to be glad or sorry. Earlier, she had almost dreaded meeting Carl, lest he hand her half the postcard. If she had known Lucy had the microfiche, would she have told him?

"I would never give it to Carl without proof," she answered herself aloud.

"Yes, I agree. We don't have certain proof of who Martin is. The question we want to answer then, is how can we force his hand?" Lucy leaned forward as though prodding Dani to reply.

Dani didn't have to think it over. "There is only one way. Force Bennig's agent to reveal himself."

Lucy nodded. "We need an angle here. Something that proves beyond any doubt which one is Martin."

Dani's mind leaped ahead. "Bennig is desperate to get the microfiche. We can offer it for sale."

"Exactly," said Lucy, satisfied. "He will send someone to pick it up. And we will know for sure."

"It will be a certain trap. He'll have no intention of paying."

They regarded each other, each reliving a personal experience. The roar of a car motor; a moment of oblivion in a graveyard.

Dani's glance returned to the diary in her hand. Was it worth all those lives, maybe their own? Did it really matter to them who got the microfiche in the end?

"It isn't right that one evil man owns all that power," Lucy decided for her. "Isn't it about time someone pierced his armor?"

Dani's eyes gleamed in agreement. "It sounds trite, but how could we go back home and continue on with our lives, knowing we'd just given up? We are between the proverbial rock and hard place."

Lucy's eyes probed Dani's expression. "You have an idea?"

"Well, now that you mention it, I do have an idea." She gave a self-satisfied smirk. "They aren't fooled by our excuse of traveling to Wales."

"I never meant to fool them, dear," Lucy interrupted. "Only to force some kind of action, like they did to us. By now, they realize we intend to head for Oxford."

Dani's eyes widened and sparkled. She raised her eyebrows. "One of these days, I'll learn to stop underestimating you. Anyway, here's what I think." She spoke at length, Lucy interjecting with arguments and counter suggestions.

Sometime later, when they arrived at an uncertain agreement, Lucy said, "Why don't we let Jeffries carry the message to Bennig?"

"Because Carl told me that Jeffries works for an Austrian company connected to that man Chetkov, as well as Bennig. And if that isn't confusing enough, Carl believes Bennig is also paying Weatherston along with Jeffries."

"Which would mean Weatherston working two ends against the middle," finished Lucy. "We have to decide how we are going to reach Bennig himself."

"I don't know yet," confessed Dani. "But the answer must lie in Oxford. I'll start there."

"Take care, Dani." Lucy's hand gripped her arm, ensuring she had her niece's full attention. "I don't mean just be observant. I mean alert. You are involved because of me. I'd feel responsible if anything happened to you . . ."

She stopped and peered at her niece. Dani's dark eyes were large and luminous, reflecting a new vitality. Lucy took a startled step backwards, her discovery turning into dreadful dismay. "Good golly! You're enjoying all this! You're having fun!"

"Hardly fun," protested Dani. "But I admit, it isn't just a puzzle anymore. It's become a challenge, and I want to win.

Somewhere, Bennig is sure of winning too, and I can't wait to let him know he's been checked all the way!"

"We're not carrying a banner for some feminist crusade. If that's what you are doing, you'd better think again, young lady."

Dani laughed and dismissed the idea with a wave of her hand. "That has nothing to do with it. Carl said I underestimate the brutality of the world. So all right, the sides to this battle aren't drawn up fairly, but they won't win without a damn good fight." Dani paused, smiling at her own intensity. "You are half right, though. The action is giving me a new high I've never experienced."

"I hope you aren't using this *high*, as you call it, as an escape from a different situation you would rather not face," said Lucy, her tone sharp. "Making decisions on the fly might be heady stuff at the beginning. Especially when you don't have to listen to Helen's opinion. But don't let your feeling of euphoria become an end in itself, Dani. If Helen only knew . . ."

At that, Dani laughed out loud. "Haven't you noticed? I'm grown up now. It was my decision to become involved, Auntie."

"Yes, I know." It seemed so simple then, thought Lucy. She let it go and said instead, "What shall I do tomorrow?"

"Stay hidden," said Dani, remembering last night's near miss, "and pray a lot."

With Saturday came the rain. It whipped in wet sheets against the window of the train heading east to Oxford. The constant sky slung low to the ground, changing the color of the landscape from spring celadon to drab olive. Against a backdrop of cold, gray light outside the window, Dani's bright optimism slowly changed to an equally gray damp. She reviewed the plan again, looking for danger points. Almost everything about it spelled danger, and she gave up. Alone in the mist, she decided they had been foolish from the beginning, starting with the moment Superintendent Proudlove had questioned Lucy. *Too late, too late,* mocked the wheels of the train, ominously emphasizing her journey forward.

Would Bennig take the bait, or had she over-estimated his eagerness to get the microfiche? She chewed her lip. What would she do when she reached the bookshop? Hope for a sudden brainstorm? Last night it seemed rational to visit the shop, but now she was here, the outlook took on an aspect of arriving at Dracula's castle looking for a blood transfusion.

At the station, she opened her street map of Oxford and located the Bodleian Library. Not quite a mile, she guessed. Outside, she turned up the collar of her coat against the wind, opened her umbrella and set off, welcoming the fresh air. At the library, unable to resist the opportunity, she signed for a guided tour through the Divinity School, The Duke Humfrey's Library and Radcliffe Camera. Awed by the first teaching room, dating back to the fifteenth century, she lingered over Bodley's personal strongbox with its intricate locking mechanism until she could no longer delay the reason she was in Oxford.

She went in search of the guide and wrote down his directions to a computer store and set off once more. When she reached the shop, she was glad to see the place empty and began a long conversation with a clean-shaven, bespectacled clerk who kept shaking his young head more vigorously the longer she talked.

"Pretty nigh impossible, but I might know of one person," he said at last, resigned to her pleas. "He'll think I'm barmy, but he does love anything to do with code." He turned to the telephone behind the counter, dialed a number, spoke at length, rolled his eyes once, listened, nodded, and gave Dani a thumbs up before returning the receiver to its cradle. He walked with her to the door and pointed down the street, giving directions. They grinned at each other while shaking hands, both aware they had agreed to something mutually beneficial.

Stretched across the storefront of the small bookshop was the word *Martin's*, and underneath, *Books.* In front was a small A-frame, naming bestsellers and a drawing of a staircase over the word, *Mezzanine.* Heart thumping, Dani strolled past, stopping half way as though the window display had caught her eye.

A sampling of books of every kind filled the window. History, art, architecture, poetry, literary essays. One corner displayed the red and black of *The Fourth Protocol*, the latest suspense novel by Frederick Forsyth. Dani peered beyond the books, trying to see into the store. Books piled on tables, and tiers of others reached to the ceiling. The shelves banked along close rows which disappeared into the dim background. She closed her umbrella with a snap and pushed the glass paneled door open inward. A bell tinkled above her head. The interior was dim, the light blocked by the tall shelves. A faint musty smell permeated the air. For a shop that was supposed to be recently vandalized, the place looked like it had been left undisturbed for fifty years. Was she in the wrong bookstore, after all?

"Need assistance, miss?"

Dani glanced above her head and saw a circular iron staircase leading to the mezzanine. A clerk perched on a ladder looked down at her.

"Just browsing for now." She smiled.

The clerk nodded and turned to whatever he had been doing.

She wandered behind a shelf, scanning the book spines.

A customer stood farther along the narrow aisle, engrossed in his reading. Or pretending? The light seemed far too dim to read by. Suspicious, she studied him while she walked forward pretending to read the signs designating categories. He half turned, and Dani saw he had a small penlight. She stepped around to the next aisle. A thin man in a sedate dark suit walked past the far end and out of her line of vision. She heard the clerk murmuring with another customer on the mezzanine. Uncertain, she headed toward the back of the shop wondering what to do. At the rear wall, there was another book shelf and a small table and chair off to one side. Beyond that, a door, leading to the alley, she supposed. Dani looked upward at the mezzanine along the side of the store and continued toward the small table.

The thin man, umbrella hooked over his arm, stood with his back to her inspecting a book. His skin stretched tight across the back of his neck. He turned his head, and she could see more parchment skin stretched over his cheekbones, pulling his mouth in a thin, straight line. Something niggled at her memory. Weatherston's description of a man with a zombie-like face who worked next to Bennig. Dani sucked in her breath. In quick reflex action she moved down the next row of bookshelves. Her stomach muscles fluttered, cramping. *He can't be. It's my imagination.* No, her mind contradicted her. Bennig had to be getting desperate now.

She moved back along the row and came closer to him. Uneasy, she glanced over her shoulder. There was nothing but the distant muttering from the mezzanine.

"Your name is Paul," she said. Her voice squeaked. She swallowed.

He turned his head toward her, his expression curious. His

flat eyes raked her face, then he lowered his head again to the book in his hand.

Dani hesitated, feeling foolish. As if aware of her doubts, he moved a step away.

Her foolishness turned into anger. "I have a certain item that is of interest to you."

It seemed to her that the man sighed, although she could detect no movement in the skin around his lips. Placing his finger between the pages, he lowered the book, crossing his hands in front of him.

"Madam?" His lips barely moved.

She gazed back at him, unwavering, ignoring his sneer. Why was he resisting her? Was he afraid he was being watched? She made a swift glance around, but could see nothing suspicious. This time she spoke in German, her voice barely above a whisper. "If you are not interested, I'm sure Chetkov is."

She struck a responsive chord. His flat eyes flickered. He placed his book on the small table and swept the surrounding area with a glance before turning back to her.

"There is a car outside where we can speak freely. I will leave now. Turn right at the door and follow to the car at the end of the block."

Dani hesitated.

"You need not worry." Paul permitted a corner of his mouth to turn upward. He turned and walked to the front of the shop. She heard the bell tinkle, and allowed the door to close before following. The clerk on the mezzanine leaned over the iron balustrade and spied her leaving. The man in the aisle placed his book on the shelf and went toward the front where he examined the window display.

Outside, she opened her umbrella and obediently followed

along behind Paul, keeping close to the store fronts. The street rose in the short block, over a small hump, before sloping down again. A chauffeur dressed in regulation gray uniform waited beside the open door of a black Mercedes. He took her umbrella before going around to the driver's side. There was a glass panel separating him from the back seat.

"Now, Miss Morden," said Paul. "I assume that is who you are? You admit the microfiche is in your possession?"

"Yes," replied Dani. Uncertainty rose again, giving her a sick sensation in her stomach. It had happened too fast. She never expected it to be easy.

"You have my agent convinced you know nothing about it."

"We didn't know we had it." She opened her mouth to ask him the name of his agent. Instinct warned her it would be a mistake.

"And what is your intention now?"

In the dim interior, his skin took on a mummified appearance, dry and brittle. He stared at her with flat eyes. Snake eyes. Deadly.

"That depends on Mr. Bennig."

He was silent, eyes raking her face.

"There is no need to give me the silent treatment, Mr. . . . ah . . . Paul," she continued. She clasped her hands around her knees to keep them still. "We both know what I want, and it seems the most beneficial solution. My aunt and I—we have been mistreated. It's only seems fair we receive compensation. In return, your Mr. Bennig gets the microfiche. Simple, really."

"What is fair compensation to you, Miss Morden?"

"We'll try to make . . . one hundred thousand dollars do."

Paul leaned in front of her and opened the car door, whereupon the chauffeur got out. Had she gone too far? The amount just popped out. It was double what she and Lucy had agreed upon last night. Shrugging to show indifference, she made as if to go. Paul closed the door again. The chauffeur climbed back in the car.

"Miss Morden, there is an old saying. To gamble against the odds is to take a tiger by the tail."

Dani smiled. "Only if one has no insurance."

"You will give me a telephone number."

Dani shook her head. "You can do better than that. I'm sure you have the authority to decide."

The line of lips twitched. "It is a weekend. It is difficult to lay hands on that amount of money on a weekend. Even for a rich man."

"Twenty-four hours," said Dani. "You can leave a message saying the terms are acceptable with the desk clerk at the George Hotel in Bath. At four o'clock. On Monday afternoon at three o'clock, I will be here in Oxford in the Radcliffe Camera. In the lower reading room, where we will complete the transaction."

Paul nodded. "Understood. But a message isn't necessary. I have agreed to the terms."

"Not quite. There is one more condition. Your agent, the one you put on the coach with us, must make the delivery."

The Mummy blinked. Dani prayed her face did not betray her.

She let her voice falter. "I find it difficult to repeat his name, at the moment." She straightened, seeming indignant. "My aunt and I have suffered a lot of . . . inconvenience. If you don't agree, the deal is off."

"You disappoint me, Miss Morden." His flat eyes flickered over her face.

No doubt he sneers at all women, Dani thought. "Tough

bananas. Let's call it our revenge."

"You want to see his expression."

"Something like that."

"Agreed." Although he gave little outward sign, the prospect seemed to amuse him. He signaled the chauffeur.

As Dani moved forward and reached for the door handle, she said, "I trust we have made a solid bargain. Don't even think of breaking faith with my aunt and me, or plan something to happen after I leave here. We have made adequate arrangements to bring your house down about your ears."

He leaned forward and put his hand on her arm, forcing her to face him. "It is not wise to make threats, Miss Morden." Even from her distance, there was no mistaking the cold steel in his eyes or voice.

Dani pulled her arm free. "Then consider it a promise," she replied, hoping her voice didn't betray her sudden chill at his words.

On the sidewalk, she took her umbrella from the chauffeur, giving him a dazzling smile and strode away, trying not to run. Her knees wobbled as though the cartilage had disappeared. *Oh God, I hope I didn't louse this one up. Curse the weekend. It gives them too much time.* A spurt of heavy rain lashed against her face, and she lowered her umbrella and hurried along the sidewalk, seeing the reflection of a dark sky in the puddles under her feet.

Inside the car, Paul lifted the telephone.

"She is walking in your direction," he said. "If you lose her, you will find death more pleasant than life. I will be at the hotel."

SIXTEEN 16

"THANK GOODNESS YOU'RE ALL RIGHT," Lucy said, her voice wavering. "My imagination has been working overtime."

Tired and cold in her damp clothes, Dani rubbed at her aching head and shoulders. But Lucy's face, pale and distorted by anxiety stopped her from making a curt reply. She recognized what Lucy must have imagined through the long hours with only morbid thoughts for company.

She sank gratefully into a chair, kicked off her soaked shoes and wiggled her toes. It seemed she had walked miles, dodging in and out of shops, eluding any real or imagined pursuers.

"I'm sorry, Aunt Lucy. It's awful to wait and worry." She peered up at Lucy under drooping eyelids. "But would you mind if I get out of these clothes and have a hot bath before we talk about it? I'm here, safe and sound."

"But—" Lucy cut herself off and sighed, her eyes glass. Her frown turned up a little on one side, and she nodded. "I'll order tea and something to eat."

Relaxing in the big tub, Dani rippled the hot water, letting her bones absorb the warmth, and tried not to think about the day's events. Not until she almost drifted off to sleep did she get out of the now cooling water and rub herself dry with a large warmed towel. Wrapped in her bathrobe, she joined Lucy to eat, glad of the bowl of tomato soup and sliced beef sandwiches.

While they ate, she related what had transpired at the computer shop, and her feelings about the bookstore, hoping she sounded more positive than she felt. Now that she was back in Bath, she swayed between amazement that she had actually faced Hoeffner and won and being unsure she had accomplished anything close to winning at all.

"They must have fixed up the book store fast, or it wasn't as trashed as Weatherston led us to believe."

"How long would it take to pick up and re-shelf a few books?" Lucy countered. "Especially if you wanted to keep your shop open for business." Dani shrugged and bit into another sandwich.

"What's he like—this Paul Hoeffner?"

"'*Cold as Blue Flujin, where sailors say fire freezes,*'" Dani replied, and as Lucy raised her eyebrows, she added. "Herman Melville. Hoeffner's face is inscrutable and difficult to read. It's all in his eyes. A rattlesnake's eyes are friendlier."

"So. Then, it all sounds too easy?" Lucy's gaze darted from Dani to the floor and back again, eyes full of doubt.

"My question too," Dani said through a drawn out yawn. She struggled to keep her mind on track, but it was slow, like the circuits in her head had fried, and she was now manually cranking the gears. "I had a look at the microfiche. If it becomes public knowledge, there'll be all hell to pay. I didn't understand what it all meant, but I recognized two names. Bennig must get it back. If I were him, I'd do the same thing. Send the only person I could trust to the shop."

"That's just it . . ." said Lucy. "If you were him."

"What?"

"If you were Bennig," she repeated, "what would you do? If you wanted to ensure the fiche stayed secret?"

"I know, I know," replied Dani. Her expression told Lucy to

quit bringing it up. She winced, remembering Hoeffner's flat stare when she left the car. "He must kill us. But then . . . maybe not, if he believes we've taken out insurance."

"What do you suppose he'll do when he finds out we have tricked him?"

"We've gone over all this before." Dani scowled, too tired to hide her irritation. "By the time he deciphers the fiche, we'll have disappeared. Besides, he's already tried plastering you to the pavement once. What have we got to lose?"

"There you go, being immortal again." Lucy shook her head at her niece. She put both palms flat on the table as if reassuring herself it was solid. "You think it will never happen to you. But when you *witness* an actual death, you see it in a different light."

Lucy's face changed. Dani saw naked terror in the eyes staring back at her. She saw the doubts, the raw imaginings flash across her aunt's face. A day alone in the hotel room while waiting for Dani to return had taken its toll.

"We'll never do it!" Lucy cried out.

"Don't!" said Dani, her tone sharp. "We've had it if we persuade ourselves we can't win. You said it yourself. We're past the point of no return now. We can't sit and play it safe, just waiting for them to kill us."

Lucy reached out and grasped Dani's hand, struggling to blot out the pictures in her mind. Out of concern and pity, Dani fought down the tears that threatened to spill over.

It took a long moment, but then Lucy's grip relaxed. "I've had it."

"Are you saying we should quit and go home?" Dani voiced the only alternative left to them. That, and despair. "Surely not!"

"No. We will not quit," Lucy's face reddened. "I'll not be persuaded out of doing what is right. Not by an evil corporation builder playing hide and seek games, nor any spook who believes he knows what is right and feeds us cock and bull advice and lies. I simply won't stand for it." Lucy's voice was close to shouting. "Nobody is going to tell me what to do anymore."

"Then we had better stay out of sight tomorrow and wait." Dani grinned. She couldn't hide her relief, even as her heart beat increased, knowing the danger they faced.

Mid-morning on Sunday, Friedrich Bennig and Paul Hoeffner sat in the dining room, just off the central hall of the house near the Grunewald Forest, with their breakfast. Conversation was limited to general subjects as they ate rolls, coffee, croissants, and jam. The butler, silent and efficient, signaled the maid to remove the plates. He placed a tray with a fresh pot of coffee on the table and withdrew, leaving the two men alone.

Feeling his age, Paul suppressed a yawn and poured himself more black coffee, waiting for Bennig to make the first move. He had arrived late from England, and had stayed awake another hour while he brought Bennig up to date, offering facts in a logical and unemotional manner. If Bennig was forming opinions on any of it, he kept them to himself. It had always been that way.

In the forty years he had known him, Paul's loyalty had never wavered for an instant. In the year before the war ended, while on leave in Berlin, there had been more air raids—each exponentially heavier than the one before it. Bennig had pulled him from the ruins severely burned, saving Paul's life at great risk to his own. Learning Paul's mother and two younger sisters had perished in an earlier raid, Bennig had visited him during his long hospital stay. He had also paid for his medical treatment, and his restorative surgery. Bennig had been waiting for him when Paul left the hospital after his last surgery. His expression curiously detached, he had watched Paul stammer out his word of thanks, then accepted his gratitude with a mere nod of his head. They never referred to the matter again.

In the earlier years of their association, Paul had attempted to analyze Bennig's reasons for such uncharacteristic behavior. He'd ruled out instinctive action done without thought, like one who rushes into danger, irrationally risking their life for another. No, it had been a calculated risk of one who attempts a goal, like a mountain climber who defies the fates on one more cliff face. Once successful, Bennig had maintained his trophy, and in an odd, impersonal way had forged an unbreakable bond between the two men. Once he had settled on his answer, Paul dismissed it from his mind. Until now.

He knew he would do his utmost to protect Bennig. His grip tightened on his cup as he thought of his agent. From the beginning, the fool had mishandled his assignment.

"This affair is taking much too long, Paul," Bennig said. "I have had to needlessly use up a favor to have that oversized policeman, Mueller, assigned out of reach." His mouth turned down at the idea. "Your agent had multiple opportunities to eliminate the two women in the beginning. Now we need to clean up." Bennig lifted his hand and let it drop to the table.

"A misjudgment," Paul agreed. "At first he was certain they didn't know what they had. He thought he could get the fiche without violence. Still, he may have succeeded but for the foolish attempt on the aunt's life."

Bennig tapped his fingers on the table. "Chetkov is getting much too restless. But again, your agent has the experience enough to easily outmaneuver him. He didn't hesitate to kill the

Schiller woman before he found the fiche. Only he now allows his emotions to cloud his judgement. Their insistence that he bring the money verifies it."

"When he completes his mission, I will have his contract terminated," Paul said without expression. He might as well have been discussing the stock market.

"I suppose there is no doubt they actually have the microfiche? Does the postcard provide a clue?"

Paul's expression dismissed the postcard. "A picture of Christ Church Cathedral in Oxford. Schiller couldn't have hidden the microfiche there, so the card was used as proof of identification." At least, he got the postcard before Chetkov found it, he thought.

"Where is the postcard?"

"I left it with him. He thinks it may still be of some use."

"But your agent made mistakes. The two women suspect he is not what he wants them to believe. The girl shows courage." Bennig smiled. "Ah well, money has a way of soothing disillusionment. Whose idea was it do you suppose?"

Paul shrugged. The psychology held no interest for him. "I'm sure she added a significant amount to the price at the last minute."

Bennig gazed at Paul for a moment and then clicked his tongue. "That could only mean she inspected the fiche."

Resulting from yet another mistake, Paul thought, nodding. They should never have been allowed to do the unexpected and change hotels. "His judgement errors left us with only one lead. The bookstore. And left me with no choice but to show myself." Paul hid his anger, but his agent would pay dearly. "The girl hid the microfiche before she came to the bookstore. Somewhere in Oxford, I would guess. Sometimes amateurs do surprising things."

"Professionals don't expect amateurs to think." Bennig smirked. "Have you considered the girl will make a copy?"

"Of course. She will attempt to pass off the counterfeit as the real item. I'll be interested to see what method she uses to convince me it's authentic."

"What is your plan then?"

Paul spoke briefly. Bennig raised his eyebrows.

"You have calculated the risk?"

"As I have said, once we have obtained the microfiche, they will all be terminated." Paul's face did not betray his thoughts. He had prepared himself for any eventuality. He would not fail.

"You have told me everything, Paul?" Bennig toyed with the spoon in his saucer.

"Yes, my friend."

At the term, Bennig threw him a sharp glance, but he said nothing. "Then I leave it in your capable hands."

Sunday afternoon at the George Hotel was quiet. Guests sipped tea in the lounge or enjoyed the welcome sunshine in the city parks. Gerald Jeffries had entrenched himself with the desk clerk in the small room behind the reception area, with only one purpose in mind—find out where the two women had gone. From where they sat, the clerk could keep an eye on the front desk. Jeffries had winked and slyly pulled a bottle of fine scotch from his pocket. With only a mild protest from the clerk, he had poured a good quantity into their teacups, adding water from the carafe on the desk.

"Here's looking up your kilt," he said, raising his cup. They drank, smacking their lips in appreciation. "I'm telling you, Wesley," continued Jeffries in an effort to put them on equal footing, "never take on the job of tourist coach driver. They would make a vicar swear. Never a minute to yourself. They think you don't deserve a spare moment, and whether you do or not, it belongs to them."

"This job is any better, I suppose?" replied Wesley. He screwed up his face and bowed in all directions. "Yes sir, yes madam. No sir, the charges on your bill are correct, sir."

"Well at least you keep them coming," replied Jeffries. "Mine just leave. And then write the company demanding their money back. The company takes it out of my pocket. Like those two women on Friday. Just took off on me they did. Left only a flipping note."

"Oh yeah, the older bird and her niece. Good looker, what?" Wesley raised his glass in sympathy and drank.

"What? Oh yes. That's them." Jeffries put a miserable twist on his mouth. "I forgot they gave you the note for me when they left. Any idea where they went?"

"Dunno." Wesley helped himself to another shot of whisky. "Like revolving doors those two are. The old bird asked for her mail. The next thing I knew, she came out of the elevator with their luggage and left in a taxi. They were in and out again in the late afternoon, this time for good."

"She didn't say anything at all?"

"Not a dicky bird." Wesley looked at Jeffries, suddenly interested. "Something the matter then?"

"Nah," replied Jeffries. "I thought I could talk them into joining the tour later on. My boss will be proper mad when he finds out."

"Bloody tourists, eh mate?" Outside on the desk, the telephone rang. "Hang on, I'm coming," grumbled Wesley, groaning as he rose.

Jeffries waited while the clerk went to the reception area. He poured half his drink into some kind of leafy plant in the corner and sat, chewing on his lip.

He had his orders. "Find those women. They are here somewhere. We lost them in the crowds."

"What about the bookstore in Oxford?" Jeffries had suggested. "We could keep an eye on it. They might show up.

"What for? They will anticipate that, and keep away. You want us all to converge on it like idiots?" The man curled his lip in a sneer leaving no doubt what idiot he was talking about.

Privately, Jeffries thought it the most likely place, but he kept his mouth shut. Men like that didn't like the competition if they thought you were too smart.

Wesley came back. Jeffries turned his watch over on his wrist to check the face. Four o'clock. He left the bottle on the table and stood.

"If you hear anything, mate . . ." he began.

"Hang on," said Wesley. "That call was a message for them."

Jeffries sat. "Oh yeah? That's great. Who was it?"

"A man. Didn't leave a name. Just said to tell the young lady he agreed. Queer sort of message. Wonder what she's up to."

"Did you tell him she wasn't here?"

"Sure did, but he said he'd leave it anyway." Wesley shook his head. "You meet all kinds."

Jeffries sat on the edge of his chair, frustrated and half scared. It could only mean she had the fiche and offered it to somebody.

Hamel or Weatherston. He'd bet on Hamel. And odds were great she expected the message and would call soon and ask for it. The phone rang again. Jeffries stopped Wesley as he rose to answer it.

"Do a pal a favor," he said. "If that's her calling, try and find out where she is. But don't let on I'm asking." He grinned, embarrassed. "Made a fool of myself over her. I want a chance to make amends before my boss finds out all the gory details."

"Leave it to me," said Wesley, and hurried out to stop the insistent ring of the telephone. He picked up the receiver just in time to hear a voice on the other end say, "No answer at that end, madam." The phone went dead.

Cursing, Wesley hung up and dialed a number. "Hullo, hullo, Eunice. I know you just phoned here, didn't you . . . ? that was your sexy voice telling whoever-it-was there was no answer, and then you went and disconnected the call before I could even speak . . . Well, give a busy chap half a minute to get here, won't you? You need more patience, Eunice. Before I forget, there's a party after shift tonight . . . Sure I'll pick you up. Now, tell me who was it calling here from the Palace Garden?"

In their hotel room, Dani hung up the telephone. She sat down across from Lucy, more to keep her knees from knocking than anything else.

"It's on."

Lucy lifted her head from her diary, then put her pen inside as a bookmark before folding the covers together. Her movements were slow and deliberate. As if the adventure ahead were just another excursion to a cathedral or museum. "All right dear. Let's go over it again."

"Monday morning, we will check into the White Lion Hotel in Oxford. At five minutes to three, I'll telephone you from the Bodleian. We'll talk until either Carl or Weatherston show. I'll give you the name of the person with Paul and hang up. Then you will telephone the bookstore and ask for Martin, this time by his real name. If you don't get a response, tell the clerk you will call again in half an hour, and every half hour until Martin answers."

Dani paused. "Use an outside telephone, not the hotel phone. I don't think you'll have long to wait. One important thing—take no messages to meet him somewhere. You must speak to him directly and then get him to pick us up. And whatever you do, *don't* return to the hotel."

"Will you be able to stop them from leaving the library?"

Dani nodded. "Don't worry. They'll need time to deal with what I've got for them. I'll stall as long as I can, then we will meet at the bus station. The librarian has already agreed to get me out of there if I need help. That's all there is to it."

Dani moved to the telephone and asked to have afternoon tea sent to their room. "After tea, how about a hard swim before dinner? Exercise will help us sleep."

"You go swimming dear. I'm going to Evening Vespers. I know we agreed to stay here in the hotel, but I need time to myself to meditate and pray. I'll take another exit from the hotel lobby, and won't be but an hour. Surely nobody will look for me in a church."

The street lights were just coming on when Lucy walked back toward the hotel. A delightful church service had left her peaceful, in mind and soul. As she neared the hotel entrance, a young man, clean shaven and neatly dressed in a somber suit, approached her. He rubbed his hands together and gave her the kind of relieved smile which said he'd been looking for her.

"It is Mrs. Trumble, isn't it?" he asked, his hand taking her arm just above the elbow. His lips clamped shut, and his face turned serious. Lucy instinctively drew away, her stomach leaping into her chest.

"Don't be alarmed." He smiled again and held his hands away

from his body, palm out. "I told them I would wait for you." He waved toward the hotel. "It's the girl with you. They said she is your niece?" Lucy stared at him, bewildered. "Oh, maybe you aren't Mrs. Trumble? Oh drat, I'm so sorry if I've made a mistake." He looked downcast.

"No. Yes—you have it right." Alarmed, Lucy started toward the hotel steps. "What is it? Has something happened to Dani?" A black hole of fear opened in front of her.

"Please, Mrs. Trumble." He looked upset. "It isn't serious. A minor swimming mishap, is all. She slipped and gave her head a nasty crack on the edge of the pool. She's gone to the hospital for tests, because she was unconscious for a time. I was in the pool when it happened, but she's all right, Mrs. Trumble, and I'm supposed to wait here for you." He talked rapidly, his words rushing over themselves. "You didn't tell her what church, is that right? And she didn't want you to worry. She asked me to bring you there. To the hospital."

Lucy hesitated, studying him. His eyes were innocent, anxious to please. *Dani. Tests? Unconscious?* Oh God, now of all times.

"It isn't far." He pointed down the street.

Still she hesitated. "Maybe I could phone from the hotel first." She took a step toward the hotel.

"Should I wait here?" He paused, face patient, unconcerned.

Lucy changed her mind. "Come on then. Please hurry."

He smiled. "My car is just around the corner. I'm sorry, but they won't let us park on the front street."

Taking her arm, he guided her around the corner to where a dusty Japanese car was parked. The small man who emerged gave her an oily smile. Lucy froze realizing her mistake. A hand tightened on her arm, pushing her. She had no time to scream.

* * *

Dani sat in the hotel room, munching on a chocolate bar and watching television. She glanced now and then at the clock on the bedside table, then became engrossed in the silly antics of a runaway groom and his bride. Sometime later her stomach growled, reminding her she had not eaten dinner. She checked the clock again . . . she didn't know where she should begin to look. *I didn't even ask what church*, she thought. With that awful realization, she sprang up from the chair. At the window, she stared down at the street. The Sunday evening traffic was thin. She took her purse and headed to the elevator.

In the lobby, fear and panic rose like bile in her throat. Dani went out the entrance and walked to the corner, staring in all directions down the streets. *I should have gone with her—why didn't I go with her?* Swallowing the hard lump of panic in her throat, she turned and headed back to the hotel. Daring to hope, she returned to the room, listened to the silence, and then went downstairs again.

The clerk checked the key slot for messages, shook his head and said "sorry miss," before he went back to sorting papers.

Dani hesitated, wanting to insist on another search, but gave up and crossed the lobby to the elevators. She'd get her coat and go search for the church. It couldn't be far.

A clerk, dressed in the dark blue blazer of the hotel staff, got on the elevator with her, shuffling a sheaf of pink paper slips in her hand. The name plate on her blazer said *'Eunice'*. She smiled at Dani as the elevator rose. Just as the doors opened at her floor the girl said, "Did your friend from the George find you yet?"

"My friend?"

"I was on the switchboard this afternoon and you called Wesley." At Dani's blank stare she added, "Wesley, from the George hotel? He said the courier from your tour was trying to reach you. I told him he could get you here." Her voice faded at the sight of Dani's stricken face.

"Oh dear. Have I gone and done the wrong thing?"

SEVENTEEN 17

SHE PRESSED HER HEAD against the window glass and stared at the street below, at the cold blue lights illuminating the faces of people passing by in front of the hotel. The speeding traffic seemed full of purpose. The pedestrians who made their way in all directions with equal concentration highlighted her own solitude and sense of uselessness.

"Please let her be all right," she prayed.

She paced the room again and kicked at a chair standing in her way.

The telephone rang.

"*Daniella?*"

Dani's knees sagged in relief. "Aunt Lucy, how could you? I've been desperate."

"I'm fine, *Daniella.*" Her voice was apathetic, drawling. "My instructions are to say little, except I am not harmed. Although I am cold, and feel rather *Lilliputian.* It's the weather, but I'm sure it will be *all right.*"

"Never mind all that. Lucy, where are you?"

"Why I'm. . ." Lucy's voice broke off.

"As you hear, Miss Morden, your aunt is well." The man's voice was high-pitched, not English, vowels pinched, the consonants drawn out. Contrived, not his natural voice. She strained to listen for any familiarity.

"You wouldn't wish anything to happen to such a harmless creature, would you? It all depends on you doing as we say."

Dani clenched her teeth, hissing out her words. "No, it's you who will do what I say! I want my aunt back in this hotel within the hour." Her voice rose to a shout. "Within one hour, do you understand?"

"You have something to trade for her?"

"I have the blasted microfiche. If you don't bring her back right now, the newspapers will get it. I assume your name is among those listed?"

The voice showed real amusement this time. "It must be true what they say about Canadians. The true north strong and free, breeds them with stamina. Publication will only ensure your aunt's demise. Even hasten it." His voice hardened. "Do *you* understand, Miss Morden?"

"Yes."

"Good. I want the document tonight."

"I can't get the microfiche until tomorrow afternoon."

"Tonight, Miss Morden."

"It's isn't here. I can't get it until tomorrow."

She heard a harsh laugh, triumphant. "Tomorrow, at one o'clock, at the Christ Church in Oxford. Go to the south transept. Someone will contact you and give you further instructions. Follow them exactly, or your aunt will pay the consequences."

"I'll do what you want, only . . . just don't harm her. Don't— " But she had spoken into the unforgiving buzz of the dial tone. Dani stared dumbly at the receiver, then she replaced it on its cradle. She gazed around the room, hearing only the echo of Lucy's presence. There were her cup and saucer on the bedside table, a slipper dropped carelessly on the floor, resting on its side. A cheer, a raucous sound of laughter and snatches of song drifting up from the street below and through the open window, only made Dani feel more alone than ever.

Who had taken Lucy? The man's disinterest in his own name on the microfiche confirmed her earlier belief that Jeffries's people were responsible. Or was she supposed to believe it was Jeffries? Would Lucy's absentminded act be able to hold them off balance?

Dani chewed at her lip. Lucy had tried to tell her something. Lucy knew her name was Danielle, so why call her *Daniella?* And why not just Dani, as she always did? She had mentioned *Lilliput* and the weather, and being cold. *Lilliput* was the land of opposites. She was cold; the opposite of hot. Was it a clue to her location? A bakery? A health spa? It made no sense. Dani groaned. There was also the pressing problem of Bennig and Paul. They expected her to be in the Bodleian Library tomorrow at three o'clock. Paul had warned her, and now she held a tiger by the tail, trapped with no way out of this mess.

Angry at herself, she made tight fists, pushing her nails into her palms, and fought against a threat of tears. For Lucy's sake, she must be able to function, not let her anxiety rise to dangerous levels, which was what these people probably wanted.

The piercing double ring of the telephone made her nearly jump out of her skin. She snatched at the phone.

"Lucy?" Hopeful.

"Dani," said Carl's voice, "thank God I've found you."

Disappointment made her snap. "You. What do you want, Carl?"

"You did a foolish thing and caused me much trouble. I'm coming over. It may take a while, but don't leave again."

"No Carl. Leave me alone." She knew she sounded hysterical.

His voice sharpened. "What's wrong? Tell me."

Dani swallowed, gripping the receiver, her knuckles white. "Nothing. I—we are both tired and fed up with it all, and we're going to bed."

She could feel his hesitation. "I'll come over to see you first thing tomorrow morning," he said at last. "This time, stay there. I'll have a man outside guarding your door."

Your man is too late, she wanted to shout, but he had hung up. She wasn't sure about Carl either, and if she didn't have the microfiche, would she ever be?

She opened her room door slightly, and looked down the corridor. A young couple stood in front of a room halfway down the hall, the man keying the door. He stood aside for the girl and pinched her bottom as she passed him. Dani heard a yelp, and a giggle sounded from inside the room before the door closed. At the far end of the hall, a short balding man stood before his door, fumbling in his pockets. He glanced in her direction, shrugged, and continued scrounging for his keys.

Carl's man?

She heard the bell of the elevator signaling a stop, and watched as the heavy doors slid open. A bellhop carrying luggage turned away down the other corridor. The man following him made Dani back into her room and close the door. *Weatherston.*

Dani's alarm and the telephone shrilled together, bringing her into consciousness. She stayed where she was, in that puzzled moment, before a jolt of recognition made her realize why her chest felt so heavy.

She looked at her watch. Six thirty. Still groggy with one of Lucy's sleeping pills, she pushed the covers aside and answered the insistent ring. Her voice sounded hollow.

"Weatherston is there, at your hotel," Carl said.

She felt numb in her vulnerability. "They've grabbed her." Her voice wavered. "They took Lucy!"

"When? Who did?"

"How do I know? Jeffries. Weatherston. Maybe even you." She was shouting again, out of control from the sheer relief of talking to somebody. "I need proof, Carl. Proof that shows you are who you say. I want her back. Do you hear me?"

"Take it easy." His tone was soothing. "There is a café not far from you called the Kicking Horse. As you exit the hotel, turn right, then right again at the end of the street. The café is half way down the block. Meet me there."

A half hour later, she found Carl sitting in a booth near the back of the café, warming his hands around a steaming cup of coffee. Dani slid along the bench opposite.

"Well?" she demanded, ignoring the other cup in front of her.

Carl hesitated, staring. She had used a good deal of makeup, trying to cover the pockets of fatigue beneath her eyes.

"You have wound your hair up." He smiled. "I like it."

Dani turned down her mouth. "How did you find us?"

"I followed Weatherston. Now what's all this about Lucy?"

She told him, only leaving out the part about her meeting with Paul.

"Did she give you any kind of clue when she telephoned?"

"Nothing. She said she was cold and something about the weather. Maybe it's a clue, but I can't figure it out."

"She's indecisive and muddled at the best of times, isn't she?"

Lucy indecisive? Weatherston didn't think so, she almost said. She remembered his calculating look when Lucy talked about trade fairs. Did he take Lucy because he realized how much of a threat she was to him?

"They want the microfiche by one o'clock today."

Carl reached out and gripped her arm. "You can't. You must let me have it. We'll think of something." The naked plea in his voice startled her.

"No."

"They will kill you both. Believe me, those kind will never let you leave this country alive. I'm doing what I can to help. People are already looking for her. Someone must have seen her."

"Even if I had the fiche, which I don't, I wouldn't give it to you," she said. "I'll do whatever they want, even for just a small chance of getting Lucy back. At this point, I couldn't care less who ends up with it. If we had known about the microfiche we would have never got involved in the first place."

"What are you going to do?"

Dani's eyes wavered then steadied on his. "Meet them. Plead with them. What else can I do?"

"I'll go with you."

"No! If they see you they'll kill Lucy." Alarmed, she shook off his arm and stood. "Stay away from me, Carl."

"Dani." Carl's jaw clenched. He reached up and pulled her down beside him. "It isn't just coincidence that Weatherston is here, watching you. You must realize by now he or Jeffries kidnapped Lucy."

"So? What can we do? Poke him with a stick? It won't get Lucy back."

A man walked by, stopping to stare at Carl as he passed their booth, he then disappeared toward the washrooms at the rear of the café. The short balding man she had seen in the corridor last night searching for his keys.

"Go to your hotel room," said Carl. "I'll meet you there."

"What for?"

"You'll see. Now just go."

"Hi! Mr. Weatherston!"

Weatherston turned. He frowned when he spotted Roberta across the street from him. Looking relieved, she dodged the traffic and came up to him.

"I missed the coach," she explained. "Shouldn't you be at the George Hotel?"

Just what I need now, he thought. He frowned again and kept walking toward the other end of Bath's Holburne Museum. Roberta switched a light nylon catchall from one shoulder to another and started after him.

"I had an errand," she said. "Gerry—Mr. Jeffries—said he would pick me up in front of that bus stop." She pointed. "At seven thirty. But he did not come."

Weatherston glanced at her. Gerry? What errand? None of the shops were open this early. "Perhaps he's late."

"I promised my English professor I would bring to his mother here, a special music record she wanted. He would not trust the postage. Yesterday she was not home, so I had to bring it this morning. Now I am stranded." Not stopping for a breath, Roberta continued talking and walking fast, dashing in front of him, trying to look him in the face. "You are going to Oxford? Would you take me with you?"

"Did you go to the wrong bus stop?" *She's anxious and going to a lot of trouble explaining everything,* he thought. Why was she really here? He turned from her, and his eyes searched the area around them.

"No, no. It is the correct one. Are you meeting someone?"

"Yes. Mrs. Trumble." Perhaps she would take the hint.

He went back over the note again. And the bellboy who had delivered it, who said Mrs. Trumble, in room 1211, had instructed him to deliver it to nobody else but Mr. Weatherston. Automatically, he registered the bellboy's description. Short, balding, middle-aged. With his hand outstretched in the usual reflex action of a hotel employee living on tips. Everything normal.

"I haven't seen you around here before," he had said anyway.

The bellboy's eyes had remained steady. "Name's Percy, sir. I'm on morning shift this week, sir."

He's telling me he knows I checked in last night, thought Weatherston. *I hope he forgets just as fast.* He had questioned the man. "I wonder how Mrs. Trumble knew I was a guest here."

"She said you'd ask that, sir, and to tell you she saw you come in, just after midnight." Percy gave him the note, smiled and kept his hand out for his tip. The note was brief. Lucy had seen him come in the evening before, and she asked him to meet her at the museum right away. Wait for her there if she was late. She had important news for him. Please hurry.

Weatherston remembered his elation. It would soon be over. His waiting tactic had paid off. Thank God he'd found her before the others had. Time was running out.

"I'm sorry if I am . . . what you say, unpopular, to you?" Roberta intruded on his thoughts. "But I have not enough money for the bus to Oxford. It's foolish but I have spent too much, and I have not seen Carl to ask him for more. So I can wait until you are free. Perhaps Mrs. Trumble is also going to Oxford? Only, could I not please ride with you?"

"Look, Roberta, I'm sorry, but I'm very busy and can't take you just now." Digging into his pocket, he pushed a banknote into her hand. "Here. Money for the bus."

He left her and headed back to the other end of the museum and his hotel to pack up his luggage, sure that Lucy had tricked him. Of course they were going to Oxford. And both had slipped away again while he was out of sight, taking the bait to meet her. Two amateurs had out-maneuvered him again. He could almost smile. Dani's idea no doubt. He had Lucy won over, until her niece had put in her shilling's worth.

He turned again and saw Roberta still standing at the other end of the museum, watching him. She looked apprehensive, small and lost. Poor Roberta. Carl won't do anything more than hunch his big shoulders now that she's been left behind. She was late, and Carl was the type to just leave her, thinking it would teach her a lesson. And Jeffries, anxious to reach Oxford, wouldn't wait an extra minute for her, thinking she would have gone with Carl.

"Come on, Roberta," he called out to her, cursing to himself. "We haven't much time, so let's get started."

Carl inspected the door to Weatherston's room, then felt around the edges before inserting a key into the lock. He opened the door and pulled Dani in after him.

"What am I looking for?"

"We won't know until we find it." He opened the closet door and pulled out a suit jacket.

Dani opened a few drawers, gently at first, then more boldly. They were all empty. She spotted his suitcase by the chest. She lifted it to the bed, and bent to the straps.

"Wait," said Carl. "Not like that. Notice the position of things, so you can replace everything accurately."

"Not that you haven't done this before, it seems," Dani said with a bitter smile.

Carl lifted the lid and studied the contents. Satisfied, he ran his hands under the first layer of clothing, then the next. He slid his fingers along an inside pocket. Halfway along the second one, his hand stopped. He pulled out a piece of hard paper.

Dani snatched at it. "The postcard!"

"Wait." Still searching, Carl pulled out the other half.

Dani fused the two. The edges matched. She turned it over, saw the address of the bookstore. It was Lucy's half.

Dani stared up at Carl, misery in her eyes, pleading. *If only I'd trusted him sooner*, she thought. Lucy would still be here.

The telephone rang once, and Dani jumped, almost letting out a yell.

Carl took the pieces from her hand. In one nearly invisible movement, he returned them to the suitcase, closed the luggage, and fastened the straps. Dani heard the elevator bell just as they closed the door to her room.

EIGHTEEN 18

IN OXFORD, DOWN A QUIET, narrow cobblestone street was an abandoned garage cum warehouse. Inside, in an area furnished with a rickety table, two chairs, and an overstuffed couch with broken springs, Lucy slowly woke, loathe to let go of her dream.

A child again, swimming on another hot summer's day, she'd climbed out of the pool, and ran with liquid footsteps to the fountain, bending to take the water in thirsty gulps until she felt wet inside too. The glorious taste of water spilling its bubbles over her chin.

Shivering, she eased her side away from a jabbing spring and licked her dry lips. The damp air was strong with the rancid odor of oil, grease, and mildew, lurking like a bad flavor in the back of her throat. She tested the strap binding her arm. The other end led somewhere under the couch, allowing her little freedom to move.

"Hell and damnation," she said out loud, flexing numb fingers.

Everything in her body ached, inside and out, and she squirmed trying to find a comfortable position. She hoped Dani had seen through her message. So far, the two men guarding her thought she was an absent minded old fool, but that didn't lull her into thinking them less dangerous because of it. She doubted her age and sex made any difference at all. But it was her only defense for now.

The older man's receding chin made his narrow nose point forward like a rat's. His eyes were small; his unwavering stare glittered with a strange light. He had a knife too, holding it like they were old friends. She knew she was looking at someone who would kill with no qualms of conscience. Lucy shivered and tried to pull her sweater closer around her with one free arm. She blinked her eyes and stretched her neck, trying to clear her dizziness. They had given her only a cup of tea since yesterday from a cracked and stained mug, but she had drank from it anyway.

She considered screaming again but decided against it. The threat in the small man's eyes warned her against uttering a sound and frightened her beyond hope.

A toilet flushed. The washroom door opened, and the young man appeared, the same one whose disarming charm had fooled her yesterday. A nice looking boy with fair, curly hair. His name was Tom. His face was the kind that could instantly trigger the maternal instincts of an older woman like Lucy, but when she peered at him now, compassion was the last thing she felt. Hate boiled up inside her from the unknown depths of her belly. She took a deep breath and closed her eyes, retreating inside to calm herself. Now was not the time for emotional outbursts. She needed to play nice. She might stand a chance if she could get him to talk to her.

"Could I wash my hands please?" she asked primly.

"What, again?"

"The damp," she explained, "and this place is cold."

He cursed and fumbled with the strap from under the couch. With a firm grip, he escorted her to the washroom containing a toilet and basin stained with rust. He reached around to the inside of the door and removed the old-fashioned skeleton key. He let her through, then locked the door from the outside.

By the time she finished and was escorted back to her seat, the little, older man was gone.

She sat on the couch while Tom redid the strap to her arm. "What time is it?" she asked.

"Almost eight."

"My nephew is about your age," she ventured, and gave him a brilliant smile. "He's a nice boy. Like you. You aren't suited to this kind of business, are you? Not really. Anyone can see you're not like *him*, your partner."

"Belt up, lady."

The conversation ended at that. So much for trying to talk to him.

Later, the door opened. The small man came hurrying in, holding a paper bag. Lucy smelt coffee and something sweet, and her mouth watered. He placed the bag on the table and turned, his face twisting.

"What's with you?" asked Tom. "You took your time getting here." He opened the bag and took out three plastic cups of coffee and three sticky buns. Lucy's innards growled with anticipation.

"I had to shake off a tail," said the little man. His tongue flicked out and he ran it around his lips.

Tom's head jerked up. "Did you lose him?"

"Yeah, but I don't like it."

"Relax, Bertie," said Tom. "There is nothing to worry about. Your little pea brain works too much overtime." Tom placed a sticky bun on a paper napkin and brought it, with a cup of coffee, over to Lucy. She restrained herself from grasping at it and held up her strapped arm, eyes pleading. Tom hesitated, then undid the binding. "We've got our eye on you, lady," he warned. He returned to the table and Bertie.

"I tell you, I know," Bertie insisted. "That guy has got me thinking, and I've figured it out."

"You think too much." Tom bit into his sticky bun.

"Listen to what I'm saying, Tom. He's going to get the cosh from. . ."

"Shut yer gob!" Tom's eyes swiveled from Lucy and back to Bertie. "What do you know?"

Bertie sat down, pushed the bag to one side and leaned over the table, whispering.

Lucy moved so she could see Bertie's lips. She would have to improvise according to the British accents, and she wasn't always accurate, but she had to try to learn what the plans were. Grateful that the large space didn't mask whispers, she put all her attention on her two captors.

"Yesterday, remember when our guvnor went to pick up his orders? Well, I followed him." Bertie grinned as Tom put his face into his hands, shaking his head.

"Just protecting our interests as you might say," Bertie continued. "It don't pay to work blind. And you never know when a bit of knowledge comes in handy. I followed him to this posh suite in the White Lion Hotel, see?"

Tom leaned back, his expression nothing short of raw fear.

"I picked the lock and let myself real quiet-like into the adjoining room while he was at the telephone."

"Now you're giving me the willies. These people don't play around. If they caught you, they would fizzle me too. Did that ever cross your nimble brain?"

"Don't worry. I'm practiced at opening doors." Bertie leaned forward until his sharp chin almost rested on the table. His voice lowered. "That man is a killer, Tom. You wouldn't like his face. His skin is stretched like the skin on a banger."

"Did you hear what he said?"

"*Leave no loose ends. As soon as the girl gets here*. That's what he said." Bertie's whisper grew desperate. "And you had better believe it means us too. We know too much, Tom."

Tom only stared at Bertie, then shook his head with vigor. "Nah."

Bertie's pointed nose twitched in agitation. "Use your blinking loaf. I know his kind. Takes one to know one, I always say. They don't leave witnesses. Bet your last quid on it. Now, I spotted some big guy following me. I think I lost him, but if he's smart, he'll figure it out. There isn't much around this place to confuse people. He'll be in here as soon as he decides it safe, and we'd better be scarce by then."

Tom paused, thinking, and the skin around his lips whitened. "What about her?" He cocked his head toward Lucy.

Lucy tried to look unconcerned, but she shivered and wrapped her arms about herself.

"I've got it all worked out," said Bertie. He glanced at his watch. "Our guv' said give him a dingle from the phone booth outside round about now, and he'd tell us when he's due here. Here's what we tell him . . ." Bertie's voice was insistent, almost panicked. He lowered his head, and Lucy was unable to make out the rest, but Tom seemed agitated. He jerked up.

"But when he gets here, she'll tell him the truth. He'll put the word out. Come after us."

"Not if we tell him the truth. Not if we put her somewhere else, for instance." Bertie licked his lips.

Lucy stifled a scream.

* * *

Dani's eyes pleaded with Carl.

"We will find her," he said again. "But we need more time."

Dani took her coat from the closet. "There is no more time."

"I'll drive."

Dani shook her head. She had never felt so wretched. "I'm going alone. Her life depends on it. I have a few tricks left." She tried to sound positive, but only succeeded in sounding doubtful.

"Like what?"

"I'm not giving them the microfiche."

"Have you been living on a banana boat?" Carl grabbed her by the shoulders, forcing her to look at him. "How many times do I tell you they don't intend to let you go, that they will eliminate all threats to their operation? The stakes are too high, too profitable. You don't understand that yet."

"Yes, yes, I know Carl." Dani waved his objections aside. "Only now, I want you to trust me. If my plan works, I'll have the microfiche for you. Just don't interfere with this, Carl. And don't follow me, or we'll both lose."

Carl's gray eyes stared at her for a moment longer, the furrow between his brows deepening. At last he slumped in defeat.

"At least give me a chance to talk to you before you go to your meeting place. I may have located her by then. Will you give me that much?"

She conceded, thankful he hadn't insisted that she tell him where the meeting place was. "But somewhere safe. If the wrong people see us, it's game over."

"There's a lane called Pusey Place, behind Ashmolean Museum. I'll meet you at the corner, where it joins St. John Street." He showed her on her map. "It will be safe amongst the crowds. At twelve o'clock."

"Can you keep Weatherston away from me?"

"You can count on it," said Carl.

At eight thirty, the day already warm under a cloudless sky, Jeffries stood by the coach door puffing on a cigarette. He couldn't wait to reach Oxford where he would disappear as fast as he had appeared. It would be over by then. He sniggered at the thought of angry tourists when they found out he had gone. Or what was left of them. At the rate people were leaving the tour, there wouldn't be many complaints.

He counted them as they came out of Lacock Abbey, one of his scheduled stops on the way to Oxford. He checked the Brookers off his list, the Griffin woman and the two old dears. Then the American who had quaffed back two liters of wine every night since he had taken over, and likely had seen the entire tour through an alcoholic haze. He saw Palmer wander out of the Abbey along with Wong and his everlasting briefcase. He needn't worry about Roberta, she'd make her own way to Oxford with somebody, since Carl didn't seem to worry or keep tabs on her. Serves him right for bringing along a bird and expecting her to sit still while he rushed another one right under her eyes. Jeffries wouldn't stick around waiting for him either.

He drew his last puff and frowned. Now the end was in sight, he was getting twitchy. He'd kept track of the girl and her aunt, but he wouldn't do it anymore. He wasn't about to have a murder charge hanging over his head. If he did, they would blackmail him forever. Jeffries swung into the driver's seat and closed the bus door. If he pushed it, he could be in Oxford two hours ahead of schedule.

Lucy finished her coffee and felt stronger. If she were to survive, she needed her wits about her. She took the last bite of her sticky bun and brought her fingers up to lick the glaze off but thought better of it and wiped them on the paper napkin instead. She eyed the remaining bun on the table.

Tom's rigid posture drew her attention. Head close to his partner's, the rat-faced man licked his lips, distraught. Tom tipped his head at her and leaned closer, talking. Bertie replied, tapping his finger against the table in emphasis. Tom shook his head. His eyes flickered over to her. Unconsciously, she pushed backwards, toward the far end of the couch, blackness flooding her mind. Nausea rose in her throat.

"Oh dear. I must—please. I'm going to be sick."

Bertie scowled at her. "Swallow it."

Lucy groaned softly, put her hand to her mouth and made a retching sound.

"Sod it!" Tom came over, seized her arm and pulled her up, causing her to stumble. Cursing, he pushed her along.

Lucy almost fell into the washroom. When Tom pulled the door shut, she put her ear up against the panel. She felt the wood shudder as Tom leaned against it, and Bertie's harsh whispering carried on.

Lucy sat on the lid of the toilet, thinking hard.

"This is the most peculiar tour," Vera Brooker said to her husband as the coach neared Oxford, "I think you must complain to Mr. Holly when we get back to London. We haven't made near the amount of advertised stops this morning. We've missed Lydiard House and Corsham Court—I particularly wanted two hours there. And these people. Most peculiar. That Mr. Weatherston, for instance. He left without a backward glance. Not a gentleman at all. At the least, you'd think he would say goodbye. And that Dani girl. What kind of a name is that for a grown woman I ask you? She and her aunt just shoved off as well. You really must complain to Mr. Holly. I insist on it—and demand a partial refund. I shall support you in that if you wish."

"Vera, for the sake of peace, shut up."

Vera Brooker gasped at her husband and closed her mouth.

Inside his room at the White Lion Hotel, Paul sat in the armchair beside the telephone desk dressed in his suit pants and shirt, sleeves rolled up and top button undone. With experienced precision, he cleaned his Mauser nine millimeter automatic pistol and checked the mechanism. He loved his old "broomhandle" Mauser and the parts he caressed had been replaced many times to keep the weapon in first class shape.

When all was done to his satisfaction, he inserted the stripper clip loaded with cartridges, pressing down and depositing them into the magazine. Finally, he removed the clip, releasing the bolt, and a cartridge slipped into the chamber.

"Hurry up in there!" A fist banged once on the door.

Lucy turned and holding her head over the dirty washbasin, pushed her finger down her throat. An empty retching followed. She groaned again.

"Please. Just leave me. Oh God, I'm so sick." She began to weep.

More whispering. She heard footsteps retreating, and her heart leaped in triumph. Disappointment followed as she heard them returning, and the key twisting in the lock. Footsteps again, then silence.

A moment later, Lucy turned the knob and pulled. The door resisted, and she leaned her forehead against it, tears welled in her eyes and started to slide down her cheeks against the door panel. Seconds later, she drew herself erect, sucked in a determined breath, and peeked through the keyhole. She saw the tip of the key. Wincing from stiffness, she got down on her hands and knees, searching the concrete floor for wire, nails—anything long and solid enough to push through the lock.

Footsteps sounded outside. She got to her feet and ran the tap water, splashing her face, moaning and weeping to herself until the footsteps receded.

Lucy reached for the tissue paper, and out of habit, she rubbed the harsh waxy-like paper between her hands to soften it. In every public washroom on the tour, the supply of toilet paper had the softness of butcher's meat wrap. Maybe it discouraged the tourists from taking a few rolls home with them, she thought, idly flexing it. She rolled it up, then a second piece around the first, twisting the two until it was the size of a pencil and tested it in the keyhole. It was too round. She mashed it flat, screwed it tighter and pushed it in. A little resistance, then the twist collapsed.

Lucy bent down and put her eye to the keyhole. The key was awry in the lock, and she considered what to do next. Standing, she mussed up her hair and tapped at the door.

"Please? Can you help me?" She waited, then tapped again.

"Now what?" Tom asked.

"If I could just have my purse—ah handbag," she pleaded. "My medication, my little pills—" The door opened. Tom looked in. Lucy sat on the toilet and grasping the basin with both hands, leaned her head against it.

"Please," she whimpered. "It's my heart." She let tears fall.

"I don't think I can stand being tied up again. Please. I have nowhere to run. I need my pills."

Tom's face stiffened, and his eyes narrowed on her.

Bertie looked in over Tom's shoulder. "She don't look half green, eh Tom?" He sounded pleased.

Lucy's fingers gripped the basin. She let her eyes roll up as she leaned forward to open her mouth.

Screwing his face up in revulsion, Tom averted his eyes. "Get her bloody handbag!"

NINETEEN 19

DANI GOT OFF THE BUS AT A4144 STREET in Oxford and walked along the street to the intersection of St. John. The sky was a mishmash of alternating clouds and sunshine, one moment teasing the people with rain, the next warmth. Standing in a casual attitude, her coat slung over her arm, she searched the area, stopping now and then to scan again in case her eyes had betrayed her the first time. She watched the bicycle traffic and imagined them moving with purpose—meeting friends, planning parties, wondering what to prepare for dinner. What could be less menacing? Two weeks ago, she was one of them, although rigid, governed by a routine of self-pity. She glanced around once more as though waiting for someone. Nobody showed any interest. Several people crossed the street toward her, and she joined the swarm continuing down Gloucester until she reached the computer store. The bespectacled young man, looking like Ichabod Crane, smiled in recognition.

"Good timing," he said and reached beneath the counter, bringing out a bulky envelope. Once more, she gazed through the window toward the street. Nobody outside stopped to look back.

"The cost is more than estimated," he said, almost apologizing. "My friend said he spent almost thirty hours, even with extra help to finish in time." He worried his glasses at the bridge of his nose with a skinny forefinger.

"That's all right," she said keeping a suspicious eye on him. "I'll pay whatever is fair." When he brightened, she relaxed. He was only nervous about her ability to pay.

He named a price. She paid without hesitation, and added three twenty pound notes to it. The young man's eyes widened.

"For a bad memory," she said. "If someone asks about my visit here, I want you to say I was only interested in the science of computers. Who makes them, are they difficult to assemble, things that any person ignorant of computers might ask. If the questions get persistent, you can admit I was also interested in imports and exports. Do not give any indication you are lying. It's important."

"Right." His eyes opened a bit wider. He pushed his forefinger on the nose piece of his glasses again.

"You must be convincing. It's of national importance. Can you do that?"

He looked determined, a bit excited at the prospect. "I can lie flatter than a sidewalk."

"One more thing," said Dani.

She gave him instructions and asked if she might use his washroom. A short time later she emerged to set off to meet Carl.

The young man watched her hesitate at the door.

"We have a back entrance."

She grinned at him. "I like a fast learner."

"Money frees up the brain." He showed her how to negotiate the rabbit warren of passageways behind the shop. He shook her hand. "Good luck."

Lying on the bare concrete and peering through the space under the bottom edge of the door, Lucy tried to judge the distance she had pushed her sweater along the floor. Was it far enough? Her long handled comb wouldn't push any farther, and they might come back at any moment.

She got to her knees and pushed the handle of the comb through the lock, lifting and forcing the key. Her breath came in short gasps against her hand. The key dipped, caught on the edge of the keyhole. Hand shaking, she rested a few seconds then reached in her bag and exchanged the comb for a nail file. She inserted the tip into the lock again, placing it under the key, and lifted. Suddenly, it was free, and she heard a plunk against the soft material. Almost sobbing in relief, she reeled in her sweater, using her finger tips to pull it back under the door and unlocked it from her side.

She took off her shoes and holding them, crept down the corridor in the opposite direction from where she heard Tom and Bertie's murmurs. Halfway across the garage, freedom within sight, a heavy thrust like a rock slammed up against her, and she fell. Lucy's first thought was to wonder why she would have tripped when the floor was clear of obstacles. But then came the pain, centered on one side, high on her shoulder.

Behind her, Tom's voice said, "Sod, Bertie, now you've done it."

"We couldn't let her get away, could we?"

Tom cursed. "You watched her work the key out of the door. Just so you could stab her."

A wrenching pain, like a poker being shoved hard against her upper back. Lucy cried out, biting her lip to keep from sinking into darkness.

Tom cursed again. "She's bleeding."

"So what do you want me to do? Tie a ribbon on my knife and

leave it for Scotland Yard?"

Bertie bent and put his hands under Lucy's arms. "Go on take her feet. We'll get her out of sight. By the time she's found, we'll be away."

"She'll bleed to death."

Bertie looked at Tom, eyes flickering. "Don't go queer on me now, mate. Not if you want to kiss the girls tomorrow. It's your fault. You believed her stupid story about being sick. Lucky I was watching the door. Now get hold of her feet there."

Bertie put his hand under her shoulders, and Lucy plunged into darkness.

Carl was nowhere in sight when she came to the corner of Pusey Place. Dani kept walking and turned down St. John, merging in with a group of tourists. As she turned to start back to Pusey, a hand pulled her around the corner and up against a wall. She let out a pitched gasp of fright, sinking against the building in relief when she saw it was Carl.

"I watched until I made sure you weren't being followed," he said. He ran his fingers through his hair and glanced up and down the street.

"Have you found her?"

"Maybe." Carl wouldn't meet her eyes.

She put her hand on his chest, trying to turn him. "What's wrong?"

"Relax. I called in a favor from a man I know. Someone whose business is knowing who in this city wouldn't mind kidnapping. He followed one of his suspects to an abandoned building. He's sure Lucy is there."

"Well, what are we waiting for? Let's go." She pulled his arm, not hiding her anxiety.

"Give it up, Dani," said Carl, not moving.

Dani only stared back at him, her eyes cold.

"All right!" He took her arm, savagely pulling her after him. "I'll take you."

"Have you seen Weatherston?" She had to run to keep up.

"Roberta is with him."

"You've told her then!"

"No. Roberta will do it for me, and she knows not to ask questions. I've told her to run into him by accident and tell him she's been left behind. She will plead with him to take her to Oxford. It will keep them both out of the way."

Dani chewed her lip. Weatherston would ditch Roberta in time to meet Paul so they could pick up the microfiche at the cathedral. How long did she and Carl have before Paul realized she wasn't coming?

As she hurried alongside Carl, her spirits lifted. She felt elated, in a rush to get to the danger point. Maybe she should take up Carl's offer to keep her safe? Some vague apprehension pricked at her mind which questioned her logic to follow him, but she pushed it down. The urge to be part of the rescue was too powerful.

Weatherston left Kingston behind and headed northeast toward Oxford. He drove with sparse movements, relaxed, looking from underneath unkempt eyebrows at the road ahead.

God, how that girl chattered. Eyes feeling glazed, he knew he had a silly smile plastered on his face. Roberta had a childlike quality about her which stopped any rudeness, but he'd prefer she couldn't speak English quite so well.

Letting her voice drift out of his consciousness he picked up the thread of his own thoughts. The day had not begun well. Although he was confident that Lucy and Dani would head for Oxford their sudden disappearance from the hotel that morning disturbed him. They were running straight into certain danger. At least he knew where Jeffries was. Weatherston calculated he was only a scant hour behind, what with the scheduled stops he must make along the way. His grip tightened on the steering wheel.

If he hadn't been at the hotel desk to hear the answer when Andrew Brooker had asked the clerk about the whereabouts of Lucy and Dani, it would have taken him longer to find them. Perhaps he was getting old, behind the times. Sighing, he wondered if he felt tired or dispirited or both. Anyone who stayed at this work lost themselves trying to live within the brutality and evil. And inside, a hard core developed which never went away. The young wizards had not experienced it yet; they were still back in the classroom training with dummies. They flourished, the first real time out, under the thrill of adrenaline pumped into their veins. The next time they were still eager. By the fourth mission, they grew desperate, craving the excitement like a drug. And like the effects of a drug, they soon grew old and disillusioned, wanting to be just another average person lost in the crowd but unable to give up what had become an addiction.

He gripped the steering wheel, and his features hardened. If only that young ass had given him Dittmahn's message the same day he'd received it. And then lying about it, saying he had sent it up the line as a routine, but not being able to account for its disappearance. A week. A bloody long week had gone by. Plus. Then more time wasted while they dithered over who to send.

". . . But then I didn't think it mattered that Carl asked

someone else in the beginning." Roberta's voice penetrated his thoughts. Her lips formed in a pout. "But he should not have abandoned me in a strange city. The tour does not even interest him."

"Yes," replied Weatherston. Feeling somewhat guilty for being preoccupied, he smiled at Roberta, his expression kind. "Being stuck on a tour with old geezers can't be too exciting for a young girl."

"Oh, that is not so," protested Roberta, china-blue eyes wide, face pink. "It is just Carl. I don't know why I agreed to come with him when I do not trust him very much, you know. He can be cruel. When I look at other men, he is angry, but then he becomes annoyed because I bother him when he is busy."

Roberta's voice faded again as Weatherston's thoughts turned inward.

The job hadn't clicked from the beginning. And on top of it all, Palmer had to show up. A one in a million chance.

Such a long time ago. North Africa. Most of them meeting the enemy for the first time. The attacks started in February, the weather blustery and cold. Miserable. Three raids behind the lines botched. All supposed to be a piece of cake, until most of the men under his command had been killed. They suspected an enemy agent. They had planned the last raid with the sole purpose of flushing the agent out. The result was successful, but costly. And Palmer, his young radioman, unconscious, almost dead from loss of blood. He wondered what Palmer would say if he knew Weatherston had carried him all the way back. The trouble started when the brass decided the agent would be more valuable left in place so they could feed him false information. And he, Weatherston, being vulnerable and idealistic, had permitted them to transfer him out before the whispers had been squelched. Dismissing his doubts, they told him all would be right in the end. But when the denouement came, Palmer had already shipped out with most of his leg gone. Now, forty years later, he turns up again, carrying a grudge as bitter as that night in Tunisia.

Weatherston's lips pinched, remembering. Palmer had been one of the lucky ones who had barely made it home. Most had not, the rest either killed, missing, or captured. No doubt Palmer's story had swelled over the years and been suitably iced, judging by the expression on Lucy and the girl's faces that night.

Roberta's high voice chattered nonstop. He heard Mavis Griffin's name, and his ears changed frequency.

"She is a strange person, too, don't you think?" Roberta was saying.

"In what way?"

"She is, how you say, undescribed?"

"Nondescript?"

"Yes, thank you. But she listens and watches, and she is nervous and fearful. She has been in Germany for a long time too, I think."

"She's pure English," Weatherston replied, startled.

"Yes, but sometimes her speaking has the sounds of German. Like speaking it so often, it has intruded onto her English. You understand what I say?"

Good lord, thought Weatherston, the girl was no fool.

Roberta left the subject of Mavis and started on Carl again, almost in mid-thought. "Carl thinks I don't listen. My teachers say the same, then I surprise them when I can repeat everything. Like this morning with Carl. Last night he was to meet me at seven, but he didn't come, and said I was wrong. But his clothes smelled like he went to see race cars, so he. . ."

Weatherston tossed her a tolerant smile. While she talked, she gazed at the scenery, eyes credulous and shrewd, but not detecting any nuance of preoccupation in him. Could anyone be so accepting of life? No, he decided, seeing her determined little chin. One of these days, she will tire of being put upon and revolt, shocking everyone.

As soon as he dropped Roberta off at the hotel in Oxford, he would go to his shop. He could forget the postcard. It was of no use now—whoever had it. Thank God Peter would recover, but that business of the postcard had been a bad idea. The new man left at the shop should have new information on Dani and Lucy by now. Also Carl Hamel and Roberta Arndt, he thought, glancing sideways. The Branch had given him poor cooperation. They either never received his requests—hard to believe—or were abominably late with replies. As though they perceived his failure, proving he was past it.

A new thought nagged at him. His expression tightened. It could account for all the slip ups, the delays, his every action anticipated. Roberta's silence grew loud, her eyes turned to him, questioning.

"I'm sorry Roberta. You were saying?"

"I said I wondered why Carl should pretend to be concerning about Dani's aunt when he never thinks about her before?"

Weatherston relaxed into a smile, thinking about Dani and Carl together. Roberta couldn't be that naive, could she? "Perhaps he wants to make a good impression," he only said.

"Oh no," Roberta was positive. "He isn't interested in Dani that way. Carl will do nothing unless it earns him money. I do not believe Dani has enough money to interest Carl."

Weatherston raised his eyebrows. "That's rather callous, isn't it, young lady?"

"It is true," she replied simply. "Carl wants people to think he originated from a wealthy family, but I know he does not. I would not say it to him, but he has lived by his cunning. It enrages him he cannot do the same as the rich people. Therefore, he has not always been honest in his business."

Something clicked over in his mind and caused his foot to ease off the gas pedal.

"It is a pity about the aunt. Being ill."

"What? Ill? Who told you that?" For the first time since their ride started, she had his unyielding attention.

"I listened when Carl spoke on the telephone this morning. He asked what happened to the aunt and was angry. He said he would pick up Dani and take her there."

They were passing through the low hills surrounding Oxford. The skyline reflected against the sun making a medieval fairy story out of the turrets and spires.

"Did he say where?" Weatherston's mind skidded near the edge. Had Roberta been leading him miles astray? He cursed the choking traffic of Oxford, wondering where he could turn around.

"Oxford," she said, and he breathed a sigh of relief.

"I wanted to go to her," Roberta continued. "Dani loves her aunt, and I thought she might like my company, but Carl said I must go with you."

"Carl wanted you to come with me?" His tone sharpened. "What did he say exactly?"

Roberta chewed at her bottom lip and gave an almost imperceptible smirk, as if the thought intrigued her. Then, double frowns marred the smooth skin between her eyebrows. She bent her head and studied her hands.

He didn't curb his impatience. "Roberta?"

Roberta lifted her head and stared at him, doubt evident in her wide eyes. And something else. Anger.

"I told Dani not to trust Carl. He has a devil inside him. Now something is making me afraid."

Inside the city now, Weatherston pulled the car over to the curb, swearing with no apology. *It was Carl.* Carl was Bennig's man. Jeffries worked for Chetkov.

TWENTY 20

THEY REACHED THE CAR, a rented Jaguar, parked by a double yellow line. There was a traffic ticket on the windshield. Carl crushed it in his powerful hands and threw it on the ground. He started the car and pulled away at the same moment Dani climbed in and shut the door.

Mouth set in a firm line, he drove fast, handling the wheel with an easy grace. He was silent, and Dani contented herself with watching their direction, studying the streets and landmarks.

She found herself pushing her foot down on an imaginary brake at crossroads when they met traffic rushing at them unexpectedly from the wrong side of the road. The car left the High, and she recognized Queen Street, and nothing until the A4144 again. After that, they crossed a bridge over the Thames. Then they seemed to wander. Through a small street, along a wider one, a bypass perhaps, turning and twisting until she lost direction.

Later, there was a narrow cobblestone lane. Dani was sure they had traveled it before, but forgot about it as Carl stopped the car at the top of the street. Hand resting on the steering wheel, he stared ahead.

"Where is it?" She was rigid, holding her breath.

Carl opened the door and stepped out of the car. She did the same, waiting for him to come around and join her. Watching him, her unease deepened. She chided herself, but pushed those thoughts aside. *He's just got the jitters too*, she reasoned.

Carl pointed at a building, halfway down the street. It looked like a garage, abandoned, the front boarded up. Dani stared at it, willing it to show her a sign that Lucy was in there. Carl reached around inside his jacket and brought out a gun.

The front entrance was a step up to a narrow windowless door set in a clapboard front. Dani led the way into a small office with dingy walls and high, grimy windows. She stopped inside, unsure for a moment, then took an automatic single step back. An overpowering uneasiness sent a shudder up her spine. She spun around to face Carl.

"Carl—"

"Quiet." He had his back to her, peering down the street through the half-closed door until finally, his hand holding the gun relaxed.

"Where's your man?" she whispered. "The one who found this place? Why didn't he meet us out on the street?"

Carl turned from the door and faced her. His back was to the light, his gray eyes were hooded, neutral.

Dani tried to ignore a queer primitive alarm ringing in her brain. "What if they've already done something to her? Maybe they spotted your man and panicked. . . . What are you looking for?"

Carl shook his head and turned back toward the door, arm bent at the elbow, gun pointing upward. "Lucy is fine. Don't *'what if'* yourself into a panic," he said. "Both of you worry too much. You about her, and she about you—Why does she call you Daniella . . . ? To answer your second question, I'm waiting. First, I need to make sure we don't have company."

His words slammed into her heightened sense of danger and

hit like hammer blows. *Daniella. He said Daniella.* Lucy's words scrambled around inside her head. The weather being all right. Weatherston and *Lilliputian,* the opposite of what Dani thought. Lucy had tried to tell her Weatherston was trustworthy and Carl wasn't. The realization roared in her head like waves pounding against the shore. She tensed, ready to spring just as Carl closed the door and shot home the bolt.

He turned again. His piercing eyes fixed on her with immediate understanding. He leveled his gun on her.

She stood motionless, blinking rapidly, her breath heavy in her chest, fighting her panic. "You . . . You planted the postcard in Weatherston's suitcase. Your man gave you the signal this morning." Self-hatred choked her.

Her anxiety about Lucy had torn her mind off balance. It was a small comfort she had only believed him *after* he offered irrefutable evidence. "You didn't follow Weatherston to the hotel. I got your phone call before he even showed up—you already knew we were there. How did you find us?"

Carl shrugged. "Paul had you followed when you left him in Oxford." He smiled crookedly. "You are an amateur at dodging people. Lucky once, but not again."

"You were with Lucy when she phoned me," Dani said. "That's why you weren't interested in where the meeting place was. Because you already decided you wouldn't wait for the meeting at the Bodleian. So you kidnapped Lucy. Do you also work for Chetkov?"

"No, Jeffries holds that dubious honor." His gun hand never wavered. "I tried every which way to warn you about the danger. You should have given me the microfiche." He came closer, his eyes intense. "Why wouldn't you listen? I liked you. I didn't want harm to come to either of you." Another step. "Now, it's too late."

He shrugged and stepped away, his expression cold again.

She let out the sharp breath she had been holding, but a fear like she'd never known gripped her chest.

"Through there." He gestured behind her.

The garage was cold, the floors dirty and smelling of oil and grease. The walls were solid brick, almost black with age. Carl waved her across the floor and through a door. He poked the gun into her back, pushing her along the hallway to another door which opened into a larger area. Cold light streamed down from a naked row of fluorescent lighting which hummed and spit in the silence. A width of black poster paper covered the only window.

Ahead of them two men sat on a ragged over-stuffed couch beside a stained table and two chairs. An older man with a receding chin, and the other with frightened blue eyes looking like someone barely out of his teens.

"What's going on?" said Carl sharply.

"How nice of you to bring the girl, Mr. Hamel."

Carl whipped around toward the voice behind them, gun arm raised.

"I wouldn't do that if I were you."

Dani's sudden hope faded at the sight of the sour-faced man from the limousine pointing his own pistol at Carl.

Without his topcoat, his shoulders looked massive, even in the well-cut jacket.

Chetkov, she thought.

A movement fluttered at the corner of her vision. She swung around and stiffened in shock. Palmer appeared behind them and took Carl's revolver. He grinned and shoved him violently over beside the other two. "Stay there," he ordered. He held up Carl's gun, emptied it with one hand and threw it across the room where it landed against the wall under the window and bounced back again. Palmer pocketed the shells, and grinned.

Carl faced Palmer, flushed with anger. "I should have wondered more why you were so anxious to discredit Weatherston."

Palmer said nothing. He looked different, thinner without his cameras swinging from his paunch. He grinned broadly at her puzzled stare. His hand hit his midsection with a satisfied whack. "The padding was a nice touch. Don't you think?"

"What have you done with Lucy?" Dani looked from Palmer to Chetkov.

The big man's eyes regarded her with an impassive coolness. He waved the pistol sideways, pointing. "Move to the table and sit down." He watched while Dani cautiously sat at the chair next to the couch, her eyes never leaving his face. "Put your hands flat on the table."

She obeyed. "Where is she?"

"Later," the man snapped. He turned to Palmer. "Take these two across the warehouse. Immobilize them, then come back here." He paused and glanced at Dani. "They can keep the woman company."

Dani gasped and lurched upward.

"Sit down." His grip tightened on the pistol. "Do not try that again."

Palmer marched the two men out. They moved awkwardly, bound together with a leather strap wound through their belts. One snarled at Palmer as he prodded them through the door. The younger whimpered softly.

The Russian stayed where he was, his gun trained on them both. Dani looked at Carl, and he stared back at her with no expression. She raised her eyebrows hoping for a sign he might have a plan to disarm Chetkov. Carl turned away.

Palmer returned, and Chetkov lifted the remaining chair. With one motion, he moved it a safe distance in front of them and sat. He leaned forward and rested his elbows on his knees, gun pointing ahead.

"Now, Miss Morden, you will hand me the microfiche."

TWENTY 1

WEATHERSTON LET THE CAR GLIDE to a silent halt, across and down from the abandoned garage. He hadn't been in this area of Oxford for close to ten years. It had deteriorated from the busy thoroughfare he used to know. A few shops farther down the street were still in business, the rest vacant, sporting sold signs and announcements of new development.

His hunch had to be on target; a hunch centered on past experience and memory that Bennig had once conducted operations in this area. That knowledge, plus Roberta's chatter about Carl being unaccounted for when Lucy went missing and smelling of cars when he returned. It was his only hope.

He trusted Roberta to do her part. Weatherston slumped down in the driver's seat, contemplated the brick building, and checked his watch again. Two o'clock. Faded lettering on the side facing him proclaimed a one-time agency for Morris-Cowley.

The door to the front entrance shifted, then opened. A head peered out from the narrow opening. Weatherston sucked in his breath and slumped further down in his seat, cap pulled low over his eyes, as though asleep, hoping he wasn't visible through the windshield. Palmer looked in both directions and lingered an instant on Weatherston's car before the door closed again. Weatherston sat up. A surge of apprehension engulfed him. He decided he shouldn't wait any longer.

He lifted the Browning from the seat beside him, cocked and locked it before tucking it into the holster under his arm, then crossed the street and ran alongside the six foot high wooden fence adjoining the building. Grasping the top of the fence, he heaved himself up, scrambling to gain a foothold against the slip of his leather shoes. Muscles quivering, grunting with the strain on his arms and shoulders, he dropped over the fence, landing in a pile of rubbish that crunched under his weight. He spent a rueful moment gasping for breath, lamenting his physical condition and telling himself he'd get into shape when this was all over. Grunting softly, he picked himself up and planned his path to the rear of the building.

Once there, he spotted a window, the panes black with grime, one broken. Back against the wall, he peered over his shoulder into the room. Two men sprawled on the floor. Carl's men, he guessed, and out for the duration. Satisfied the room was otherwise empty, he pushed his arm through the broken pane and felt for the window clasp. It was rusted shut. Cheeks turning pinker with the effort, he continued working at it.

Thwack!

Dani's answer to the Russian earned a quick reply. Palmer's cupped hand smacked Dani hard against the ear, and her whole head rang. She had never been prouder of her snide wit, even if it came with a headache and bitten tongue.

The Russian uncrossed his legs, and leaned forward again. "Come now. Miss Morden, be civilized about all this. You are only delaying the inevitable."

"Palmer and your strong arm tactics aren't what I call civilized," Dani said, trying to sneer through the pain. She touched her bruised and swollen mouth and wiped a dribble of blood and saliva away with the back of her hand.

The Russian's massive chest heaved with silent laughter. He turned to his muscle and directed him out of the room with a silent gesture. Palmer, wringing his hands together, leered at Dani and gave her quick, single up-down flash of his eyebrows.

"I've got someone I need to check on anyway," he said before striding out the same door he had taken the two men through earlier.

"Palmer watches too many of your police television dramas. Demonstrative proof that North American television does more to teach brutality than any organization ever could."

"Bring my aunt here before I tell you anything," Dani said through her teeth. "I've already told you, I didn't bring the microfiche. Let me see that Lucy is all right, and I'll take you to where I've hidden it."

Without a word, Chetkov stood. He ambled a few steps forward, grasped an arm and wrenched Dani to her feet.

Browning in hand, Weatherston heard his own breath coming in slight gasps through his open mouth. He closed it, listening. Nothing. Twisting his head, he searched the whole area, peering into the dark corners, where the light from the high, smoke-stained windows didn't quite reach. Most of the large area was bare. At one end was an old grease pit, covered now with plywood. In another corner stood a high stack of wooden crates, dark with age.

Satisfied he was quite alone, he moved across the floor and stopped beside a small door. Keeping his back flattened against the wall, he grasped the knob and hoping the door didn't squeak, eased it open. The door opened noiselessly, and he slid into the hallway and listened. He could hear a murmur of voices from a half-open door ahead of him. Staying on the balls of his feet, he started toward it, moving past another partly closed door showing a sink. A washroom. Ahead, he heard Dani's protesting voice, her words muffled and high.

A soft scrape of a shoe against concrete sounded from behind him. Too late, he thought of the washroom door he'd passed. He tried to turn, leaning into the arm wrapped tight around his throat and the knee in his back. The arm constricted, and he lost his grip on the revolver.

With his arm still tight against Weatherston's neck, Palmer pocketed the Browning, then gave a vicious poke with his own pistol against Weatherston's ear.

"Bloody Nazi."

Dani arched as the Russian gripped her hand, spinning her around, savagely wrenching her arm up behind her. Pain shot through her elbows and shoulder. She bit her lip, choking off a cry.

"Perhaps you would like to show what you have hidden on your body," he hissed. He pushed her forward, propelling her up against Carl on the couch.

"Search her," he ordered. "Strip her. Do it so I can see if you find the microfiche." He raised the pistol. "Now!"

The door opened. The Russian moved to the side. Weatherston tumbled into the room and landed hard on his knees, pushed from behind by a swaggering Palmer.

"I spotted him before in his car outside," Palmer spat with pious triumph, "Still hanging about with his German friends.

Aren't you, Weatherston?"

Chetkov considered Weatherston for a moment, curiosity in his eyes, then he relaxed. The Russian waved Palmer away, his gesture indicating he should watch Carl and Dani.

"But you are wrong about Mr. Weatherston, Palmer," Chetkov said, watching the Englishman rise to his feet. "I know of this man well. He was never a traitor. He is a member of MI5." The Russian smiled and nodded to Weatherston. "The Home Office sending in their best, are they?" He grinned, mocking, but his eyes were watchful, and he kept a respectable distance.

Weatherston took the time to casually dust off his trousers. "It seems you had the advantage of me," he said, bitterness creeping into his voice. "Of course, you've been getting information all along, isn't that right?" Weatherston's stare probed into the Russian's eyes.

Chetkov's confident smile confirmed it.

"I thought so," said Weatherston.

"No!" protested Palmer in a strangled voice. "He's a bloody traitor! Sacrificed his own men."

"If you'd stayed in touch with the other survivors, you would have learned the truth of what happened." Weatherston looked him square on, pity in his eyes before ignoring him. He turned to Dani, taking in her bruised face. "All right, Miss Morden?" he asked gently.

Dani nodded. She massaged her aching arm and moved to the far end of the sagging couch, away from Carl. "I'm sorry. About all this, I mean. They've got Aunt Lucy somewhere."

Chetkov shrugged and turned down the corners of his mouth. Weatherston's eyes were not nice to see as they flickered from him and centered on Carl. His hands clenched.

"You're just in time, Weatherston," said Chetkov. "Hamel was just about to assist the lady in finding the microfiche."

Carl made a foul allusion to the Russian's ancestors.

Chetkov's face darkened. "We're wasting time," he said. "I suppose Palmer will have to do the job. Unless Miss Morden prefers to oblige." He turned to Dani who didn't move. She sat up straight, defiance plain in her face.

Palmer stepped in front of her and reached out to grasp the lapel of her shirt where it met in a V at the front. She watched his face as he leered through his glasses at the creamy expanse of her neck.

"Wait." A disgusting, sour taste filled her mouth. "I'll do it."

Chetkov nodded as she stood, turning her back. With fumbling fingers, she undid the waistband, then the zipper of her linen slacks. Weatherston heard the sound of tearing tape. While all eyes were on Dani, he shifted his position toward her and Carl.

Palmer snatched at the wafer-thin envelope and handed it to Chetkov, beaming in triumph at Weatherston.

Chetkov opened the envelope and pulled out a square of microfilm and held it up to inspect it. His smile faded. Taking a round magnifying glass from his pocket, he moved closer to the light and repeated his examination. He opened his mouth dumbly, then closed it and pinched his face into a scowl.

"What's this? A trick?" he asked.

Carl turned his head and glanced at Dani, eyes narrowing. Dani kept her own on Chetkov.

"You've got what you came for," answered Dani. "Now where's Lucy?"

"Where is she, Chetkov?" echoed Weatherston.

The Russian's jaw grew rigid. His nostrils flared in anger.

"There is nothing on this microfiche but numbers," he said, waving it at Dani.

Dani shrugged. “So get a computer to read it.”

Carl laughed. Chetkov turned toward him, his face red with fury.

“Ignorance is bliss, Chetkov.” Carl sat up straight and moved to the edge of the sofa. He laughed again, mocking.

“I advise you to keep your mouth shut, Hamel.” He aimed his pistol at Carl, who raised his palms and sank back again. Chetkov turned back to Dani, aiming at her this time.“

“A computer to read it? What does that mean?”

“You figure it out. You deal in computers, don’t you?”

Palmer traded places with Chetkov, and held the microfiche up to the light, squinting. “She’s right,” he reported. “A low level assembly language. It’s no problem.” He shook his head as he continued inspecting the film. “My God, pity the poor programmer who had to write all this.”

He looked up from the microfiche at Dani, speculation in his eyes. “It’s cumbersome. I’m surprised whoever did this for you didn’t suggest something else.”

Dani didn’t hide her surprise at his remark.

Palmer chuckled happily at her expression, showing the gap between his front teeth. “Surprised, little lady? Electronics is my real business, not photography. Being a radioman lost me my leg. Now, electronics provides my living. No thanks to the Pommy bastards,” he added. “The Russians, now, they’re different.”

Dani kept her expression impassive, but learning Palmer was no stranger to computer programming made her heart bounce a forbidding wobble.

“Never mind all that, Palmer,” interrupted Chetkov. “Take the microfiche. Verify it.”

“I can’t right now.” Palmer lifted a hand in protest. “I’ll need a disassembler package. Then I have to work out the instruction and argument to operate it. We'd be here for days."

Chetkov grunted in disbelief. "Are you waffling for time, Palmer? So we'll pay you more? It can't be that complicated."

Palmer's face puckered as though he'd sucked on lemons; like a teacher who discovered his pupil was deficient. He waved the microfiche above his head. "This is not basic stuff mate. I assure you, it is complicated."

"She could have substituted the documents," said Chetkov, not hiding his anger. "I gave you an order. Obey!"

"Smarten up, Chetkov," interrupted Carl. "I guarantee it's the correct fiche."

Chetkov turned on him, "Shut up, Hamel. Planting the wrong information would be in Bennig's best interest."

"You're a fool!" said Carl. "The two women didn't know they had the microfiche until Friday. There was no time for them to examine it or find something to switch with it."

Dani stared straight ahead.

"I hate to trouble you with the facts," broke in Weatherston, his tone resigned, weary. "But he's right, you know. When I questioned them about the microfiche, they didn't know what I was talking about. They weren't lying. Why beat a dead horse, now?"

Behind the pile of crates in the corner of the garage, a small figure moved. Teeth chattering in fright and cold, she rose and began flexing muscles cramped with pain from long moments of absolute stillness. First, she moved her feet encased in stout walking shoes, followed by increasing the circulation in her legs, arms, and torso. Afterward, she checked her patient, lying under the thick bundle of an Icelandic sweater. Good thing she had obeyed a sudden impulse to bring it along with her. She debated for another moment whether she should stay with her patient, but told herself she could do no more here. A doctor was needed, but there was no time to search for one and the police too. The wait was over, and action was now imperative.

Fearful that an inadvertent touch might set the piled crates tumbling, she hugged the wall, moving across the garage as if crossing a minefield and prepared for the eventuality of an explosion at any moment.

From her hiding place she had watched Carl push Dani across the floor, before Palmer had taken the two men to the small paint shop attached to the garage. She had flinched at each muffled shot, holding her hand over her mouth, barely daring to breathe.

First, Palmer had gone to the front entrance then returned to the hallway. A short time later, she heard the faint sound of breaking glass. Her relief at the sight of Weatherston had almost made her cry out, but one glance at the still form on the floor beside her reminded her that to move too soon might earn her the same fate. Weatherston could handle himself.

Dani watched Chetkov hesitate and then let out her breath when he replaced the pieces of the film in the envelope. It disappeared into the inside of the tailored jacket. He nodded at Carl and gave the pocket an extra pat. "You've made a mess of this one, Hamel. Unfortunate for you and Bennig. But then I don't blame you." His smile took in Dani. "It is not so easy to kill this one, someone much younger and prettier than the last, eh?"

Dani jerked her eyes around to Carl.

"Oh yes, he killed the Schiller woman, and the man, Dittmahn, without getting the microfiche first. He couldn't make the same mistake again. Lucky for you, Miss Morden."

Oh fool! Dani told herself. *Roberta warned me about Carl. Lucy did too. But I was too full of myself, my own superiority to listen to them.*

Her eyes locked on Weatherston's. His were full of compassion. She stared back at him—shock and pain, raw and bleeding. A sudden thought struck her.

"Where is Roberta?" she mouthed silently. He smiled, as though acknowledging the hope in her eyes.

"But this time, he waited too long," continued Chetkov, oblivious, and effusive in his victory. "There is a Russian proverb that says *'Innocence is the best makeup.'* You should never become involved with your quarry. It's harder to kill when you have looked at her every day."

Carl's own face was a study in impotent human hate.

"Palmer."

The change in Chetkov's tone brought Dani's head up. Carl straightened. Only Weatherston remained the same. He watched Chetkov with a strange curiosity in his eyes.

"I'm leaving now," said Chetkov to Palmer. "You have made your own arrangements for transportation?"

"That depends," replied Palmer.

"Ah yes, I almost forgot. Your proof of deposit." Chetkov took a slip of paper from his pocket and still keeping the pistol trained on the others, handed it to his accomplice.

Palmer examined the paper and grinned. "Right then."

"What are you going to do?" Dani asked, aware that fear was evident in her eyes. *Is this the way it feels? Am I going to beg?*

"Here." Chetkov handed his pistol to Palmer. "It is full. I suggest you use this. It is not traceable." He scanned the three watching him. "You understand I do not want any shell casings left behind which would connect to Russia?"

Palmer nodded and pushed Chetkov's hand away. "Don't need it mate." He reached behind to the small of his back and inserted his Makarov into his belt, then held up Weatherston's Browning. "May as well blame the English. Leave everything to me." He looked directly at Weatherston. "You will be the last." Palmer's fist thunked against his leg. "I will enjoy making you pay for this."

Chetkov eyed him and shook his head in a regretful way. "I see you will do as you must, but don't delay too long." Chetkov's eyes swept over the group one last time. Dani saw a momentary flash of satisfaction in them. "Bennig should thank us for cleaning up."

Carl shot out and grasped Dani, pulling her in front of him.

Weatherston cursed.

The walls and floor tilted, and Dani closed her eyes. She felt a hard shove and fell forward. Another arm threw her up against the couch. A shot, then another. Something pulled at her sleeve. She opened her eyes. People moved in a confusing blur. Later, she would recall it all as a kind of slow moving video.

A weight fell over her legs. She heard herself screaming.

Carl was lying across her knees, the surprise still showing in his eyes. Blood dribbled out from a tiny but precise bullet hole in his head. Dani's scream ended in a gurgling sigh. Her gaze fell on the open door, just in time to see Mavis Griffin point the gun in her hand; this time at Chetkov.

TWENTY 2

IN THE SAME INSTANT THAT MAVIS GRIFFIN SHOT CARL, Weatherston dived toward Palmer. Palmer brought his gun up and Weatherston blocked it with his hand. They both fell to the floor, and the Browning slid across it. Dani saw Chetkov go for the light. In the sudden blackness, there was a sound of a body rolling, followed by a crash as the table fell over. Another shot, and glass shattered somewhere near. Realizing she would have to move or risk being shot, she pushed Carl's body away and crawled along the floor using the couch as a guide. Her knee struck something solid, and she winced in pain. She put her hand down and snatched up a pistol.

Dani felt her way around the end of the couch, her fingers clawing the wall for the window. She choked back the taste of bile in her throat as her foot nudged Carl. Her fingers caught at the edge of the heavy black paper on the window and she pulled hard. The moldy paper came away easily in one piece, letting in a stream of afternoon light. Mavis was lying by the open door, and Dani couldn't see Chetkov anywhere. Palmer straddled Weatherston, lips drawn back from his teeth in a hideous grin with the effort of keeping his hands tight around the Englishman's throat. He banged Weatherston's head against the concrete floor until his body sagged. Palmer rose on one knee, staring down at him. Dani brought up the gun with both hands, pointed it at Palmer, and fired.

The click sounded loud in the silence. Palmer turned. Wild eyes staring as though in search of his own lost soul, he started toward her. Dani stared at the pistol and recognized it as Carl's gun. Palmer relaxed then patted his pocket where the shells were and laughed. Reflexively, she brought up the gun again, backing away, and fell over Carl's body. The gun slipped from her hand. He reached behind him and brought out the Makarov. Holding it down by his side he walked slowly toward her.

Eyes wide in terror, she looked past him for signs of help. Mavis raised herself, then collapsed again. Dani saw her gun beneath her. A movement behind Palmer's right gave her some hope. Keeping her face neutral, she made herself look at her tormentor.

Palmer laughed in pure delight. "There is no help there, little lady. They're out for the count. Perhaps permanently. Now it's just you and me."

She stared at him, raised hands palm out. Could she make a run toward Mavis and try to get her gun? "Wait. Please. At least tell me what you've done with my Aunt. I deserve that much."

"You will see her soon." Palmer pointed the Makarov at her, waving it back and forth, enjoying the moment.

Dani cautiously rose to her feet, hands still in the air. Palmer aimed the gun at her, and for a moment she thought he looked apologetic. She wondered if she would hear the gunshot before she died. A little more time, she prayed.

Her eyes flickered over his left shoulder toward Mavis and faked a look of surprise.

Palmer swung left, gun raised, then turned again to the right. But it was too late. Weatherston had already executed a classic roll, and in one graceful movement grabbed the pistol, raised himself on one knee and fired. Palmers face exploded.

Dani stared at Palmer, then over to Weatherston.

"Okay. Right then," his voice rasped. "Not too old after all."

He came over to stand in front of her. "You kept a cool head, Dani. Gave me time to get myself together. He would have used my gun to kill Mavis, then me, and make it look like suicide."

Dani hardly heard him. Whimpering, she sank down, pulled up her knees into a tight little ball and began to rock back and forth. A stinging pain shot through her arm.

"She's all right," Weatherston called back, now bending over Mavis at the doorway. "A bang on the head." He cursed. "The Russian got away."

He came over to Dani and sat beside her on the floor. He lifted her torn sleeve away. "Flesh wound," he grunted and tied his handkerchief around it, stopping the ooze of blood. His voice was hoarse. He pointed toward Mavis, speaking in a conversational tone to bring Dani back.

"Joseph Dittmahn was her husband. Griffin is Mavis's maiden name. She was in England visiting relations when they killed Joseph."

Dani stopped rocking and stared mutely up at him, trying to comprehend.

"She and Ida Schiller planned everything." He touched his throat and cleared it again. "They would use the tour as a cover. Once in England, Ida assumed it would be a simple delivery, and nobody would even think of looking for them among a group of people on a tour." His face showed what he thought of amateurs. "I tried to get Mavis to return home, but she was determined to find the man who killed Joseph."

Light streamed through the window, illuminating particles of dust in the air. Weatherston absently rubbed at the bruises on his throat. Dani looked at Carl and the man that was Palmer who now had no face. She started rocking again.

"I waited until I heard the big man say that Carl killed Joseph and Ida." Mavis winced and groaned as she sat up. "It's the reason I came here."

"I can't say I enjoy your timing much, Mavis." Weatherston shook his head in wonder. "But I'm grateful just the same."

There was a growing noise of traffic outside, a slam of a car door, then voices. The faint sound of Roberta's high chatter urging someone to hurry.

"Roberta and the police," assured Weatherston. "Better late than never. We'll send out an alarm for the Russian and Jeffries." He reached for Dani's hand.

At his touch, Dani stopped rocking. The heaviness in her chest steadied into pain. A darkness had fallen around her, and she doubted it would ever go away.

Roberta burst into the room. "The police would not believe your note at first." Her eyes widened at the sight that greeted her. Both hands over her mouth, she ran forward and sank down beside Carl.

"Lucy," croaked Dani to Weatherston.

Mavis rose and came near, kneeling on the floor and put her arm around Dani's shoulders, making soothing sounds which Dani couldn't understand.

A constable showed up at the door, supporting a small plump figure wrapped in the folds of a bulky Icelandic sweater thrown across her shoulders. One arm supported another peeking out from under a bloodstained wrap. Face pale, and expression bewildered, her hazel eyes swept around the room. The constable looked sympathetic.

"Auntie!" Dani cried out and scrambled to her, weeping now.

The policeman helped Lucy settle on the couch, easing her into a sitting position. He removed his jacket and placed it over her knees, while three startled pairs of eyes looked on.

"The ambulance will soon be here, mum."

"So kind, young man," said Lucy, smiling up at him, as though thanking him for an extra lump of sugar in her tea. The constable blushed.

"I'll meet your chief now, please, constable," said Weatherston.

The constable shot a reluctant glance at Lucy and left. Weatherston winked at Dani and followed him.

Dani touched Lucy's cheek. "Oh Auntie, are you all right?" She gazed at her aunt's pale face, dark circles under her eyes, then at her arm. "Can you ever forgive me?"

"She's lost a great deal of blood," said Mavis. "Her shoulder has a nasty knife wound. I repaired it as best I could, but she should see a doctor to prevent infection."

"I owe my life to you, Mavis." Glassy eyes peered at Mavis with near unfocussed gratitude.

Dani glowered at Mavis. "You found her?" Anger flashed across her face. "You knew she was here all the time? Hurt? And you didn't get her to a doctor?" Her voice was near hysteria. "All that time lurking for God knows what reason, Carl, a murderer . . ."

Dani stopped. She swallowed hard and whispered, "Oh God, please forgive me. I'm so sorry, Mavis."

Mavis nodded. Lucy put her hand on Dani's arm. "I'm sure if she had considered it serious enough, she would have taken me to a doctor, Dani." She considered the woman for a moment. "Patients must trust their nurses. And I believe you are a nurse, aren't you. Mavis?"

"It was my profession, yes." Mavis grinned at Lucy. "I met Joseph after the war when I was a nurse at the hospital in

Germany."

"Someone also used to nursing the wounded in the front lines, I imagine," Lucy smiled back.

"Yes. We had much experience in patching up terrible wounds until we could get them to a doctor." They gazed at each other in complete understanding.

Roberta made a small sound. She laid her hand against Carl's chest, rose and walked from the room without a backward glance, her arms stiff at her sides.

Dani finished inspecting Lucy's damage and opened her mouth to speak.

"A bath and a shampoo will do nicely, thank you," Lucy said in the same tone of feigned bewilderment she used to avoid topics under discussion. This time, Dani happily obliged.

The Russian hurried around the corner and crossed the street. On the other side, he stopped and brushed the dust from his suit and combed his hair with his fingers. He checked his pocket for the fiche and continued to the middle of the block where his chauffeur had parked the limousine. His hand on the door handle, he looked back along the street. All was quiet. Sucking air through his mouth with relief, he opened the door and climbed in.

"Herr Chetkov," said Paul.

Chetkov made a move toward the glass panel dividing them from the front seat.

"Relax, Chetkov," Paul said. "We have replaced your chauffeur with our own." The car doors locked with a soft click.

Chetkov turned down his mouth. He shrugged his large shoulders more into his jacket. "Why are you here?"

"The fiche."

Chetkov put his palms out and then let them drop into his lap. He looked regretful. "We are both fortunate. Palmer destroyed it before he died, protecting us from Weatherston. Carl is also dead, killed by Dittmahn's widow. The police are all over the area, and I just barely escaped. It has not been a good day."

Paul's face did not change. The tight skin over his cheekbones had become more shrunken in the last few days. "You would not dare to leave the field without your prize, Chetkov. Even sacrifice your own men to cover your escape. I will not ask again."

"Listen. You are mistaken this time. I—"

Paul pressed the Mauser against Chetkov's side, near the heart, and fired. As Chetkov fell sideways. Paul caught him and arranged him against the car seat as if he were resting there. Paul searched him and removed the envelope. He held up the microfiche to the smoked glass window. A puzzled frown creased his skin. Again, for a long moment, he inspected the microfiche and then allowed a faint smile to stretch one corner of his mouth. He considered the dead man. "You Russians never learn, Chetkov. You destroyed the entire house when only the door squeaked."

Chetkov stared back at him in startled death.

Paul signaled the chauffeur. Before he got out of the car, he pressed his thumb on the butt of the Mauser and dropped the gun on the floor. Ignoring the unspoken question in the chauffeur's startled face, Paul led the way down the street.

Mavis and Weatherston sat in the police car, not speaking. They watched two mortuary vans take away four covered stretchers. A small crowd stood about, curious but silent. A television camera pointed toward a man speaking into a microphone. Two newspaper reporters tapped on the window of the car.

A police constable and Dani came out of the garage beside Lucy, who was lying on a stretcher. Dani made to get in the ambulance, but the police constable took her arm and pointed toward the orange striped car containing Mavis and Weatherston. Dani protested but the constable was firm. After the ambulance pulled away, she went to the car, ignoring the hovering television interviewer and reporters.

"She looks so helpless," Dani said to Mavis, and her eyes filled with tears.

That helpless look bought her time and likely saved her life, thought Weatherston, staring straight ahead. They wouldn't get away, he vowed. Chetkov. Bennig. Paul too. Plus the mole in his own organization. *We could have prevented this whole miserable mess.*

"It's too bad he got away with the microfiche," he mumbled aloud and brought his hand down on the dashboard with some force.

"He didn't." Dani smiled. "It was a phony."

Weatherston's cheeks turned a shade pinker. Dani reached up and removed the pins holding the tight roll to the back of her head. Her hair tumbled down, and something rolled past her leg. Weatherston caught it before it hit the floor. A small roll of microfilm.

"I went to a computer shop, and the boy in charge put me in contact with a programmer. He programmed the whole document for me. He called it LaTeX. He laughed at me, said it was all crazy and inefficient, but he liked a challenge. I told him the main purpose was to confuse. I also got him to make a phony duplicate, flat like the original microfiche."

"Ingenious," said Weatherston. "But what would Chetkov

have found if he'd checked?"

"A game." Dani glanced up at Weatherston, a disinterested glaze covering his eyes. She shrugged, "I didn't count on Palmer. He would have known within a few minutes if he'd had time to check."

"Luck," muttered Weatherston.

"But he didn't check, did he?" said Dani. She was tired. "It wouldn't have made any sense to him anyway. If Palmer *had* checked, he would have thought he'd made an error and started over, giving us time to get away. It has a code."

"Eh?"

"Remember the first day at dinner we spoke about computers and how the instructions must be very specific to get the response we want. Well, the programmer programmed his numbers, and then I asked him to make a small change in them, something only I would know and remember.

"Like what?"

"Something simple. Like do a minus one from the end decimal number for example. I had a bad moment when Palmer noticed how incompetent it was. Thank whatever is good in the world that Chetkov didn't give Palmer time to think about it." Carl had known immediately but backed her up when Chetkov questioned it, she remembered. Was she supposed to thank him even though he didn't do it for her safety? Carl had only grabbed at a chance he would get the real one later. "I never paid much attention in the computer course I took, but I couldn't think of another method which would appear authentic. Grasping at straws really."

"Never mind," said Weatherston. "You've lost me already. I'm not up on these new personal computers, but they seem to be catching on with people who love numbers. Don't tell me anymore, you can explain it all to the boys in the know. One question though. . . . What happened to the original? There were signatures on it."

"I had them printed off and mailed to our hotel in London. Just in case. It was Lucy's idea."

Weatherston closed his hand around the roll, and gave a triumphant shake.

"At least I didn't louse that up," muttered Dani under her breath. She felt let down, bitter. "It's my fault they kidnapped Lucy. She could have died."

Weatherston saw her fists tighten. "You're ashamed it wasn't you."

Dani's eyes widened. "How did you know?"

He shrugged, knowing a good deal. "It always happens, but it will pass with time, and Lucy will be fine, believe me. She's a tough lady underneath. A magnificent job, both of you." His main thought was for Lucy. Defiant, never believing she couldn't escape.

Mavis squeezed Dani's hand. "My dear, you could not have prevented it. The order was to eliminate you both. Those like you and I cannot believe such evil people exist. But they do." Her chest rose and fell with labored emotion.

Weatherston agreed, adding, "You can only guess about evil when it isn't staring at you bang on. When you can still hope it will never be as bad as your worst fears."

Except for Weatherston's friend Charlie, Dani wanted to say. "When Charlie was killed, Lucy tried to tell me that when you see such death, you think about it more. She accused me of behaving as if I were immortal, and she was right. I didn't think about it. About dying, and not being here. You know?"

Weatherston nodded.

Dani gazed hard at Mavis. "Your husband stood up to them, and it killed him. You saved our lives, Mavis. You should feel vindicated."

"I admit," Mavis replied, "that I have no twinge of guilt about killing Carl. Joseph's death made me so angry." She paused, her vision still colored with memory. "I hated him for leaving me that way. Then Ida told me why he had died. Together, we decided we would finish what he started. Her murder frightened me half to death, but I could not give up. Now I have buried my dead. I can face the months ahead." It had been a long speech for Mavis, but her voice was strong. Her habit of trailing off had disappeared.

"How did you know about Palmer?" Dani asked Mavis.

"Jeffries became worried. It was all too much for him—more than he bargained for. He got careless. When we arrived in Oxford, he told Palmer he was running away, and they argued. Neither paid any attention to me standing right there, listening to every word. I simply followed him. I simply got a taxi and followed him. Palmer didn't even check, he was so anxious to get here." Mavis leaned back against the seat and closed her eyes.

"Your performance was most convincing throughout the whole trip," Weatherston said.

"What performance?" Mavis opened her eyes. "It was no act. I was running out of time and almost crazy with fright."

TWENTY 3

TEN DAYS LATER, Dani and Lucy stared up at the east window of the south transept of Christ Church in Oxford, admiring the bright confusion of colors around the stained glass and background of trellis, worked in blues and reds.

Weatherston quietly came to stand beside them and rubbed his hands together. “Shall we get a spot of lunch before the inquiry begins?”

Lucy turned, her face still pale, but the black circles beneath her eyes had disappeared. She favored her stiff shoulder. “How will the inquiry work? Is it like a court?”

“A closed inquiry. You’ll just tell your story to a panel of men and answer their questions. Nothing too strenuous.”

“Have they found out who murdered Chetkov?”

“Paul Hoeffner. A gun with his fingerprints all over it was still in the car. He also signed a statement claiming the whole plot of shipping the computers was his idea. Hoeffner said he used Bennig’s name and authority without permission, and he provided documents showing Bennig was not in the country at the crucial dates. The signatures all belong to the corporations where Paul has complete power of attorney. The companies in which only Bennig has full authority are clean.”

“Do you believe him?”

Weatherston sighed. “Paul would never be careless enough to

leave evidence of his crime. Nor would he pull a stunt to harm Bennig. But there it is. The evidence speaks."

"And the others?"

"They picked up Jeffries at the airport." He looked satisfied. "A lot of others as well, with the cooperation of police in other countries. Electronic research company officials, customs officials, a parliamentary figure." His mouth drooped. "Including a person in my department, which will be kept quiet. But we've cleaned house."

He traded glances with Lucy, his eyes apologetic. "That one kept me from getting to the truth much sooner, and could have caused your death. But everyone is on their toes now, with changed attitudes and noses to the grindstone. You'll read everything in the papers tomorrow. Then you'll see."

Dani paced in front of the windows, looking at them. "I'm still trying to figure out which of you followed me at Brighton. Somehow, I don't think it was Carl. He had nothing to gain, except to frighten me."

"It was Charlie," said Lucy. "And I believe he engineered that purse snatching episode to put us on our guard."

Weatherston nodded, eyes twinkling. "He didn't know you had seen him following Ida. He'd have been intrigued to know you suspected him of the murder. He was suspicious of you, until he spoke to Dani in the hotel lobby. After her murder, he dared not see you again, and I couldn't blow my cover, so he followed to protect you."

Lucy nodded. "If whoever followed Dani in Brighton was there to do her harm, he could have kept off the path and stayed on the grass to avoid being heard. The man following was just walking behind her and nothing else." Hindsight is always so perfect, she thought, sad again.

"Don't mind me," said Dani, laughing. "Talk to each other as if I'm not here." She gave Weatherston a sideways glance. "I for one, would like to know the true story about Palmer."

"Dani!" said Lucy, shocked.

Weatherston frowned and said nothing for a long moment. "What would I tell you? A bitter war that makes bitter men? Wars that take the world's future away, lying buried on a battlefield, un-lived dreams buried with it? What would any of those men have given for Palmer's chance at a future? Even with one leg?" He stared them down, waiting for the answer.

Lucy lowered her gaze and sighed. Dani could think of nothing to say and tapped the toes of her shoes on the floor, hands clasped behind her back. She felt a trifle embarrassed. She smiled at Weatherston and gave a small shrug to tell him she was sorry.

"Lunch?" he suggested again.

"Give us ten minutes?" Dani asked.

"I've tried to think of a way to apologize," said Dani when they were alone. "About taking my anger out on you. The best way is to come right out and tell you I recognize what a damn fool I was. The fact remains, I prolonged the whole mess. I persuaded you my decisions were the right ones. It was my fault that you were kidnapped."

"No, it wasn't, Dani. We got careless and gave them their chance when we separated. You went swimming, and I went to church. From the very beginning they determined to stop us."

"But I had to be so right, didn't I? And it could have ended with disaster. I'm so sorry." At Lucy's patient expression, Dani smiled and sighed, then looked up at the window again. "I'm still dodging, aren't I? What I want to say is, well . . ." Dani faced Lucy square on. "When we get back, I'll tell Mother about my lack of judgement and how things might have ended. I misread all her messages and turned them upside down. All this time, I believed she made me an actress and gave me a role to play." She rolled her eyes at Lucy. "Now, I can hardly believe myself. Together, we'll work things out."

"Dani, I've always had a simple philosophy. People who aspire to heights which remain forever out of reach become impatient. Wishing isn't enough. Yet, Helen was always sincere in wanting the best for you. It doesn't matter how or why you become what you are if you're satisfied with yourself at last. Are you?"

Dani continued to stare at Lucy, first in puzzlement then in wonder. "You certainly have a knack for boiling things down, don't you? I've never asked myself that question. Perhaps I wouldn't have answered it anyway, because it was easier not to face it. I think I was a prisoner in my own black hole. It's hard to face the truth isn't it?"

"Maybe you just have to work at it. And Edward?"

"Edward?"

Lucy's smile broadened. "You know, Edward Pierce? Are you going to marry him?"

Plodding, secure Edward. "No," she said. Relief flooded through her, and she laughed at herself with genuine merriment. "We're just a habit—comfortable with each other. The kind of relationship that friends have, really."

Lucy smiled and rummaged in her purse, bringing out a package of hard candy.

Dani took a deep breath. "Are you aware Weatherston approached me about a place here? Well, it was more a warning."

"No. What place?" Lucy asked, absorbed in opening her package and inspecting the contents.

"A job, Auntie. He said outwitting those men made a few

people in his office sit up and take notice." Dani shuddered at the memory. "Such evil. I made some huge mistakes, but with the proper training, they believe I'd be a good candidate."

Lucy's total attention fixated on Dani, her candy forgotten. Her eyes narrowed. "What are you talking about?"

"Weatherston warned me that someone would offer me an opportunity to join the *Firm* as he called it. He said that a German policeman, his name is Mueller I think, will be here for the inquiry. Weatherston said when they all learn of what I did with the microfiche, I would be asked."

Lucy's face turned red. Her eyes flashed with anger. "And what did Martin say about it, exactly?"

"If I was as smart as he knew I was, I'd turn it down. That it was an ugly, unthankful job. They would talk about serving mankind, but it was all rubbish. He told me to go home."

"Take his advice for goodness sake, Dani," Lucy declared, her face dull with fear.

"Yes, but I admit the whole situation gave me a high I've never experienced before. A feeling of purpose and intellectual exercise almost like euphoria." She stared at Lucy, her chin tight, defiant and pleading at the same time. "Can you understand what I mean?"

"I understand that once is enough for a lifetime," Lucy said, memories etched on her face.

But was there more she could do, Dani wondered. "So much evil. If we had known everything at the beginning would we have done the same?"

"Left it to the police," Lucy determined.

Dani nodded. But they both knew nothing was that easy, because not knowing about the microfiche had them running blind from the start. In retrospect, things seemed different. She thought about the part of her conversation with Weatherston which she wouldn't repeat to Lucy. She'd become less human and would lose all trust in people. Those in the profession became so immersed in role playing, they lost themselves. He had laid a hand on her arm and smiled, saying if she needed excitement, to look for it in another occupation. The statement had aroused an anger in her, and she hotly declared her involvement had been for a search for justice, not excitement.

"Last week's lessons are still bleeding, Mr. Weatherston. From now on, I'll weigh the pros and cons of proposals which affect my life. But thanks for the advice."

They had left it at that. But she felt incomplete, as if something were unfinished. Had he exaggerated to put her off? Or was she falling into her own trap again?

"I guess," she admitted, reassuring Lucy. "From now on, teaching History and its people will be more exciting. Which means more in-depth research for my students and myself. Research will be my specialty." She laughed. "No more yawning in my classes. I'm ready to go back and see what happens."

"A wise choice," agreed Lucy. But Dani felt Lucy's eyes searching her face, which she kept neutral while her thoughts waged a war inside her. Moving toward danger had taken all her courage, but at the same time she had never been more alive. Still, the events in the warehouse, her brush with death, and the shock of facing her own weaknesses, were fresh enough to convince her that constant exposure to violence would harden her or worse.

"What I'd really welcome is a whole new location to widen my experience and interests. . . . Montreal for instance. What do you think? Would it be too alarming for Mother?"

Lucy's face lit up. "Yes, it's about time you had your own

place. Until you decide where you'll live, you can stay with me. As for Helen, you'll find out she will grab at the chance to lead her own life."

"I hope you're right." Dani's reply was doubtful, but her spirits lifted in anticipation. "It's great to have choices, isn't it? But let's talk about the here and now. Next on the agenda is another week in Oxford while you recover. Only light shopping and sightseeing until the doctor gives the all clear. There's no rush to return home right away is there? You know, that last tour was a bust, so what do you think of signing up for another before we leave? Scotland would be nice." She gave Lucy a gentle prod on her uninjured side. "I always wanted to see the Highlands. All those men in kilts."

"Sounds like a plan," Lucy agreed just as Weatherston joined them again.

"Wong is out there. He wishes to join us for lunch." Weatherston grinned and turned to Dani. "Well, really, he just wants *you* to join him for lunch."

Dani pulled her mouth down at the corners and shuddered. "Have lunch with a briefcase? I know you like him, Mr. Weatherston, but must we have him along? Is he still carrying that thing everywhere?"

"I'll offer to hold on to it while you lunch if you like." Weatherston's face was innocent.

"What does he carry in that case anyway? He never lets it out of his sight."

Weatherston glanced at Lucy. "I bet it's no mystery to you, is it?"

Lucy gave him her best befuddled smile. "Why I imagine he carries his new business acquisitions."

"Cute, aren't you?" Dani scowled at Weatherston before

turning to Lucy. “Okay, I should know better than to ask, but how did you know that?”

“I told you, I saw him switch his briefcase with another Chinese man at the computer store in Winchester. I saw him do the same thing when we were at the Cheddar Caves. I assume the person was his nephew, whom he is training to take over his business. I expect he doesn’t trust the telephone or the mail or any public system and wants to relay all his instructions by hand.”

“He has good reason to believe that the Reds are spying on him,” Weatherston joined in. His head had bobbed delighted nods at each of Lucy’s statements. “Less than ten years before China takes over Hong Kong, and many Chinese must think ahead. It’s a very big deal.”

“I should have known.” Dani stifled a giggle as the sound echoed eerily through the cathedral.

“He’s got good taste, I’ll say that for him,” Weatherston said, looking all the more like a placid country vicar. “He thinks it’s about time you married, and he’s ready to offer himself as the prospective groom.”

Dani’s strangled cry of disbelief bounced off the empty spaces, startling a few worshippers in quiet prayer.

Weatherston nodded, face sober. “He says you already told him that no woman would turn down a chance to have a husband like him, unless they were blind.”

“That’s just woman-speak for choose some other woman, not me. Besides, I would never say that. When did I ever tell him that?” Her stomach turned turtle and nosedived into her sneakers.

“At a disco place. You danced with his nephew. A most innovative and provocative dance, he said. You turned his heart into pudding."

Weatherston's lips turned up at the corners. "They both think you will be the perfect assistant in his business. But of course, marriage comes first."

Dani waved both hands in desperation. "No-no-no, not me. There must be plenty of other girls in Hong Kong more suitable than I am. Homestyle girls, the same culture and all that. She could look after the children or something while he was away on business."

Weatherston pushed his agenda, enjoying every moment. "I suggested the same thing. But he vetoed that. The exact words were, *'It is like buying new overcoat and leaving it hanging in closet, is it not?'"*

Lucy laughed out loud, and Dani shot her a *et tu Brutus* glare.

Weatherston wasn't finished. "He's going to ask you today. Or rather, he is going to ask Lucy's permission as your guardian at hand, so to speak." He tried to smother his chuckle, but failed.

"I can't believe I'm listening to this." Dani took both Lucy's hands in hers, careful of her injury. "Listen, Auntie, I won't have lunch with you after all. I'll see you at the inquiry. I have the address right here." She patted her handbag, backing away. "Two o'clock did you say? You can tell Wong—well, explain to him that I'm not civilized, and I'd make life miserable for him." She ran back and gave Lucy a kiss. "You're a dear. You'll know what to say."

Dani turned and scurried down the aisle toward the far door.

THE END

Dani kept her resolution to move to Montreal. She stayed with Lucy until she found her own apartment and taught history at a collegiate. After a year, the routine began to pall, and she entered the RCMP at Regina. Her high intelligence got her transferred to Vancouver on the fraud and money laundering desk. Dani thinks Weatherston may have had a hand in her assignment. Lucy believes that one day, Dani will be the first woman to become Commissioner of the RCMP.

Weatherston retired from the Service. He and Lucy kept in touch, and they trade visits often enough to make Dani wonder why it doesn't become permanent.

Wong moved to Australia where he set up lucrative business enterprises ranging from fishing boats to technology with his nephew. He married and now has three sons.

After the USSR fell apart in 1991, Bennig pulled strings and had Paul Hoeffner released. Hoeffner immigrated to Arizona and lives on a ranch purchased by a grateful Bennig, the title given as a gift to Hoeffner. By mutual agreement, they rarely speak with each other.

In Germany, Roberta Arndt obtained a first-class honors graduate degree in social work.

Mavis Dittmahn moved back to Stuttgart and sought out Roberta. They consoled each other and eventually became good friends. Together they established a hostel for troubled youths which has been successful in helping young girls and boys move toward rewarding careers.

After bad publicity, and lawsuits by the Brookers and the American lady, Mr. Holly decided there was no profit in the luxury bus tour business.

NOTES AND OTHER THINGS

Perpetual Check began with a news item about computer sanctions against the USSR. While clearing out my file cabinets, I found the yellowed article, saved for some unknown reason, along with my travel diary from a tour of the UK with my daughter. That started me on a journey of imagining *'what if?'*

There are differing opinions on why the Cold War ended in 1991. One of these opinions argues the downfall of the Soviet Union was caused by computers. If one thinks about the freedom the internet allows, it might be so. Certainly the USSR was far behind the U.S. in technology, software, and the internet which the Soviets viewed with deep suspicion. For instance, in 1987, not one software program could be found in Czechoslovakia, or other satellite countries unless smuggled from the West. As early as the 1970s, the Soviets made an organized and sustained effort to procure banned Western technology to use for military advancement.

As secrets go, a spy in Japan leaked the news that between 1982 and 1984, Russia had obtained a number of sensitive technical products, software and on-site expertise from the Toshiba Corporation of Japan. As a signatory to the NATO sanctions, the consequences were huge for Japan. Heavy fines, sanctions, and resignations of Toshiba executives almost finished the company. The U.S. used the case as proof that the Soviets used the technology for military ends when Soviet submarines suddenly acquired the ability to go undetected, aiding their espionage missions.

By 1985, some of the NATO sanctions pertaining to certain types of small desktop computers was lifted, perhaps because by that time, the ban was almost impossible to police. For purposes of my story, I have kept the total ban in place.

Last, if the reader searches for that certain deserted warehouse in Oxford, it won't be found. I needed a rundown area, so I made it up. The same can be said for Bennig's corporation and his residence on the edge of the Grunewald Forest in Berlin. It resides only in my imagination.

~ Flee

ACKNOWLEDGEMENTS

Once again, appreciation for my editor, Tessa Barron, who has no limits. She has an eagle-eye for editing and zeros in when something is missing or in the wrong place, or needs more research. I often need reminding that while I take for granted ordinary life and history thirty years ago, younger readers may require explanations and demonstrations in the show, not tell, area. I thank her for the many hours she must have spent re-living my story. Over and over.

My husband, George, obediently sleeps when I have to do research or type out the next chapter. Of course, at his age he loves to sleep anyway, and seems as grateful to stretch out as I am to let him. Although his memory is not great, he knows that I have a story to tell, and he thinks I am a wonder to think one up. So I am grateful to him and thank him for the encouragement, and his continued trust that I can achieve it.

Thanks to my daughter, Brenda, who reads with fresh eyes and looks for grammar and spelling. Thanks to Martin Dignum, my distant relative in Cheshire, England, who cheerfully researched things I was unable to find on Google. And not least, I am grateful for the people, you know who you are, who encourage me and tell me they look forward to reading my next book.

F. Nelson Smith spent her career submerged in the numbers, working as a Certified Managerial Accountant. She now lives in Red Deer, Alberta, drowning in words, writing mystery novels. *Perpetual Check* is her second novel through Bear Hill Publishing.

ALSO BY

F. NELSON SMITH

"With its vivid atmosphere and unforgettable characters, *No Straight Thing* is a treat for fans of suspenseful historical fiction."
~ BlueInk Reviews, Starred

"Ultimately heartwarming despite its macabre circumstances, *No Straight Thing* is an engrossing historical mystery."
~ Clarion, Foreword Reviews

AVAILABLE NOW

---

bearhillbooks.com

www.ingramcontent.com/pod-product-compliance
Lightning Source LLC
Chambersburg PA
CBHW030334310726
48979CB00001B/19
* 9 7 8 1 7 7 5 0 7 4 1 7 5 *